1

2

KEEPING ON

ON

Janet Hunter

4

SUGGESTED SOUNDTRACK

1. Um, Um, Um, Um, Um, Um – *Major Lance*

2. Be Young, Be Foolish, Be Happy – *The Tams*

3. I'm Gonna Run Away From You – *Tami Lynn*

4. A Little Bit Hurt – *Julian Covay and the Machine*

5. Here I Go Again – *Archie Bell and the Drells*

6. Picture Me Gone – *Evie Sands*

7. Right Back Where We Started From – *Maxine Nightingale*

8. Back Stabbers – *The O'Jays*

9. You're Mine – *The Vibrations*

10. It Really Hurts Me Girl – *The Carstairs*

11. Land of 1000 Dances – *Wilson Pickett*

12. Interplay – *Derek and Ray*

13. Nobody But Me – *The Human Beinz*

14. Get Ready – *The Temptations*

15. Seven Days Too Long – *Chuck Wood*

16. A Little Togetherness – *The Younghearts*

17. You Don't Know Where Your Interest Lies – *Dana Valery*

18. Come on Train – *Don Thomas*

19. I'm Not Built That Way – *The Hesitations*

20. What – *Judy Street*

21. Ain't Nothin' But A House Party – *The Showstoppers*

22. These Things Will Keep Me Loving You – *The Velvelettes*

Chapter One

I woke up with the feeling that the world was caving in on me. A wall seemed to have ballooned in towards me and was swearing quietly under its breath. I tried to put my arm up to protect myself but found I was trapped across the chest. The wall wriggled about a bit. I made out the words 'effing guy rope' and the situation became clearer. The tent resumed its regular shape and whoever it was on the other side of the canvas regained his feet momentarily then tripped over another guy rope near my head. I lay still as I listened to him get up and stomp off, still swearing loudly about the stupidity of people who pitch their tents in his path.

For a moment it was quiet. I assessed my surroundings. I was lying on my back with a sleeping bag beneath me. It appeared that I was fully clothed: socks, jeans, t-shirt and jumper and had an arm draped over me. The hand seemed to be placed quite deliberately just below my left breast. The fingers were pleasingly long, they looked as though they could belong to a pianist, or they would if the nails weren't chewed and ringed with black oil. The owner hadn't been disturbed by our intruder. I shifted slightly so I could look at him.

As ever, Lance was dressed head-to-toe in army green. He wore combat trousers and still had his flight jacket on. Several of his scooter rally badges and patches were visible, as was the stitching – large uneven black stitches that were unravelling in several places. The words 'SeaDogs S.C.' had been written on the jacket in black marker pen. I had heard that at least one club member had got a tattoo to show their club affiliation but Lance had never mentioned whether he'd had it done. So far I'd not examined his body sufficiently to be able to say for sure that he hadn't. We hadn't bought patches for this rally yet. Only Dave had managed to acquire one and he'd pinned it to his jacket so he could let the world know he had attended Isle of Wight 1984, whilst he was still on the island.

Lance was lying on his side with his mouth slightly open. I thought he was good looking but he wasn't the sort of boy that girls went silly over, probably because he didn't care at all about how he looked. His dark brown hair was just messy. Pretty much everyone who wears a crash helmet runs their fingers through their hair when they take the helmet off. They might use a wing mirror to check their appearance. Anyone with unnecessary mirrors on their scooter probably has them for the purpose of making sure they look good. They'll probably have a comb handy and maybe an eyeliner pen. It didn't look as though Lance owned a comb. He did have long thick eyelashes that girls were jealous of though and so didn't need the eyeliner. He was one of those people who look completely different when they smile but that didn't happen very often. I reckoned I'd seen more of them than most people though and that thought made me smile to myself.

I thought back to the previous day. The ride down to Portsmouth had been my first experience of a proper scooter run and I'd found it exhilarating. Now I was a member of the Sessex Girls Scooter Club I had a ready-made group to ride with. We joined up with the SeaDogs, minus Lance, making up a group of nearly a dozen scooters. We took the A roads, using Sam's map, bunching up in places and stretching out in others. It felt good to have the protection of the others as well as the friendly rivalry over whose scoot was performing best. At times we got split up but we made frequent stops to regroup. The closer we got to Portsmouth the more scooters we joined up with and at one point it felt like everyone with a scooter was heading down to the south coast.

We were just looking for the ferry terminal when we came across someone by the side of the road fiddling with an upended scooter. We'd have stopped anyway but when we discovered it was Lance we were all relieved that we hadn't ridden past. I was happy to see him and nervous to speak to him at the same time. I hadn't seen him for several weeks and had only received one letter from him which just said he'd see me on the ferry. In the letter he had said to 'wait for him' which had a number of possible meanings. As he'd left for Manchester without any plans to come back to Essex I was left not really knowing where I stood with him.

When the boys decided that they weren't going to get the scooter fixed in time for the ferry crossing it was agreed that as I had passed my motorbike test two days before, I should ride two up with Lance as my pillion passenger. That broke the ice and before we'd arrived on the island we'd cleared the air and somehow come to the conclusion that we did want to be together. I'd ridden off the ferry, with Lance's legs hugging me on both sides, feeling about as happy as I'd ever felt. I hadn't known how much I'd wanted him until I saw him by the side of the road.

We followed the stream of scooters heading for the campsite. Dave and Ben kept alongside us. Ben, on the back, kept grinning and giving the thumbs up. Lance held on tight around my waist. I could tell he wanted to offer advice on my driving ability but luckily the wind rushing past us made it impossible.

It was mid-afternoon by the time we arrived at the campsite. There was a big mass of people waiting to get in and a wall of sound and fumes as riders idly revved their engines. I wondered if Lance would get any stick about riding pillion to a girl but no one seemed to notice. With all my layers on it probably wasn't easy to tell my gender anyway.

Once on site it seemed as though thousands had arrived and set up camp already. Sam took charge and led us to a space at the edge of one of the fields. We parked up, trying to claim as much space as possible. Lance dismounted and I immediately missed his presence behind me.

'I enjoyed that,' he said.

'What? My driving?' I asked.

'Yeah, that as well,' he replied.

Sam was already organising tent layout and construction, to much groaning from everyone else.

'Look, when we've done this, that's it,' she said. 'Do what you like for the rest of the weekend, I won't say a word.'

'Is that a promise?' asked Dave.

'We've got to work out who is sleeping where first,' said June.

'We could. Or we could just see how the mood takes us later on,' said Perry, giving her a wink. 'I've got plenty of room alongside me.'

June had mentioned it, I knew, because she hadn't brought a tent and probably Ben didn't have one either. I'd said previously that she could share mine but clearly she was thinking that this was a bit unlikely. Lance and I were both stood there holding our tent bags.

'You two don't need one each, do you Salty?' she said pointedly, looking at Lance.

We both watched as his ears and cheeks turned red. I knew he hated June's directness. This time though she decided to take another tack.

'Look,' she said, 'how about Ben puts up one of those tents while I go get some food? Annie and I can share her tent and maybe Ben can squeeze in with you?'

We all knew that wasn't how Lance wanted it and everyone looked on to see how he'd answer. I decided to save him.

'Well I only really want somewhere to put my clothes right now,' I said, removing my jacket and one of my jumpers and my over-trousers. The boys starting humming the tune to The Stripper.

'You can still go and get some food though,' Lance said to June. 'Pie and chips, for me.'

I wasn't sure it was a good idea sending June, she had a tendency to get distracted and might not be back before dark, but she wandered off with everyone's pound coins and we got to work with the tent poles.

Ben came over to help me.

'What do you think?' he asked. 'Do you reckon you can let June and me have your tent?'

'Maybe. Probably. I don't know. Is it that important?'

'Yeah,' he replied. This is a defining moment in my life. I've lived next door to June since I was seven and I've been in love with her since I was ten. I can't believe she's interested in me. I need to get in there while I can.'

'Hmmm, actually I think if she really likes you, you don't have to rush.'

'That's what my mum said. You know June though, what do you think?'

I did know June. She wasn't known for long-lasting relationships. Her attitude attracted lots of attention and she tended to get carried away in the moment of attraction. I wondered how much

12

Ben was aware of this. I decided to think positively on his behalf though.

'You know what,' I said, 'it's about time she fell in love properly and it might as well be with you. You'll have to keep on your toes though, don't let her out of your sight for too long.'

He looked over worriedly in the direction she'd gone.

'Not now, you idiot, I said kindly. 'She's only gone for chips. Right now if you have any hope of using my tent you'd better help me put it up.'

In fact June did turn up, almost exactly as the final tent erection was completed. She was laden down with plastic bags full of polystyrene boxes from the chip van as well as cans of lager and coke. We'd left a circle in the middle of the tents and everyone collapsed there to eat.

Bertie told a very long and boring story about his journey back from the Torquay scooter rally and I could see everyone drifting off, even the boys who might have been interested in the intricacies of the electrical problems he had had on his Vespa PX200.

I looked around the group. It all seemed a little too settled, with most coupled up. I was sat next to Lance and he was idly playing with the seam of my jeans along my thigh. Next to us were June and Ben. Across from us were Dave and Sam. Dave was lying on his back and Sam had her head on his chest. Both had their eyes closed. Next to them were Suzy and Perry who were sitting closer than they might have done and were whispering quietly to each other.

Only Andrea looked interested in Bertie's story. She was asking questions in the right places and nodding at his answers. Andrea and Sarah seemed to be looking more and more alike. They were dressed similarly in jeans and denim jackets and both had their hair cut short.

The spare SeaDogs in the group seemed to have disappeared, perhaps in search of single girls. As Perry had explained, you had to strike early if you had any chance of hooking up. The imbalance between boys and girls though suggested that this wasn't the primary motivation for attending scooter rallies and most lads seemed to enjoy getting away from girls for a bit. That's what made our group look a little odd and I did think at the time that it couldn't last.

The sun was beginning to go down and it was starting to get a bit cold. Bertie had made it to fifteen miles from home about thirty minutes from when he'd started his story.

'But you did get home eventually, didn't you?' asked June. 'I'm just thinking, 'cos you're here now.'

'Oh, right, . . . yes,' replied Bertie, and shut up immediately.

'Right,' said Sam, making a move, 'I'm going to see what's going on. I don't know if anyone is coming with me.'

'What do you want to do?' Lance asked me, standing up and holding out his hand to pull me up.

Part of me wanted to crawl into the tent, any tent, and go to sleep but I also felt that if we found some music then I could dance for hours. 'Go and dance?' I said.

We headed towards the central area of the campsite. Lance and I walked together at the back of the group.

'Are you okay?' I asked.

He nodded. 'I'm annoyed about my scooter. I'd rather have it here than at the ferry terminal. At least I could be working on it. I feel like part of me is missing.'

I sort of understood. Once you got into scooters they became far more than a means of transport. We gave them names and personalities. We put expectations on them and took out our frustrations on them.

'By the way,' he continued, 'do you mind not asking me about what I'm going to do after this weekend? I don't know what I'm going to do yet, but I don't really want to talk about it. I sort of want to lose myself for a bit and see what I think when I come out the other end.'

I knew he didn't mean getting drunk. Lance was a very careful person. He liked to keep a clear head in case he needed to ride somewhere so he barely drank and he seemed to have no interest in drugs. His means of escape seemed to be riding or working on his scooter so it made sense that he was feeling the loss of it.

'Okay,' I replied, 'but I'm quite a good listener if you change your mind.'

As we got closer to the central area we begun to hear the music coming from the stage. The bass line could be heard first and it immediately lifted my mood. Ahead of me I saw June do a little shuffle and I could see she was itching to find some room and get dancing. The area in front of the stage was already heaving with scooterists anxious not to waste a minute of the weekend.

We squeezed in along the edge of the crowd. June was the first to move in amongst the dancers with Ben in tow. I'd never seen Lance dance so I didn't expect him to follow me.

'I'm going with them,' I said to him.

He nodded. 'Be careful. I'll see you back at the tent if I lose you.'

'You could dance?' I suggested.

He shrugged. 'Maybe.'

Dave overheard this part of our conversation. 'Salty doesn't dance,' he said. 'Never been known to step onto a dance floor, so don't even try.'

I laughed. 'Then he doesn't know what he's missing.'

I squeezed through the dancers until I got to where June, Ben and some of the others had found a bit of room for themselves. I found the beat and began to move my feet in time. No one was looking closely at anyone else so you could pretty much do what you wanted. You could try out one move and if it worked you could repeat it and if it didn't, it didn't matter. Some dancers were trying out Northern Soul moves but there wasn't really the room for exuberant leg kicking so we kept our steps short and neat.

One track merged into another. The familiar ones were met with a huge cheer and rarer ones were given a bit of thought until everyone found the rhythm. After some time June mimed to me that she needed a drink and so we worked our way back out of the crowd and found Lance exactly where we'd left him.

'He must think a lot of you,' said Sam to me, 'you'd never find him staying in this tent otherwise. He'd be off finding people with broken scooters to offer advice to.'

'You can't beat a good mechanical discussion,' he shouted to her over the music.

We headed over to the beer tent. The rhythm of the music was still pounding in my head and a felt quite dizzy.

'Who's pulling an all-nighter then?' asked Dave.

No one looked keen. The early start and the ride down was clearly beginning to take its toll. I stood up ready to make a move back to the tents and Lance made a move too. Ben tugged my sleeve.

'Annie . .' he started and I remembered the conversation about the tent sharing. I decided to be bold.

'Um, Lance,' I said, 'if you had anyone sharing with you would it be me, or would it be Ben.'

He looked at me and one of his rare smiles broke out across his face.

'Well it wouldn't be Ben.'

'Can I let them have my tent then?'

He nodded and everyone smiled. Ben almost hugged Lance but stopped himself in time and hugged June instead.

'You knew it was always going to happen that way,' he said, as we made our way back through the campsite.

'I did,' I replied. 'It was good to keep them in suspense though.'

In the tent we did what we could to make ourselves comfortable. We were very gentle with each other, understanding that we still weren't sure of each other. The canvas felt very flimsy and we were very aware of people moving between the tents.

'Perhaps we should have booked a B&B,' he said.

'Maybe one by the ferry terminal so you could have nipped back now and then to check on your scooter,' I suggested.

'That wouldn't have been such a bad idea,' said Lance, and I knew he wasn't joking.

Chapter Two

Lying next to Lance that Saturday morning I felt really content. The hardness of the ground and the lack of covers really didn't seem to matter. I knew a lot of people found Lance grumpy and hard to get on with but also that those who knew him well had a real affection for him. He was unswerving in his loyalty for his friends and that gave him a strength that people were really attracted to. He also had a softness for me that I didn't see him show anyone else. I could have stayed there for ages watching him and listening to him breathe if I hadn't needed the loo so badly. That, and the fact that the air in the tent seemed to be suffused with the smell of his socks, made me decide to get up.

I wriggled out from under his arm. I cursed my choice of footwear as boxer boots with all their eyelets are so fiddly to put on. Eventually I was dressed sufficiently and set off for the ladies. These were horrible of course so I was finished quickly. I decided to buy some teas to take back. Waiting in the queue I was surprised to see Ben come along. No one else was up when I had got up and I had thought that he and June would be the last to show their faces. I looked at him closely. His eyes were veined with red.

'Good night?' I asked.

'No, not really,' he answered. 'I didn't realise how much she snored. Is she always like that?'

'In my experience, yes,' I said. 'You can prod her until she shifts position but it doesn't make any difference, she just starts up again.'

'Not that I've slept with her that often you understand,' I added hurriedly, 'sleepovers, one night in Morecambe, that sort of thing. If you get married though you'll have to get separate rooms or you'll never get any sleep.'

'Yes, I am already having second thoughts about that. There must be something wrong. Maybe she could have an operation,' he mused.

Ben helped me with the teas. Between us we bought eight on the grounds that this was as many as we could carry, and also some Kit-Kats as these seemed more suitable for breakfast than crisps. We stuffed the Kit-Kats in our pockets of our jackets.

'You know,' I said conversationally, 'I don't ever want to wear clothes that don't have pockets. Lots of women's clothes don't have pockets for some reason. I mean, where are you supposed to put your stuff?'

'In a handbag?' suggested Ben.

'A handbag? That's no good. What am I supposed to do? Hang it from the handlebars? My scooter doesn't have a glove-box you know. I don't think anyone's thought it through.'

Ben shrugged. He clearly couldn't care less. 'Better keep with the pockets then,' he said.

Back at the tents Lance and June were both up as were Sam and Dave so we distributed the teas and chocolate into thankful hands. Dave made some impressive yoga shapes whilst we looked on bewildered. Scooter rallies were obviously great places for discovering things you didn't know about people.

No one spoke for a while. More people emerged from tents and wandered off to the loos. Eventually June broke the silence.

'So, what are we doing today?' she asked.

'Parts fair,' said Lance. 'I reckon I know what I need to fix my scooter.'

'Then Ryde?' said June hopefully.

'Ride where?' said Dave. 'The ride-out is on Sunday isn't it?

'Not ride, Ryde. You know, seafront, cafes, pubs, shops, that sort of thing.'

'Followed by an all-nighter?' said Sam. 'I feel the need to dance till dawn.'

Now we had a plan we all lapsed into silence again. It was a bright, dry morning, almost too good for a scooter rally.

Finally Dave spoke up, 'Anyone know what time it is?'

Only Sam was wearing a watch. 'It is,' she said 'nearly half past ten.' Lance jumped up in a hurry.

'Shit, I didn't realise it was that late,' he
said. 'I need to get the parts.' He glanced over at
Dave. 'You coming?'

'Yeah mate,' Dave replied.

'Can I come too?' asked Ben. Lance didn't
look too keen.

'You can,' he replied, 'as long as you shut
up as soon as you realise you don't know what you
are talking about.' Ben nodded but didn't say
anything.

'Shall we see you over there later?' asked
June.

'You can try, or you can see us back here,'
Lance replied.

'We need to get patches anyway,' I said.

The boys wandered off leaving just the girls.
Sam looked around at all of us.

'You know,' she said, 'you don't usually see
groups of girls together at a rally. Let's go and
cause a stir.' There were seven of us altogether:
Sam, Suzy, Karen, Andrea, Sarah, June and myself.

'We ought to look as good as possible,' said
Suzy, 'do your eyeliner and whatever.'

'Oh and if you've got something that says
'Sessex Girls', wear that,' added Sam.

June who had seemed a bit deflated when
the boys made it clear she wasn't welcome on their
parts shopping trip, perked up immediately.

'Come on,' she said to me, 'you do my face
and I'll do yours.' She unearthed her make up bag
and set to adding black lines around my eyes and

piling on the mascara. I repeated the favour for her, adding swoops to the edges of her eyes. We admired each other's handiwork in the mirrors of the closest scooter and I surreptitiously used my finger to wipe off some of the colour I thought was excessive.

While the rest of us were dressed in clothes suitable for riding a scooter, Karen appeared in a stretchy black and white dress. We all looked at her with admiration. She tugged at the hem a bit self-consciously.

'You look great,' said Sam, 'you get to go in the middle.' She positioned Karen between us.

'Now,' she continued, 'think about your attitude. Look like you're ready for anything.' She bounced on the balls of her feet. I tried copying her.

'I feel like an over-confident boxer about to be knocked out in the first round,' I complained.

'You'll be okay,' she said, 'adjusting the collar of my jacket. 'Just remember you're a Sessex Girl. No one can touch you.'

We threaded our way through the tents single-file but joining back into a group once we hit the pathways. Some boys, three-up on a 50 Special, passed us slowly.

'Alright, girls?' shouted the one driving. He raised his fist, nearly toppling them all off in the process. 'Doing anything later?'

'We'll see you on the beach,' shouted Suzy. 'You can buy us all an ice cream.' They all looked interested and might have turned back if it hadn't have been an impossible manoeuvre in their current situation. More scooters passed us and we got a few honks and a few comments.

As we walked past the food and parts stalls the level of attention increased. The comments were mostly complimentary and it felt fantastic to be noticed and admired. June put her arm through mine.

'This is great, isn't it' she said, waving regally to onlookers and blowing kisses. Up ahead of us, someone with a professional-looking camera aimed it at us and took a few shots. He gave Karen his card.

'Give me a ring next week and I'll send you proofs,' he said. 'Plus, if you're ever in the Taunton area, let me know and I'll arrange a studio session, if you know what I mean.' He gave her a nudge. She did know what he meant.

'Bugger off right now,' she said, 'or I'll break either your camera or your nose, whichever makes the best sound.' We watched as he made a hasty exit.

'No one messes with the Sessex Girls,' she said. 'Although I would like to see those pictures.' She made to tear up the business card but then changed her mind and pocketed it.

At the Paddy Smith stall the crowd parted for us and we all bought our rally patches. Andrea got distracted by a parts stall and we left her there discussing the relative merits of Polini and Ancillotti exhausts.

'Doesn't this make you want to buy a scooter?' I asked June. While no one had said anything officially, it looked as though she had been accepted as an honorary member of the Sessex Girls.

'No, not really,' she replied. 'While I've got my charm and good looks I reckon I'm better off cadging lifts. It's probably safer.' I agreed that, in her case, it probably was.

'I wonder where Ben and Lance are,' she said. I had been wondering the same thing. We found Lance sat at a table by one of the tea stands. He had a plastic bag on the table in front of him and was looking pleased with himself. June went off to look for Ben.

'Hello,' I said. 'Did you get what you wanted?'

'I did,' he replied. I had a peek in the bag which contained various cleverly shaped pieces of metal.

'So, what do you think is actually wrong with it?' I asked

'Do you want me to explain?' he asked. 'Because I can, in great detail.'

'Does it involve the carburettor?' I asked, 'because as soon as someone mentions that word I switch off for some reason.'

'It does.'

'Don't bother then,' I replied.

'I won't,' he said. 'There is another bit of good news though.'

'What's that?' I asked.

'Well I got talking to the bloke running the stall. It turns out he's got a garage somewhere just outside Portsmouth and he's offered to give me a lift back in his van tomorrow. He said we can pick up my scooter and take it back to his place and I can fix it there.'

'Tomorrow. But that's Sunday. You're not leaving early are you?' This news hit me hard for some reason.

'Yeah, well that's when he's going. It's too good an opportunity to miss.'

'But I can give you a lift back to the ferry and you can pick your scooter up then.'

'What? And fix it by the side of the road?'

'No, I suppose not,' I said grumpily, 'but you can't leave me on my own.'

'You're hardly on your own are you,' he said gently. 'You've got June and all the other girls and Dave will keep an eye out for you.'

'But still . .'. I knew I was being unreasonable, I could see the benefits for Lance but it didn't really help.

'Look,' he said, 'why don't we have a special night tonight? Screw the all-nighter, we'll find a restaurant somewhere and have a proper meal. Pretend we're adults. How about that?'

'Yeah, okay.' I thought about it for a bit. 'But will anywhere let us in looking like this?'

'What do you mean, 'looking like this'?' he asked. 'You look fantastic. I reckon I'm about the luckiest bloke here.'

I wasn't used to compliments like that. I could feel myself blushing. 'Thanks,' I mumbled.

Chapter Three

Later back at the tents everyone was making plans to ride into Ryde.

'Do you want to drive my scooter and I'll ride pillion?' I asked Lance.

'Can do,' he said. I handed him the key.

It felt strange getting on the back of my Vespa. I watched how Lance handled it. I could feel him testing out the range on the gears and the turn on the handlebars. The ride down to the town was a laugh. He seemed to get more power out of it than I ever had and didn't seem to be hampered by having a passenger. There were hundreds of scooters already displayed along the front so we rode along slowly until we found a gap and parked up. Across the path a ramp led down to the wide sandy beach. June let out a whoop and ran down on to the sand. Most of us followed. I sat down to remove my boots and socks. The sand between my toes felt good.

Across the water we could see the buildings of Portsmouth. It seemed so close and yet so far away, as if we were in another world. I could see why Lance didn't want to talk about his plans for when the weekend was over but he did seem keen to get it over with rather than make it last as long as possible.

June, Ben and I and some of the other girls walked along the beach towards the centre of town. The boys made their way at a much slower pace along the pavement, stopping to admire scooters and speak to their owners. Once we got to the centre there were gangs of scooterists standing outside pubs and ranks of scooters displayed on an area of grass at the bottom of the hill. June and I queued up for ice creams and then sat on a wall licking our 99s.

'You know Lance is going back tomorrow?' I said to her.

'No. Why's that?' she asked.

'He's found someone with a van to take him and pick his scooter up.'

'Oh, well. That's best, isn't it?'

'Do you think? I don't know when I'm going to see him again.'

'Why not? Is he not coming home?'

'He doesn't know what he's doing.'

'Didn't he ought to by now? How old is he, twenty one?

In a way it was easy for us at seventeen to say that someone four years older ought to know what to do with their life. But I'd spent the whole summer thinking about what I might do after I finished college but I still didn't know.

'I don't think he did too well at school, so he just got a factory job when he left, but he says you can't be a forklift driver all your life,' I explained.

'Well you can, but it'd be pretty boring wouldn't it.'

'Yeah,' I said, 'also you shouldn't be stuck with the decision you made at sixteen, should you?' That reminded me that my mum had had a college interview the day before. I wondered if I should find a phone box and give her a call.

Ben spotted us sitting on the wall. 'You've got to come, June,' he said, 'have a look and choose your favourite scooter.' They walked off and left me on my own. I looked around for the others. I could see Dave and Perry but I couldn't see Lance. I finished my ice cream and was just wondering what to do next when I felt a tap on my shoulder. It was Lance carrying a bag from a men's outfitters.

'I've booked us in at an Italian place up the hill,' he said, 'eight o'clock. And I bought a shirt so you wouldn't be ashamed to be seen with me.' He showed me the button down cream shirt he'd bought.

'Really? I'd better buy something too,' I said. 'Will you wait for me? Meet me here in an hour?' Lance nodded.

I walked up the hill where the shops were. There were still a few scooterists buzzing up and down the hill but otherwise this felt more like a regular High Street on a regular Saturday afternoon. There were no chain stores though so after walking to the top of the hill looking in windows I decided to go into a shop selling vintage clothes half way back down again. I only had jeans, t-shirts and jumpers with me and only boxer boots for shoes so I needed a complete outfit. The shop owner was obviously having a slow day so having engaged me in conversation I had told her what I was looking for. She recognised me straight away as a scooterist, perhaps the crash helmet had given it away. I came out half an hour later with a bluebell linen shift dress and some grey soft suede court shoes. I wasn't sure about changing in to them in the tent but I reckoned I would look pretty good once I'd got them on.

I found the others sat on the wall where we'd been sitting earlier.

'Where'd you go?' asked June.

'Shopping,' I explained, 'I've got a date tonight.'

'Wooooh, get you,' she said, giving me a nudge.

Dave appeared with a scooterboy I didn't recognise.

'Is everyone here?' he shouted. 'I want to take a photo.' He gave his camera to the boy who'd obviously been drafted in as photographer. Dave began to organise us into a group. Some of the boys stood on the wall. Lance, June and I sat on the wall with some of the others. Ben and Suzy decided to stretch out sideways on the pavement in front. Lance put his arm around my back. Somehow I'd ended up in the middle of the group, a position I wasn't familiar with. I was usually somewhere on the edges.

The photographer took up his position in front of us.

'Right,' he said, 'after three, shout out the name of your favourite scooter club. One, two, three.' We all called out 'SeaDogs' or 'Sessex Girls' except for one lone unidentified voice who called out 'A12 Maniacs' and we all looked round to see who it was.

We posed for a couple more shots and then Perry fell off the wall on to the sand below and the group broke up.

'I'll make everyone prints when I've finished the film,' called Dave. 'They'll be good value, only three pounds each.'

We hung around for a bit longer. Groups of scooters idled along the sea front road, enraging the car drivers stuck in between them. The engine sounds and the smell of the two-stroke seemed to sum up what being a teenager was all about. It was being excited and excitable at the same time. The experience was almost dreamlike in its repetitiveness and yet it felt like anything could happen. I tried to explain it to Dave who was sitting nearby.

'Yeah, you know what that is, don't you?' he said.

'No, what?' I asked, expecting some deep philosophical answer that would explain the meaning of life somehow.

'Carbon monoxide poisoning,' he said.

Back at the campsite I zipped myself into the tent to change. I could have done with a shower but Sam lent me her dry shampoo and I did the best I could with a damp flannel. Although Karen had shown earlier how putting on a dress could be a confidence boost, I felt exposed in my outfit when everyone else was in denim and khaki. I had hoped to escape without the others seeing me but I had to wait for Lance who'd disappeared off to the loos and took an age to come back. I therefore had to suffer the attentions of the boys who were all lying around catching the last of the sun.

'Looking good, Annie,' said Dave kindly.

'I'd give you one,' said Perry.

'Is that a compliment?' I asked. He thought for a moment.

'Well, you know, I'm not that fussy,' he mused.

'You can't be, or you'd never get any at all,' said Dave. Perry shrugged and nodded in agreement.

'Doesn't mean to say Lance isn't a lucky bastard though,' he said.

Eventually Lance showed up and was equally admired by the boys.

'I have never seen you look this good mate,' said Dave, 'particularly not halfway through a rally.' He did look good. He hadn't shaved but the stubble sort of suited him. Getting up close, his breath smelled minty and fresh.

'I'd fancy you myself,' continued Dave, 'if I wasn't already in love with the most beautiful person in the world.'

'You mean me, of course,' said Perry.

'Of course,' said Dave and made a lunge for
Perry. They rolled around on the grass for a bit and
we were able to slip away quietly.

We'd decided to take the bus into town and
get a taxi back. Without our helmets or clothes
displaying rally patches there was little to identify
us as scooterists. We could have been locals or
holidaymakers. It felt quite strange after a couple of
days of having an obvious identity, a bit as if my
personality had been wiped clean. I wondered if
this was what Lance had meant about behaving as
adults: becoming an anonymous member of society.
I wasn't sure I was very keen.

In the restaurant we were given a table
against the back wall. It looked like every other
Italian restaurant I had ever been in. I felt nervous,
being on my own with Lance and being expected to
make conversation. Luckily he looked nervous too.
I kicked him gently under the table and he caught
my foot between his ankles and held it there. We
grinned stupidly at each other for a bit until the
waitress came over to take our order. She rolled her
eyes in a way that suggested she'd seen many
instances of this sort of behaviour before. She
rattled through the specials and we chose some
pasta dishes, some garlic bread and carafe of house
red.

'So,' I said, 'what are we going to talk
about? If we can't talk about what you're going to
do after this weekend, that is.'

'But I do know what I'm doing,' he replied.
'I'm picking up my scooter, taking it to this bloke's

garage and fixing it.' This plan seemed a bit short-term to me.

'But after that,' I asked, 'what then?'

'Ah, well, that's the bit we're not talking about.'

'Really?' I didn't want to push it but I thought he must have some idea of which direction he was going to point his scooter in once he'd fixed it. If the two choices were his Mum's or his Dad's then he would either be going to Essex or Manchester.

'Yes,' he replied. 'Really.'

'But you'll let me know where you go, when you've gone, won't you?'

'Yes. But I'll see you at Weston won't I?

'Weston Super Mare? When is that?' I asked.

'Mid-September. Three weeks away.' I had known about it, but I hadn't made any plans for it.

'Yeah, maybe,' I said. 'I'll be back at college by then.'

'Not at the weekend though?'

'No, but on the Friday. And the Monday.' I wasn't sure I was up for such a long journey over such a short period of time.

I thought for a moment. 'But if you were in Essex you could take me, couldn't you?' I was going to add 'if your scooter's fixed', but thought better of it.

'Yeah, but I don't suppose I will be.'

'Why not?'

'Because my Mum doesn't want me.' He breathed out heavily. 'See, this is exactly what I didn't want to talk about.'

'How about Maureen?' Maureen was his aunt.

'No. She's got too many cats. And she'll side with my Mum.'

'You don't know that.'

'Oh. And you do, I suppose?' He glared at me. The waitress arrived with our bread and wine and I saw her trying to suppress a grin. Presumably she enjoyed warring couples more than happily in love ones.

Lance poured out the wine and I took a massive gulp of mine, wincing at the taste.

'You're not going to end up sleeping rough, are you?' I asked. I had thought about asking my Mum and Dad if he could stay with us, but very quickly decided against it. There were lots of reasons that was not a good idea. Lance did have a good few friends who thought well of him and would no doubt put him up, but I didn't know of any that had their own place, everyone was still living with their parents. That was okay for June, Ben and me, we could still be at school. But some of the others, like Dave, were old enough and probably earned enough to be renting somewhere. I wondered if Dave was saving up for something, like getting married to Sam. The thought was intensely depressing: once you got married you'd have to start thinking about having kids and then your life was basically over.

'No,' said Lance, 'I'll go to my Dad's if I have to. I haven't actually fallen out with him yet.'

So there it was, he would end up back in Manchester, and I'd be stuck in some long-distance non-existent relationship. It all seemed a bit hopeless.

'I'm thinking of trying to get some work abroad when I finish college,' I said in an effort to change the subject a bit. Lance looked shocked. I was a bit shocked myself at having even spoken this idea out loud. It was something I'd been thinking about for a bit, especially since going to Ibiza. Julia getting a job as a kids' rep had shown me that ideas like this didn't have to be unachievable and I could aim for something out of the ordinary.

'Wow,' said Lance, 'where?'

'I don't know yet. I'll have to do some research, there are books about working abroad so maybe I can write off to some places. My college qualification ought to help. Maybe I'll try the cruise lines.'

'I'd never see you,' said Lance.

'You could fly out to meet me when we come into dock,' I suggested. 'Barbados or somewhere.'

'I've never been on a plane.'

'Neither had I until I went to Ibiza. Just because you haven't, doesn't mean you can't.' I didn't tell him that my Dad has been petrified by the experience.

'I'd have to have a good job to be able to afford the ticket though.'

'Yeah,' I said shortly, 'you would.' There was no way round that.

Later, we walked down the hill to the front. We stood for a while looking at the lights across the Solent. Behind us, scooters were still buzzing along the coast road.

'I'm quite a simple person, you know,' Lance said, breaking the silence. 'I don't have any great ambitions. I have the things that interest me, like scooters, but apart from that I've never thought I could aim for something beyond what I've already got.'

I kept quiet, not wanting to interrupt whatever it was he wanted to say.

'It's not an excuse,' he continued, 'but I suppose no one ever made me think I could. But you, you scare me. You scare me and you make me feel excited at the same time.'

'How do you mean?'

'Well, you're sort of . . . restless. As if you're not happy with what you've got. And that makes me think I shouldn't be either. Especially right now when I haven't actually got anything. I've never thought much beyond the next week before but you're always looking far ahead, imagining what that could be like.'

'Well, I do like to daydream,' I admitted.

Lance took a deep breath. 'You know I fancy the pants off you?'

He said this as if it was a question requiring an answer, so I nodded.

'Well I do, but I don't know what you think,' he paused for a moment, but somehow I can't see this working. You know, you and me.' It took me a while to realise what he had actually said. Then it felt like he'd taken all the breath out of me. I could feel my face warming and the tears forming in the corners of my eyes.

'It's like,' he continued, looking out across the water 'neither of us know what we're going to do next but we're not heading in the same direction. I feel like I might hold you back, and I don't want that.'

I tried to answer but couldn't get any words out. Maybe this was what he meant about behaving like adults, deciding between us that we didn't belong together. Lance turned to look closely at me. He had a tear in his eye too.

'You know I'm right, don't you?' I nodded. He took hold of my hand and held it tight.

'You'll be the one that got away,' he said. 'The one I'll compare everyone else to.'

He moved in close, put his arms around me and kissed me deeply. I couldn't help but respond. I clung to him, shivering and feeding off his warmth.

'What now?' I asked, when he broke away. 'What happens now?'

'I'm not giving you up just yet,' he said. 'We've still got tonight. If that's okay?'

I was still shivering. The night seemed to have got suddenly cold and neither of us had jackets. I wanted to be somewhere safe and warm where no one could see me, no one could look at my face and ask me what was wrong. The town felt crowded and the campsite would be too.

'I'm going to have a walk down to the sea,' I said, wrapping my arms around myself.

'I'm coming with you then,' Lance replied. 'Remember we're not splitting up, I'm giving you up. That's important.' I wanted to argue against his decision but I didn't have the energy.

I took my shoes off and we walked across the sand, wordless now. We stood by the sea and watched the tiny waves ripple in front of us. Lance stood behind me and wrapped his arms around my waist and rested his chin on my shoulder. I held on tight to his arms and hands.

'We can change our minds,' he said. 'Not now, but in a year, two years', twenty years' time.' I wondered if I hadn't said about wanting to work abroad, if we wouldn't be standing here having this conversation. Whether it was just my ambitions that had put him off, or something more, something about my character. I felt very small.

'Can we get back, do you think,' I asked, 'without anyone seeing us?' Then I thought about our sleeping arrangements. I'd given my tent up so potentially had nowhere to sleep.

'We can try,' Lance replied. It seemed as if he had read my thoughts. 'Do you think we can still share the tent tonight?'

'Yes,' I said. 'Please.'

Eventually the cold became too much. We walked back on to the front and got a taxi back to the campsite. Music was thumping from the stage and we could see the crowd jumping along in time. I wished it were possible to find June somewhere in the middle of the crowd where I could lose myself in the dancing.

Instead we walked back up to our camp. We didn't see anyone else although there seemed to be rustling from one of the tents.

'I'd be going for a ride now,' said Lance, 'if I had my scooter. It helps to calm me down and cheer me up.' I knew what he meant and I thought about offering to lend him mine. I didn't want to be a passenger though, or be left alone, so I decided to keep quiet.

We crawled into the tent. I pulled on my jeans and as many jumpers as I could find. They kept me warm but I still spent an unsettled night. I heard the others come back at various times and I also heard Lance leave the tent and speak in a low voice to someone else although I couldn't work out who.

Later when I woke up it was light. We were almost in the same position as we'd been the morning before, with me laying on my back and Lance lying beside me with his arm across my chest. It seemed as though nothing had happened and yet at the same time everything had changed.

I could hear movement outside and so I stayed where I was. I didn't want to get up and have everyone ask me how the evening had gone. I lifted Lance's arm off me. I felt as though I wanted to make the break up mean something as the night

41

before our actions hadn't matched what we'd talked about. The movement disturbed him though. He opened his eyes and we looked at each other for a bit.

'I told them,' he said after a while. 'Well, I told Dave anyway. He'll tell the others so they won't ask you any awkward questions.'

'Thanks.'

'He said I was an idiot, by the way. Although that wasn't the actual word he used.' I smiled. 'They'll look after you,' he continued, 'make sure you get home okay.'

'When are you going?' I asked.

'About lunchtime, I think. I ought to go and check I suppose. I don't want him to leave without me.'

Once he'd gone I lay on my own for a while. Then I heard the sound of the zip and June popped her head in.

'Room for a not very small and slightly smelly one?' she asked. I could have hugged her.

'Of course,' I said. She took Lance's place beside me.

'I heard,' she said. 'How are you?' I shrugged, as much as you can do when you're lying down.

'I feel like I was just given a prize and then had it taken off me straight away, because they made a mistake.'

'You know it's only because he thinks so much of you.' She rubbed her finger down my cheek picking up a stray tear. 'It's like he doesn't think he's worthy of you.'

'Well that's a stupid reason,' I said. I wasn't in the mood to think rationally.

'Yeah, I know,' she agreed. 'Look, I expect Lance is taking his tent so shall the three of us all squeeze into yours tonight?'

'If I won't cramp your style.'

'We'll survive.'

'I could just go home now,' I said.

'No. You can't do that. Edwin Starr's on tonight.'

'Is he?' I perked up a bit.

'Yeah, you don't want to miss that, do you? We'll get down there early and get up the front somewhere.

'Thanks June,' I said.

'What for?'

'You know, just being you.'

She smiled and kissed the tip of my nose. 'You know everyone's on your side,' she said. 'Now let's shift your stuff into your tent and go and get a coffee and the biggest bun we can find.'

Chapter Four

We managed successfully to avoid the others for the rest of the morning. June had thought that most of them were going on the ride out anyway. It did seem as though the campsite was quieter than it had been. We got breakfast from one of the stands and found a sheltered place to eat it.

'So how was your evening?' I asked.

'Oh, you know, I just danced all night, well for as long as I could. Ben only lasted about four tracks though. He wandered off and I never saw him again. It wasn't an all-nighter so when it ended I went back up to the tents and he was already inside asleep.'

'I suppose he's alright is he?' I asked, 'you know, with this head thing. His Dad did tell him to take it easy.'

'He says he is, but I don't know.' June looked a bit worried.

'It's not really a good place for fragile people is it?'

'Most of them are fragile though, this morning,' she said, looking at a boy walking past looking very unwell, 'just in a different way. In the end you have to be kind to yourself.'

'And to others.' I added.

'Yeah, that's probably how it works best,' June agreed. 'Talking of which, me being kind to you, how about we take a trip out somewhere on the island? Get away from all this for a bit. And, you being kind to me, can drive us there.'

'Yeah? Where are we going to go? Not Ryde again.'

'No. How about Alum Bay, they've got a chair lift and rainbow rocks.'

'Okay. Rainbow rocks sounds good,' I said. 'I'm fed up of all this khaki. Do you know how to get there?'

'Not as such but it's right by the Needles so if we just head west we should get there eventually.'

Such an outing did mean we had to go back to the tents and I was nervous in case Lance was there. I'd decided it was best to avoid him if I could. It was a bit cowardly but it was quite possible he was doing the same thing. He wasn't there but his tent was still up so I figured that he was probably still on the campsite somewhere.

I got the keys for my scooter and kick-started the engine. June said she'd walk until we got off the campsite as the ground was so uneven so I idled alongside her, letting my feet drag through the grass. When we got near the trade stands I kept a look out for Lance. Although I'd felt as though I wanted to avoid him there was something that made me want to see him too. I knew that this probably wouldn't be the last time I saw him but somehow it felt like it. We could have gone to look for him but it mattered somehow if I did bump into him that it had to seem accidental.

June was looking for someone too and suddenly veered off the path. 'Won't be a mo,' she said. I pulled my scooter off the path and parked up for a moment. June had gone over to a stall selling bacon rolls and came back with Ben who was holding a large steaming polystyrene cup in one hand and a roll in the other. He looked very tired.

'Salty's looking for you,' he said to me.

'Where is he?' I asked. Ben waved his roll vaguely behind him.

'Over there somewhere. I'm not sure I could find him again.' I looked at June to see what she thought about this information. It didn't look as though she was up for a long search.

'To be honest,' said Ben, 'I am not sure he was looking for you. He just asked me if I'd seen you.'

'Right,' said June, taking charge, 'we're off to Alum Bay for the afternoon.' She would have dragged me away if I hadn't been sat on the scooter. I pulled it off the stand.

'What are you up to?' I asked Ben.

'Going back to sleep, I hope,' he replied. 'I'll see you for Edwin Starr later.'

'Okay. If you see Lance, tell him I said 'Bye''

'Just that?'

'Yes. Yes, I think so.' I couldn't think of any more meaningful message to pass on.

Once we'd got to the campsite entrance, June levered herself onto the back of the seat and we set off towards the west. June wasn't as good a passenger as Lance, she didn't anticipate the bends as well as he had and she kept twisting to wave to people we passed along the way.

'Alum Bay?' she shouted hopefully to a few of the better looking ones and they mostly replied with gestures that suggested we should keep going straight on. Eventually we began to see the signs for it and at what felt like the end of the road, found a large car park. We parked up alongside a number of other scooters.

'Well that was fun,' said June. 'More fun than with one of the boys.'

'Yeah? Why's that?' I asked.

'Well, they're always trying to show off, aren't they, taking risks when they don't need to, just 'cos they think it'll impress me. I prefer your style of driving.'

'Slow and steady?'

'Yeah.'

We walked over to the buildings in front of us. There seemed to be a number of shops selling souvenirs of one sort and another and a tea rooms with lots of outside tables. I was suddenly really hungry. We got some food and took it outside.

June sat where she could check out a group of lads who were sat a few tables away from us. From their crash helmets and clothing I took them to be the owners of the scooters in the car park. I couldn't look without being seen to be looking so I relied on June to describe them.

'There's five of them,' she said. 'Approximate age: nineteen. Two with shaved heads, three with hair, one curly, one ginger, one wearing a hat. I bagsie the curly-haired one.'

'Why's that?'

'He's got the jolliest looking face.'

'Fair enough. Who should I go for?'

'Hmmm, let me think. Neither of the shaved heads, I don't why anyone thinks that's a good look. They must be trying harder to intimidate other blokes than they are to attract girls.'

'So that leaves the ginger one and the one with the hat.' I said. I did have a bit of a soft spot for boys with orange hair. It tended to give them delicate, freckly skin which made them look quite vulnerable.

'Yup. The one with the hat looks a bit more dangerous, more of a challenge.'

'What sort of a hat?' This was important.

'Hmm, sort of a sailor's one with a peak.'

'Dark blue?'

'Yes.' The hat passed the description test, I was interested. I risked a glance round.

'Don't look!' hissed June. 'They're moving. Act normal.' I turned back quickly. I could feel them heading our way and I tried my best to pretend we hadn't seen them. They passed us behind June and I could see them clocking our crash helmets which we'd left on the table. I looked for the one in the hat. He was tall with skin-tight bleach-splashed jeans, canvas shoes and a sleeveless jacket over a stripy top. His hair spilled out from under the peak of the cap. He did indeed look like something of a challenge. He caught my eye as he went past and we exchanged smiles.

'Woaah,' said June. 'Lance? Who's Lance?'

'I'm just looking,' I said. 'Presumably that's allowed.'

'If you and Salty are no more, then everything's allowed,' agreed June. 'Maybe not this quick though.'

We finished our lunch and wandered over to the chair lift. As we went over the cliff the land dropped away below us and we could see over to the Needles and the red and white lighthouse. I felt a bit dizzy and clung on with unnecessary strength. At the bottom there was a lad with one arm in a sling. He helped us off the chair with his good arm.

'Ah,' he said, 'you must be the nurses. I've been waiting for you.'

'We're not nurses,' replied June, 'but I'll give you an examination if you like.'

'Umm.' He looked a bit scared. 'Perhaps I'll wait for the real nurses.'

June and I spent some time exploring the beach and admiring the colours in the rocks. We found a spot in the sun and sat and watched the other tourists for a bit. The boys we'd spotted earlier were clambering over rocks way over to our left. Everyone else appeared to be in family groups and there were hundreds of kids shouting and screaming as they dashed about the place. A group of young girls in front of us turned cartwheels over and over.

'Do you remember when you used to do that?' I asked June. I did remember and it hadn't been that long ago.

'There's a point, isn't there, usually about when you start secondary school when you start being concerned about showing your underwear and it becomes something you don't do any more,' I said.

'I'm not sure I've reached that point yet,' said June and she stood up, tugged down her top and launched herself into a cartwheel. The first one was a bit lopsided and she landed heavily on the second but by the third she'd got into the rhythm. She did a few more and then came and sat back down.

'That was great,' she said. 'We shouldn't ever give up on stuff like that. You have a go.'

I agreed it did look fun. I checked to make sure no one was looking and then got up and, finding a suitable flat area of beach, put my hands up and threw myself into a cartwheel. I felt muscles I never normally used stretching as my legs went over my head and I landed neatly with one foot following the other. I laughed out loud with the pleasure of it.

'See what I mean?' said June. 'We used to be able to do those without thinking. It didn't matter where we were, as long as we had enough space.'

'Yeah, but we take up other things instead, don't we?' I argued. 'We didn't used to be able to ride scooters on the roads, well not motorised ones anyway. We didn't used to be able to drink. We didn't used to be able to sleep with boys. Perhaps you have to give some things up so you can take on other things.'

'You mean you can't do cartwheels and have sex at the same time? Haven't you ever read the karma sutra?'

'No. Have you?'

'Well, I looked at some pictures once.'

Not wishing to have June describe the pictures, I changed the subject. 'Have you phoned your mum since you've been here?'

'No! Why would I do that?'

'So she doesn't worry.'

'It's if I did phone that she'd worry. She'd think there was something wrong with me. Have you phoned yours?'

'No, but I think I should.'

'There's a phone box at the top, you could use that.'

We made our way back up to the chair lift. At the bottom the same lad was still there only he had his other arm in the sling. 'Ah you must be the nurses. .' we heard as we made our way back up.

At the top we pooled our two pence pieces and I shut myself in the phone box whilst June sat on a bench outside.

As I dialled I wondered what my mum would be up to. Half way through a Sunday

51

afternoon, on a Bank Holiday weekend, I guessed she'd be sat down with the crossword from the paper. The phone rang for a long time. Eventually she answered it.

'Hello Mum,' I said.

'Ooh, hello love,' she replied, 'I was hoping you'd call.'

'Why?' I wondered if something had happened.

'Oh, you know, just wondering if you were okay. It's very quiet, we're missing you.'

'I'm fine.' I said. 'Tired, you know.'

'But you're keeping safe?' She asked. 'Friends are okay? June? Lance?' This wasn't a question I was prepared to answer at this point although I knew I would have to eventually.

'Yes, everyone's fine. June and I are at Alum Bay.'

'Oh, I went there once, when I was about ten, I think.'

'Did you cartwheel on the beach?'

'I don't know, it's too long ago. Why would you ask that?'

'Oh, no reason. How did you get on with the interview?'

'Yes, fine, I think. I don't think they're too fussy. They mostly seemed to want to check that I knew what I was letting myself in for. They're going to let me know next week.'

'That's good.' The pips went so I shoved in another 2p. I watched June who was over by a shop entrance talking to one of the boys we'd spotted earlier.

'So, you're back tomorrow?' Mum asked.

'Yes, I don't know what time though.'

'Doesn't matter, I'll put a stew on and you can have it whenever.'

'Sounds good,' I said. 'I'll need a bath too. Or perhaps a shower first, then a bath.'

'That bad is it.?'

'Worse,' I said, feeling grubbier even as I thought about it.

'Oh well, enjoy your last evening.'

'Will do.'

I pushed open the door. June was on her own again.

'Who were you talking to?' I asked.

'Didn't catch his name. That was just one of those lads, asking if we were at the campsite.'

'And?'

'And, I said we were.'

'You've not arranged to meet them then?'

'No! Why would I do that?'

I didn't know why she would, but that didn't mean to say that she wouldn't.

We had a wander round the shops and both bought a small glass jar in the shape of lighthouse filled with the coloured sand. I thought I'd give mine to my Mum. Back in the car park my scooter was left all on its own. On the flyscreen I spotted a greasy smear which on closer inspection appeared to be a kiss mark made with the help of lip salve.

The mark was wide and thin so looked like boy's rather than girl's lips.

'That's weird,' I said, pointing it out to June. 'Was that there before, do you know?'

'Don't think so, although I'm not sure I'd have noticed.'

I wiped it off with a tissue, figuring it would just collect dirt off the road if I left it.

Chapter Five

Back at the campsite I felt sufficiently removed from the whole situation with Lance to face the others. I wondered if that had been June's intention, she always seemed fairly disorganised but underneath it all I got a sense of a keen mind at work. She made things happen but didn't reveal her workings.

Most of the boys were lying around by the tents. There was a flattened rectangle of grass where Lance's tent had been and there were lager cans lying scattered around. Sam appeared from her tent with a bin bag which she forced on Dave.

'Clear it up.' she said. 'When we leave tomorrow, apart from the grass, no one's going to know we've ever been here.'

'How's the grass going to know, it's just grass,' replied Dave. She looked at him crossly.

'Oh, you know what I mean.'

Dave reluctantly stood up and began picking up cans.

'See,' he said to us, 'this is why we're better off not coming with girls. Us boys will leave the cans and never think of them again. You, meanwhile, will spend the whole journey back worrying that you've left a crisp packet unaccounted for.'

June and I sat down next to Ben, who was looking a lot fresher than he had done earlier.

'I slept all afternoon,' he said happily, 'I've only just got up.'

'Ready for Edwin Starr, then?' I asked.

'Yes, although if we'd wanted to get up the front Perry says we should have gone down there already.'

'We're small, we can push our way through,' said June.

'I think I'll be happy on the edges,' I said.

We went down to the stage area together, the whole gang of us. Suzy came and walked beside me.

'I just wanted to check you're okay,' she said.

'I am now, I think,' I said. 'It was a bit of a shock though. I thought he really liked me.'

'He does really like you, you know that,' she replied. 'I've never known him be the way he is with anyone else but you.'

'But,' I said.

'Yes,' she agreed. 'But. You could say a lot of things after that and none of them would really get to a right explanation. You've just got to accept with Salty that once he's made his mind up, that's it. He might change it but only very slowly. And he'd never admit he was wrong in the first place.'

Suzy thought for a moment. 'You'll find someone else,' she said, 'and you'll wonder what you saw in him.'

I tried to imagine being in that position. It suddenly came to me that what I saw in Lance was what he saw on me. He made me feel like a better person. I wondered if that was what love was: being with someone who made you feel good about yourself. It all seemed very selfish all of a sudden.

'Some people are better off on their own,' continued Suzy. 'I am. I've tried being in a relationship and I didn't like it. Maybe Lance is like that?'

'What didn't you like about it?' I asked.

'Well mostly I didn't like having to agree what we were going to do. If I decide to do something I want to just go ahead and do it, not have to ask permission.'

'I don't think Lance and I were like that. We weren't together long enough.'

'No, I didn't mean that. There might be lots of reasons. I just think it's a bit odd that people are expected to be in this male-female couple.'

'Yes, I suppose. It's like you learn that that's normal and then that's what you look for, never mind if it works for you or not.'

'Yeah,' said Suzy, 'I'm planning on living on my own, to hell with what everyone thinks.'

'Won't you be lonely?'

'No. I like my own company. I'm quite happy reading a book. This rally's doing my head in to be honest, I'll be glad to get home for a bit of peace and quiet.'

I laughed. She sounded like an old woman but I understood what she meant.

'It's not like I don't enjoy this sort of thing,' she said, indicating the crowd and the stage in front of us, 'it's just I like to have lots of space in between.'

It seemed as though everyone on the campsite and several thousand others had amassed in front of the stage. There was a group already playing and a few people were dancing but it was clear everyone was really waiting for Edwin Starr. Someone only had to shout 'War!' for a large section of the crowd to reply 'What is it good for?' and an even larger section to respond with 'Absolutely nothing.' The quieter ones amongst us then muttered 'Say it again y'all,' even if we didn't mean it.

There was no way we were getting to the front of the stage and I didn't want to, it looked as though we'd get squashed. At the outer edges though the groups were more sparsely spaced and we found a gap to the right of the stage. Someone had brought a case of lager and handed them out. June began dancing to the band on stage and everyone cheered her on. Half an hour later the band finished their set and the crowd excitement levels went up a notch or two.

Edwin Starr came on to a huge roar, almost drowning out his opening cry of 'War!' and everyone immediately started jumping up and down. I kept close to June for a while but she was intent on getting nearer to the front so I soon lost her. I was waiting for 'Stop her on Sight' and when the group launched into that I got lost in the rhythm and when the song ended I couldn't see any SeaDogs or Sessex Girls at all. I didn't matter, the band played 'Agent Double-O Soul' and I lost myself in the music again. The sea of people dancing pushed me further and further to the centre of the crowd and when I stopped dancing for a moment I felt like I needed to come up for air and started working my way to the back of the crowd. There was a lull in the music at this point and I heard someone shout out:

'Look, it's one of the cartwheel girls from the beach.' I looked up and one of the boys we'd seen earlier was pointing down at me and looking in the direction of the one with the hat. I looked up at him and grinned.

'Are you dancing?' he asked and held out his hand. I took it and he led me into some sort of jive that was completely inappropriate to the beat coming from the stage. I joined in as well as I could.

'Actually I was just trying to get out for some air,' I said pointing in the direction I had been trying to move in.

'Mind if I come with you?' he asked.

'Watch out for Jools,' shouted one of his mates, 'you can't trust him.' I looked up at him questioningly.

'You can trust me,' he said. 'We're only walking and talking. Come on.' He led the way through the crowd making far better progress than me. When we got to the edge he stopped.

'Would you like a drink?' he asked.

'Water, please.' I hadn't realised how thirsty I was. We found a stall and queued up.

'So,' I said, 'I'm Annie. And you are. . .Jools?'

'Jules, with a softer J,' he said. 'It's French, my mother's French. But what do they know? Philistines.' He waved his hand dismissively.

'But you don't sound French.'

'No, I could if I wanted.' He rattled off a long explanation in French. 'But I find everyone's happier here if I don't.' He seemed quite jumpy, his long limbs in constant motion.

'Where are you from?'

'North Devon. On the coast, almost into Cornwall. And you, Annie?' He said my name in a way that made my knees cave in a little underneath me.

'Essex,' I replied. 'And yes, I've heard all the jokes.'

'Jokes?' he asked. 'No jokes, it's a beautiful county. With beautiful women.'

'Keep going,' I said. 'Flattery will get you everywhere.'

We both got a bottle of water and walked back towards the mass of dancing people. At the back small groups of people were sat around and so we found a clear spot and joined them. Jules bent his knees up so they came almost under his chin.

'So were those your friends? The ones at Alum Bay?' I asked.

'Friends, colleagues, maybe. Fellow travellers I call them although they prefer to go under the name 'Moretonhampstead Marauders'. We're not from Moretonhampstead, we just liked the alliteration. Plus it gives us an in-built point of conflict with the 'Moretonhampstead Mudslingers', which means we can always find a ruck if we want one.'

I wasn't sure how much of this was made up so I just nodded to show I was listening.

'It's a bugger to get on a badge though,' Jules continued, 'no matter how much space you give yourself you always end up running out of room by the time you get as far as 'Mara'.'

He took a tin out of his pocket and, opening it, stuck his finger in and wiped it across his lips.

'Oh, it was you, was it?'

'Me?'

'You who left the lipstick mark on my flyscreen?'

'Lipstick? This isn't lipstick.' He was mock outraged. 'I don't know, you'll have to do some forensic tests.' He took my hand and planted a kiss across the back of it.

'There,' he said, 'does that look like your lipstick mark?'

'I can't see it there,' I said. 'I'll have to rub sand over it or something to see where it sticks.'

'Maybe, or I could try another part of your body.'

'Or a flyscreen.'

'Perhaps, although in my experience flyscreens aren't nearly so responsive.' He wiped his arm across his mouth in a way that suggested the disgustingness of a flyscreen.

'Ah, you see, it must be you,' I exclaimed. 'I don't know anyone else who would go round kissing flyscreens.'

'Just because you don't see them do it, doesn't mean they don't. In private. You should try it sometime.'

'So,' I said, changing the subject, 'which scooter was yours?'

'The coolest one of course.' I hadn't really inspected them in great detail. There were a couple of PXs I thought, a Lambretta and a cut-down.

'Not the cut-down?'

'No. I like my scooter to look like a scooter. Try again.'

'It would have to be the Lambretta then.'

'Correct. You can double your money if you identify the model.'

'Oh, I don't know.' I threw a few letters out: 'SX, GP, TV, Li?'

'One of those was correct. It is, in fact, a TV175, Series 2.'

'Wow,' I said for the lack of anything else to say.

'Wow, indeed. As I tell my league of acquaintances, you may admire her from afar. You may not touch, you may not breathe close to her.'

'How do you get anywhere then?' I asked. 'Every piece of road dirt must feel like a flint gouging the paintwork.'

'Her paintwork,' he corrected. 'And it does, we just have long recuperative sessions in the garage afterwards. Just me, Florentina and a vat of T-cut.'

'Your Florentina should meet my Luigi,' I said. 'They might get on well.'

'You forget they already have met,' replied Jules. 'Flo felt she was a little too refined for your Luigi although she was open to the idea of taking him under her wing to teach him a few things.'

'Cheek,' I said. I was enjoying myself with Jules. He seemed to have a whole fantasy world in his head that he found indistinguishable from the real world. In front of us the band seemed to have launched into their second encore of 'War!' and the crowd were half in a frenzy and half giving in. More and more people began to drift past us in search of the beer tent. I felt a small kick on the sole of my foot.

'That didn't take you long, did it?' I looked up to see Perry glaring down at me.

'What do you mean?' I asked.

'Well Salty's barely left the campsite and you're already . . .' He pointed between the two of us.

'Already what? We're talking.' I was furious. 'You don't know anything about it.'

'I know what I see.'

Jules got up at this point and stood threateningly over Perry.

'While I don't think Annie needs my support,' he said, 'I would just like to say I think you're taking an antediluvian attitude there.'

'A what?'

'An antediluvian attitude. You don't need to understand it to know it's not good.'

Feeling a bit left out, I stood up too. I saw Sam come up behind Perry and quietly assess the situation. She grabbed hold of his elbow.

'Come on Perry,' she said, 'let's leave them to it.'

'But . . .' he argued.

'Look,' she said to him, 'I'll explain it on the way back.'

'Sorry,' she said to Jules and me, 'he's just a bit drunk.' In a side whisper to me she added 'Nice catch.'

'Right,' said Jules when they'd gone, 'I'm not even going to ask what that was all about. Do you want to come back to mine for a bit? We've got a camper van.'

'Really? Do you have a shower?'

'No, sadly not. Although can you imagine how attractive we'd be if we did? Even Billy would pull.'

He led the way to the opposite side of the campsite from where our tents were. I worried a bit about how I was going to find my way back later. In a way, I was hoping I wouldn't have to.

I recognised Flo when I saw her again. I stopped to admire her for a second.

'Don't touch,' warned Jules, 'and definitely don't sit on her. No bottom touches her except mine.' I imagined that this would be what Lance would be like if he had a scooter like Jules's. They were very different in one way: Lance never told anything but the absolute truth as he saw it, but very similar in another.

Behind the scooters was a VW camper van. It had an awning with a table underneath at which a couple of the boys were sitting. The side door was open and there was a light on inside. It all looked very welcoming.

'Alright Billy, Sandy.' Jules nodded to the boys at the table. They were the two with shaved heads. 'This is Annie.'

'Pleased to meet you, Annie' said the one I presumed was Billy very formally. He stood up and held out his hand. I took it and he shook it very firmly. The other one rubbed his hand on his thigh and held it out too.

'We saw you doing cartwheels earlier,' he said and blushed bright red. Jules patted him on the shoulder.

'He's not got much experience with girls,'' he explained. 'Right shall we go inside?'

Inside there was a stove and a sink and a table at the end with bench seats on either side. I sat down.

'Coffee or tea?' asked Jules as he lit the stove and out a kettle on.

'Oooh, tea, please,' I said.

He produced a packet of bourbons and some jaffa cakes. 'Help yourself.'

'This is all very civilised,' I said. 'I could stay here all week if I had one of these.'

'We have done,' said Jules. 'We came over last weekend. The camper van belongs to Billy's dad. It's his pride and joy. Billy has to phone home every evening to report on how he's looking after it so his dad can sleep at night.' He produced a deck of cards.

'Right,' he said shuffling them, 'tea, biscuits and a game of cards. If that's okay with you?'

We played cards until late. The others: Curly, with the ginger hair and Fred, with the curly hair, joined us. I ended up squashed at the far end of the bench with Jules opposite me.

'Did you lose your friend?' asked Fred.

'Yes, somewhere in the Edwin Starr crowd. You could probably find her, she'll be the last one left dancing.'

'Even after the music's finished?'

'Very probably.'

It was all very easy. I got the sense that Jules was just interested in people. He didn't have particular intentions towards me and that helped me relax. It wasn't that I didn't fancy him but I found it hard to get into the mood sexually when there were so many people around. Not everyone was

66

that sensitive, there were plenty of tents you went past that clearly had people getting it on inside.

'So are you leaving tomorrow?' I asked.

'Got to,' said Jules, 'I'm back at work on Tuesday.'

'Oh? What do you do?'

'He thinks he's an artist,' said Fred.

'I am,' Jules responded. 'Art doesn't just have to be on walls.'

'You don't do graffiti do you?' I asked.

'No,' said Jules slowly, 'that's generally on walls. I work with Billy's dad, spray painting vehicles. I helped do this,' he indicated the van, 'and I did Flo. I'm hoping to pick up more scooter work, maybe some custom stuff.'

'Are you a spray painter too?' I asked Billy.

'No,' he replied. 'I'm studying metallurgy at university.'

'Oh.' I said.

'Yeah,' agreed Jules, 'No one knows what to say in response to that. His dad feels very let down. I had to step in to shore up the family business. I'm like an honorary son.' He dealt another hand of cards. 'And how about you, Annie? We know very little about you except you have a very pretty nose and a lovely smile.'

'And she can cartwheel,' said Sandy.

'I wish I'd never done that now,' I said. 'I wasn't doing it for an audience.'

'Maybe not, but you certainly found one,' said Jules. 'Anyway, about you.'

I gave them the edited highlights: 'I'm seventeen, I'm studying hotel and catering at college, I live with my Mum and Dad in Essex and I ride a Vespa 100.'

'Seventeen,' said Jules, wistfully, 'I remember being seventeen, you're uncorrupted at that age.'

'How old are you then?'

'Nineteen. And with a wisdom beyond my years.'

I had no idea what the time was, but I was getting tired. 'I'd better be going,' I said. 'I've got to find my way back yet.'

'You could sleep here,' said Jules. 'But you'd have to turf one of the boys out.'

'No, it's okay,' I said. 'My friends might be worried about me.'

Actually I didn't think they would. Sam might have described Jules to June and she would probably be willing me not to come back. She always thought you should take up any opportunity offered to you.

'I'll walk you back then,' offered Jules. We extricated ourselves from the back of the van. Jules picked up a torch, 'so we don't trip over guy ropes' he explained. 'I've already done that once this weekend and I don't intend to do it again. Now where are you parked?' I indicated the general direction I thought our tents were in and we set off.'

'I think Fred quite fancied your friend, by the way,' said Jules.

'June.' I said. 'She has a boyfriend.' At least I thought she did, I wasn't exactly sure what was going on with her and Ben.

'And you?' he asked.

'Well I sort of did but as of yesterday, I don't.'

'Oh well, that's good. Or bad.'

'Yeah, well, I was upset at the time,' I explained, 'but doing cartwheels on the beach helps you get it out of your system. And meeting new people.'

'That can help,' said Jules. 'What was he like, your sometime boyfriend?' I hesitated. 'You don't have to tell me,' he continued. 'It just sometimes helps to get your head straight about a person if you talk about them. Sometimes it's really hard to describe them positively and you know they're not good for you.'

I thought for a bit. It was hard to know where to start.

'Well,' I began, 'he's a mechanic. Well, he's not, he doesn't have a job at the moment, but that's what he is by nature. He understands metal better than people, I think. He can put things together and make them work.'

'Sounds like my sort of a person,' said Jules.

'And I guess he likes the certainty of metal and he'd like people to be the same way'. I thought a bit more. 'He's a loyal person. You can trust him. And when he makes a decision he sticks to it.'

'Is that what you love about him?'

'What makes you say I love anything about him?'

'Because of the way you talk about him. Not what you say, but the way you say it.'

'Oh,' I said. I was lost for words.

'Do you think he'd talk about you the same way?

'I don't know. Yes. Probably.' That was the softness in his voice that he seemed to reserve for me.

'Well,' said Jules, 'I'll let you work that one out.'

I thought I'd change the subject. 'You're very smart. . .' I began.

'For a spray painter?' he asked.

'Well, yes.'

'I like to read,' he explained, 'and I like to study people. I like to paint because I've been doing it since I was twelve. I'm good at it and I can be creative but it doesn't mean that's all I know.'

'I like to read,' I said, 'but I don't think I'm smart.'

'You're probably smarter than you think,' he said. 'I hated school, I hated being treated like a child so I've mostly taught myself. That way you can choose what you learn.'

We'd almost reached our tents. I was a bit nervous of bringing Jules any closer in case Perry was about and looking for trouble.

'This is me then,' I said. 'Thanks for walking me back.'

70

'S'alright,' he said. We stood awkwardly for a moment.

'I really enjoyed your company,' I said.

'Yes. Me too,' he replied. 'Maybe we could keep in touch?' He dug in his jeans pocket and pulled out a pen. 'Shall we exchange phone numbers?'

I told him mine and he wrote it on his hand and then wrote his on mine.

'Are you going to Weston?' he asked.

'I don't know yet, it's quite a long way for a weekend.'

'Yeah, it's a local rally for us. Give me a ring though if you decide to go, and we could meet up.'

'I'd like that,' I said.

Suddenly he moved in and wrapped his arms around my back in a hug. I had my face in his chest and breathed in his dark, musky scent. When he let me go I almost fell over.

'See you, Annie,' he said and with a wave he was gone.

Chapter Six

Engine noises woke me early the next morning. June surfaced too and we wandered down to the food stalls together.

There was a clear space next to our tents where a group had packed up and left already and there was a steady stream of scooters heading for the campsite exit.

'I didn't hear you come back last night,' said June.

'No, it was about 2am I think,' I said. 'You and Ben were asleep. I just squashed in beside you.'

'Sam said you were chatting to a tall bloke wearing a hat,' said June.

'Yes. That was Jules. The boy from Alum Bay, the one I liked.'

'He found you in that massive crowd?'

'Yeah, I know. Seems a bit unlikely doesn't it?'

'So did he help you get over Salty?'

'No, not really. Sort of the opposite. He made me think about what I liked about him.'

'Weird.'

'Nice guy, though. Really nice guy. I've got his phone number.' I showed her my hand where the numbers were starting to smudge into one another.

'You'd better write that down before you lose it,' said June, producing an eye pencil and a cigarette packet from the depths of her jacket pocket.

'I could always get it tattooed on instead,' I suggested.

We queued for coffee and I scrubbed my teeth with the corner of a tissue I'd found in my pocket. Basic hygiene had been quite difficult over the weekend and I was beginning to see why khaki was such a popular clothing colour choice as it could withstand being worn for days on end without looking very much worse than it did at the beginning.

'Imagine people like Dave,' I said, 'who are going to have to put a shirt and tie on tomorrow. They won't know what's hit them.'

'Yes,' agreed June. 'It's like a double life.'

I had another week before I was due back at college and had nothing at all planned for that time. At that point it felt as if my life only existed in a field on the Isle of Wight and that everything that had gone before and would come in the future was just a mirage, a dream. I put the feeling down to a lack of sleep playing havoc with my senses. For a moment I could see myself as if I was an onlooker. I watched myself order coffee and fumble a little when taking it and I wondered what I thought of me. I shook my head and luckily the feeling passed.

June and I sat down and I told her a bit more about Jules and his friends including the fact that Fred had shown an interest in her.

'Maybe we should go and find him,' she said. 'Ben's being a bit off with me.'

'They live in Devon though,' I said.

'Almost like being abroad.'

I wondered about that. I was so keen on getting a job somewhere exotic but maybe somewhere like Devon would be different enough. I'd be able to speak the language and get home for Christmas if I wanted to.

'We could go and find them if you wanted,' I said. Even as I said it I knew I didn't want to. It would be really obvious and a bit too keen. Jules could phone me if he was interested.

'Nah,' said June, 'let's leave it. I'm ready to go home. Let the dust settle for a bit. There are plenty of guys out there.'

Back up at the tents Sam was back in charge. Everyone had a job and half the tents had already been packed away. Ben had made a start on mine and looked relieved when I came along to help.

'There's still loads of stuff inside,' he said, 'but Sam was bugging me to start taking it down so I thought I'd better look busy.'

'Well you hold it up while I'll crawl in and sort the stuff out,' I said. 'I'm not keen on suffocating.'

'I saw Lance yesterday,' Ben said as I was sat in the tent, putting all our things into piles.

'Oh?'

'I think he was going to leave you his tent, but he saw you'd moved your stuff. I said we were all going to share yours. I think he wanted to see you before he left.'

'It was probably better this way,' I said.

'Yeah, maybe. I said you'd said bye. He said to tell you to take care of yourself.'

That small thought made me very sad suddenly and I was glad Ben couldn't see my face. I busied myself in the tent for a bit longer.

'Are you going to give us directions for the way home, Sam?' asked Bertie as I eventually emerged.

'No Bertie,' Sam replied. 'Where do you think I've been keeping those? Anyway if you've kept the map for getting here you can just work backwards can't you?'

I saw Bertie's face fall.

'Don't worry Bertie' she said, 'we're sticking together on the way back, aren't we?'

Packing up successfully was difficult. Everything seemed harder to compress down into a size that could fit onto a scooter. I'd also got the dress and shoes I'd bought for the meal out with Lance. I wasn't sure I'd ever wear them again, they felt a bit tainted. I thought about shoving them in one of the bin bags Sam was handing round. My Mum would never agree with me being so wasteful though and eventually I managed to get them rolled up inside my sleeping bag and strapped onto my scooter.

Perry's scooter was parked up alongside mine. We had bumped into each other a couple of times. We each apologised politely but he was clearly being cool with me. I couldn't be bothered to start up a conversation about it, I decided that he could think what he wanted.

Finally, after much swearing and after Sam had confirmed she was happy with the cleanliness of the site, we were ready to go.

We joined the great mass of scooters leaving the campsite and headed in a stream to the ferry terminal. I pitied any car drivers also trying to get across the Solent as they were completely outnumbered.

At the terminal we had just missed a boat and there were already queues for the next one. There seemed to be hundreds of police hanging about although there was little for them to do. I pulled my scooter on to the stand and just sat quietly, taking in the conversations around me. Spirits seemed to be more subdued than on the way over but I heard the word 'Weston' several times and it was clear everyone was making plans for the next rally.

The trip back across the water seemed to take a lot longer than the journey there and I almost dozed off only to be rudely awakened by what seemed to be several hundred scooters firing up in unison. We'd planned to regroup a few hundred yards outside the terminal at Portsmouth and so I took the opportunity to have a look for where Lance had left his scooter. Of course it was nowhere to be seen. I hoped that he was on his way to fixing it and had decided where he was heading once he had.

The journey back to Essex was long and slow. Sam had designated Perry the leader again but he kept having electrical problems and at one stage it seemed as though we were stopping at every single lay-by.

'Can't I ride with you?' whispered June who was riding pillion, 'he's driving me mad.'

Eventually we came across a Little Chef and we all piled in except for Perry who we left outside to continue working on his scooter. I took pity on him and took him out a cup of tea but he barely acknowledged it. Sitting inside I took some pleasure in watching him drink it though.

On the road almost blindly following the scooter in front was the perfect time to think things through, but I felt too close to the weekend's events and needed more space and time. Instead I concentrated on the changing surroundings: tree, hedge, house, house, tree, car, junction, tree. Above us a dark cloud threatened from the west and a couple of times showers broke out, sufficient to wet the road and make me wish I had another layer of clothes on.

Once we got through the Dartford Tunnel we were on home turf and the sights were more familiar. Even the road signs seemed friendlier somehow. Finally we arrived back at the Red Cow car park where we'd started from three and a half days before. It had only been a long weekend but it felt like a lifetime. We made plans to meet at the next soul night and went our separate ways.

At home, my parents were in the garden, Dad digging over a patch of earth that had previously contained potatoes and Mum deadheading and generally worrying over her roses. Mum took one look at me and shoved me upstairs to the bathroom, turning the shower on full and hot. My clothes seemed to have gained the ability to stand up on their own. I left them outside the door and Mum immediately put them in the wash. I stood for a long time under the shower and then put the plug in the bath and sat as the water slowly rose around me. Eventually fearing I was going to fall asleep and drown, I got up, wrapped towels around my body and hair, lay down on my bed and fell into a long and deep sleep.

Chapter Seven

'We missed you,' said Mum. I was sitting at the kitchen table, eating slice after slice of toast with marmalade whilst she was doing the ironing. 'You seemed to be gone for an awfully long time.'

'It seemed like a long time to me too,' I agreed. 'You should come with us next time,' I said. 'There's no age restrictions. There were definitely some Mods from the sixties there, I'm sure.'

'I'd need a scooter,' said Mum, 'and a sidecar, Dad would probably want to come too.'

She pulled something blue out of the pile of washing and held it up. 'What's this?' she asked.'

'It's a dress,' I said. 'I needed a dress.'

'On a scooter rally?'

'Yes.' I hadn't been intending to tell her much about the weekend although I was sure she'd want to know how I got on with Lance.

'Lance took me for a meal,' I explained. 'I needed an outfit.'

'Oh? And did you have a nice time?'

'Sort of yes and sort of no,' I said. It seemed to start out alright and then he broke up with me.'

'Oh, love.' Mum put the iron down and came over to give me a hug. 'Did he say why?'

'Well, yes. It's very long and complicated though. I think he thought I was too much for him.'

'Maybe you are, you know,' she said, smoothing back my hair. 'You're not very demanding, but your mind is off up there,' she indicated the ceiling, 'sometimes. And that can get a bit much for some people.' She saw the look on my face. 'That's not a bad thing though.'

'Anyway,' I said to change the subject, 'he didn't know whether he was going to be at his Mum's or his Dad's or whatever, so he said he might phone. Although that was before. .' I stopped short. He'd also said we might meet at Weston but that was also 'before'. 'So maybe not,' I finished.

'Sometimes these things just take a bit of time,' said Mum.

'I did give our number to someone else though,' I said, brightening at the thought. 'A boy called Jules,' I pronounced it the French way, 'from Devon.'

'So if the phone rings, it might be for you?' she asked. I nodded.

'Or, more likely, it won't ring at all.'

'Look,' said Mum, 'I might get my college letter tomorrow. If I do, do you want to go shopping? They've given me a book list and I'd like to get ahead on the reading.'

The post came early to our house so I woke to find my Mum sitting at the end of my bed waving her college acceptance letter.

'I start next week,' she said. 'The same time as you, I think.'

So we went for a celebratory trip to the shops. Mum spent ages choosing some skirts and blouses from Marks and Spencer for her new role as a student and then we went and had a giggle at what passed for clothing in Top Shop.

'I suppose you'd rather go to the Army Surplus,' said Mum.

'You say that like it's a bad thing,' I replied.

Afterwards we hit the bookshop. I left Mum with her book list in the Business and Accounting section and I settled down in the travel section. Hidden on the bottom shelf I found the book I was looking for.

Later, as I slurped on a strawberry milkshake in a café, I showed Mum what I'd bought.

'Working Your Way Around the World,' she read.

'Yes.' I showed her the inside of the book. 'See, it's all divided into countries and they tell you the kind of work you can do and give you some addresses to write to.

'So what do you want to do?'

'I don't know yet. I'll tell you once I've read the book.' We settled down to read, me with my book and Mum with 'Travel and Tourism, Level 1'.

I spent the next couple of days with my head in the book. There was lots of advice for University students wanting to work over the summer holiday but I was looking for longer term work so I discounted those. No grape-picking and definitely no winter sports. I thought I ought to look for something that made use of my college course and so I ticked anything that looked as though it would require catering or customer service skills. By the end of the week I had narrowed the choice down to four options and began writing letters requesting further information.

On Monday morning, Mum and I were both getting ready for college. She was on a day release programme so was only doing one day a week. She'd been into the travel agents and they'd offered her a Saturday morning shift to begin with. She was happy and nervous in equal quantities. Luckily her college was the other side of town to mine, so there wasn't any suggestion that I'd give her a lift in. She left the house before me and I gave her a wave as I passed her at the bus stop.

At college, June was sitting on the wall of the motorbike park waiting for me.

'Are you ready for this?' she asked as we pushed our way through the year's new intake who were all gathering nervously in the entrance to the building. 'We're the big guys this year, everyone will have to look up to us.' I saw a couple of boys notice my crash helmet and whisper to one another.

82

In our form room, everyone was comparing their summer holidays. Some were talking excitedly about their trips abroad whilst Steve was boasting about his work experience in a London hotel, 'Kensington, you know,' he said. 'It's all Middle-Eastern royal families, I made tons of dosh in tips.'

'I thought you were looking a little pale,' said June. 'You can't have got much sun with all that brown-nosing.'

'I got enough,' he said defensively. 'What exotic places did you make it to then?'

'Debenhams' coffee shop and a weekend in a tent on the Isle of Wight,' she said. 'Beat that.'

'How about you, Annie?' asked Steve.

'Ibiza, and a weekend in a tent on the Isle of Wight.' I replied. 'It was the place to be.'

'Obviously,' he said. 'Oh, by the way, I would invite you both to my 18th, but it's at Revelations and you have to be eighteen to get in.'

'That excludes most of us then,' said June. 'Who are you inviting, your new royal friends?'

'Well some of the people from the hotel might come down for the night and both Andy and Paul are eighteen already.'

'No girls then?'

'No, we'll meet some in there, I expect. Grown up girls, not kids, like you two.'

June and I both had birthdays in December so we weren't that much younger.

'Do you have any plans for yours?' June asked me and, when I shook my head, 'Maybe we should do something together?'

'Yeah, good idea,' I said. 'Julia had a meal in a posh restaurant for hers. But that's because she's boring. Maybe we should go somewhere we can dance. Not Revelations though.'

'No.'

'Ben wouldn't be able to get in, for one.'

'No, although he's been very cool to me since we got back. He made some comment about my snoring, we had a big row and I've hardly seen him after that.'

'And you both looked so happy on the Friday.'

'Yeah, that's what a weekend in a tent on the Isle of Wight will do to you. They should make every couple do it as a test of their relationship. I wonder how many would survive.'

'Talking of which,' she continued, 'have you thought about Weston?'

'I've thought about it,' I replied. 'I've even looked it up on a map. Do you know how far it is?'

'No.'

'Dad reckons it's almost two hundred miles. That's going to take us five hours even on a good day.'

'Oh, I was going to ask if you'd take me if you were going.'

'That'll take even longer, with your weight on the back. Six hours.'

84

'We could leave here at lunchtime on Friday, be there in time for the evening, come back on Sunday afternoon.'

'Well, maybe,' the thought of going with June did make it more appealing somehow. 'I'll think about it.' I said.

The week passed in a flurry of new timetables, new subjects and talks on 'greater expectations' and 'career planning'. I was pleased to see that Friday afternoon was labelled 'personal study period' on our schedule as this meant we would be able to sneak off to the rally without anyone noticing that we had gone.

On Wednesday when June and I were sitting in the common room, we were approached by two boys.

'Is that your scooter outside?' one of them asked me. Since I had my crash helmet on the table and was wearing a jacket with rally patches sewn on this was an easy assumption to make.

'Yes,' I said hoping to give a sense of 'what of it?'

'It's only you don't see many girls on scooters.' They were clearly impressed.

'Well, you do if you know where to look,' I replied. 'There's quite a few of us.'

'That was why we were asking. You see Phil and me, would like to . '

'Meet girls on scooters?' June interrupted. The boy who wasn't Phil blushed.

'Well, yeah. Not just that though, we'd like to know where everyone hangs out.'

'Apart from here, you mean?' I said, indicating the seats June and I were occupying. 'Well there's the motorbike park in town, you must have seen some scooters there and then there's a soul night at the Red Cow. Every second Wednesday, next one's tonight.'

'Oh, okay. Thanks.' They went to leave. 'Maybe see you there then?'

'Maybe,' I agreed.

'Oh God,' said June when they'd gone, 'you've just got yourself your first groupies.'

'Do you think?' I couldn't say I wasn't flattered.

I went round to June's after college finished and I took her up to the Red Cow. I was getting used to having a pillion passenger now. It did slow us down but once I'd got over the fear of toppling over with us both on-board, it was nice to have a companion.

We parked up with the other Sessex Girls and hung around the car park for a while. Dave showed up with Perry riding pillion.

'I had to take my scoot into the garage,' he said mournfully. 'I'm just hoping they can fix it in time for Weston.'

'It does make you miss Salty, doesn't it,' said Sam. 'He might have grumbled a bit but he would still have fixed it for you and would have stayed up all night to do it if necessary.'

'You're talking about him as if he was dead,' I said and then had a sudden worry that it was because he was and I hadn't heard about it.

'Well, no one's heard from him,' said Dave. 'Unless you have?' I shook my head. 'So we have to assume he's alive until we hear anything different. He never was one to pick up the phone.'

'You watch,' said Sam. 'We'll all be sat around at Weston and he'll just show up.'

'Yeah,' agreed Dave, 'and we'll all be really pleased to see him even though we're all really annoyed with him.'

'So everyone's going then?' I asked.

'It looks like it,' said Dave. 'How about you two?'

'Thinking about it,' I said. 'June's trying to persuade me.

'Well, you should,' said Sam. 'It'll be your last chance until next Easter.'

'When are you all going?' I asked.

'Thursday evening, I think,' said Sam. 'Dave and I have taken Friday off work.'

'And I'm pulling a sickie,' said Perry.

'Andrea and I can't get going until Friday evening,' said Sarah. 'We'll be showing up at midnight and stumbling around looking for you all in the dark.'

'Looks like it's just you and me then,' I said to June. She wasn't listening. She was looking at the other end of the car park.

'Don't look now,' she said. 'I think your admirers have just arrived.'

'Oh God,' I said and grabbed June by the arm. 'Quick, inside now.' We ran across the road and up the stairs. 'Hopefully they didn't see us.'

'You can't avoid them forever,' said June, heading straight for the dance floor. 'At some point you're going to be presented with a declaration of adoration and you're going to have to let them down gently.'

'How about,' I said, joining her on the floor, 'saying that a girl scooterist would never go out with someone without a scooter and is unlikely to even consider anyone with a 50 Special. That ought to put them off for a bit.'

'Yeah,' said June, 'It's worth a try.'

Over the next couple of days the boys seemed to have claimed our spot in the common room. 'Phil and non-Phil' we'd named them since we didn't know the other one's name. We didn't even know what course they were on, 'Secretarial, I'm guessing' said June. We could have just talked to them and found out, but avoiding them had become a bit of a game. On Friday therefore we went into town at lunchtime.

I was queuing up in Smiths to pay for a magazine when I felt a tap on my back and someone say: 'Annie, isn't it?' I turned around to see Lance's Mum queuing up behind me.

'Oh, hello, Mrs Morales,' I said, 'How are you?'

'Oh, you know, getting by,' she said. 'It's ever so quiet now Lance has gone. I have to keep myself busy.' She waved a stack of women's magazines at me.

'He didn't come back then?' Even as I asked it, I knew he hadn't. Someone would have seen him if he was back in town.

'No, I haven't seen him in weeks. Haven't heard from him either.' It was my turn to pay. I put the magazine on the counter and delved into my purse for the money.

'I don't suppose you . . .?' she continued. I shook my head but didn't really know what she was asking. Had I seen him, heard from him, did I know where he was? The answer to all of these was no, but I didn't know how much she knew. Mrs Morales counted out her money, she only seemed to have just enough. I waited for her and we walked to the exit together.

Outside we stood there awkwardly. June hovered for a moment and then went to sit on a wall nearby.

'I saw him at the Isle of Wight,' I said. She looked confused. 'The scooter rally.'

'Oh, when was that?' He clearly really hadn't been in touch for a bit.

'The weekend before last,' I explained. 'The Bank Holiday weekend.'

'And you're still . . .together?' she asked.

'No.' I shook my head.

'See, I told him,' she said. 'I said he wasn't treating your properly.'

'Actually it was he who broke up with me,' I explained. That confused her.

89

'Look,' she said, 'I've got to go catch my bus, but would you come round sometime? I could do with having a chat about Lance. Maybe there's quite a bit you could tell me.'

'Um, yes. Yes of course.'

'I work in the mornings but I'm home every afternoon and evening. You can just drop in. You know where we .. sorry, I live?'

'Yes, I remember. Sometime next week?'

'Yes, any day.'

With a wave she was off at a run towards the bus park.

'Who was that?' asked June, watching her departing back.

'Lance's Mum. She clearly doesn't know where he is. She invited me round.'

'Are you going?'

'I said I would.'

I was actually quite curious and decided to go and see Mrs Morales on Tuesday when we had an early finish at college. I think she must have heard the sound of my scooter as she came out into the front garden to meet me.

'I thought you were Lance for a moment,' she said. 'But I'm not disappointed it's you. Come on in.'

She led me through the kitchen and into the front room and went to make a cup of tea. I sat down for a moment but then spotted a frame of photos on the wall and went to have a look at them.

They were Lance's school photos, seemingly one every year from the age of about five to fifteen.

In the first photos he looked scared, then he moved through cheeky, then cute, then finally surly. His hair started off short, got progressively longer and messier until the age of about twelve when he was suddenly shorn bald before returning to long and messy again. At seven he was missing his front teeth and at six, eleven and fourteen he had scabs in different places on his face. In the early photos he wore home-made shirts, including one very bright floral one, and in the later ones a white or grey school shirt and a tie with a variety of differently sized knots.

I wondered what I would have thought about him if we'd been at the same school. In the early years he looked like he'd be everybody's friend but by the end he looked like the problem pupil, the one who's forever sitting outside the Head's office.

Mrs Morales came in with the tea and a packet of digestives. She saw me looking at the photos and came over.

'That's my Lance,' she said. 'He used to be such a lovely boy.'

'He does look sweet here,' I said, pointing to the early photos.

'Yes, he was until he went to secondary school. He was such a mummy's boy. We'd do everything together. And then he grew up.'

'You don't know when the point is that they stop listening to you,' she continued. 'It just happens and then you spend all your time arguing.'

She sat down in defeat. 'I do miss him. I even miss the arguing.'

'You'd have him back?' I asked.

'I would. Of course I would. But he won't ask because he's so bloody-minded.' She paused for a moment. 'That was why I asked you round, Annie. I thought you could tell me what you knew about what he's been up to. You said you'd seen him.'

'Yes.' I didn't know how much she knew so didn't really know where to start.

'We had a row,' she said, 'I don't know if he said.'

'He did . . . mention it,' I admitted.

'I can't remember how it started but I do remember telling him he wasn't treating you right. He's not had a lot of girlfriends, and I was trying to help him out, give him some advice, you know?'

I nodded.

'Anyway he took against that. And he was going anyway, I was jealous, I suppose. You know his Dad can't do no wrong in his eyes, even though he's a piece of . . .' She stopped herself. 'And maybe I said some things I shouldn't have.'

I liked Mrs Morales. She had an honesty to her that reminded me of Lance. But I wary of revealing things that he might have told me in confidence. 'He did think he wouldn't be welcome back,' I said.

'Was he thinking of coming back then?' she asked hopefully. I realised that of course if she hadn't heard from Lance since he went up to his

Dad's she wouldn't know how he had got on up there.

'Well, yes. I don't think it was working out up in Manchester,' I said carefully. I watched as her face lightened.

'Oh? He didn't say why, did he?'

'He did,' I said. 'But I'm not sure it's my place to say.'

'No. No, of course not,' she replied. 'See, I knew you were classy, most people would just have wanted to gossip.'

'So,' she continued, 'he came down south and you saw him then?'

'Yes. And his scooter broke down and so he was going to someone's garage to fix it at the end of the weekend. But he didn't know where he was going to go after that.'

'But he hasn't come back here.'

'No. He said you didn't want him. I thought you probably would have him back but he wasn't prepared to phone up and find out.'

'Too bloody pig-headed,' she said. 'We're both as bad as each other.'

'So,' I said. 'I've seen his friends, Dave and Perry, and no one's heard from him. So we don't know where he is right now.'

'Perhaps back up at his Dad's?'

'Maybe,' I said. 'He was thinking of going to Weston-Super-Mare. It's another scooter rally, on this weekend.'

'Are you going?'

'I'm thinking about it.'

93

'And would you see him if you did?'

'I expect so. I don't think he's hiding from anyone on purpose. I don't think he's hiding from me.' I wondered if he'd thought about me at all and if he had if he thought of me with longing, the way I was increasingly thinking about him.

'Well, if you do, would you tell him to phone me?'

'Yes, of course.'

Mrs Morales and I talked a little more. She offered me tea but I thought I ought to go. I left with promises to keep in touch and to let her know if I heard from Lance before the weekend.

Chapter Eight

Having made so many promises, I felt that I had to go to Weston. I told June of my decision on Wednesday morning and she immediately began making excited plans.

'It'll be more fun going just the two of us, won't it?' she said. I wasn't sure. I had enjoyed the safety of a group going down to the Isle of Wight and the knowledge that someone would be there to help if we broke down. Luigi had been pretty reliable until now, but there had to be some point where he started to go wrong. I had clocked up a few thousand miles on him now and I made the most of not having to plan my transport ahead of time, I could just go where-ever whenever.

I did though, have to think about how much stuff June would bring and how we would fit it all on. I packed as much stuff as I could in with the tent and sleeping bag and hoped for the best. On Friday morning I brought all the stuff into college and crammed it into my locker.

'So much for leaving without anyone noticing,' I said to June when she arrived.

'What's this?' asked Steve. 'Don't tell me, Outward Bound. You're both going for your Duke of Edinburgh's award.'

'Yeah,' said June, 'I'm going for 'Endurance on the Dance Floor' and Annie's trying to break the record for two hundred miles two-up on a 100cc scooter.'

'That's the slowest time,' I said, 'not the quickest.'

'Well, good luck,' he said. 'I won't be surprised if you don't show up on Monday morning although I will rat on you to the Principal.'

'You would as well,' said June.

'Yes, I have my reputation to protect,' he replied.

'What's Ben up to this weekend?' I asked June when Steve had gone.

'Oh, who knows?' she replied. 'I told him I was going with you and he just muttered something and stormed off. I think he's jealous of you.'

'Of me?'

'Yeah, cos we get on so well,' she explained. 'So, anyway, last time we were all coupled up and this time we're footloose and fancy-free. We'd better make the most of it.'

I wasn't bothered myself about getting off with anyone. I hoped to see Lance and I did think I'd like to spend more time with Jules if I got the chance but I didn't expect anything from either of them.

'Did you phone your French friend?' asked June, reading my thoughts.

'No, but I've brought his phone number,' I said.

'That's not much use, if you're both in Weston, is it? I was hoping you'd introduce me to his friend. Especially if they've come with the camper van.'

'Well if they have, they'll be easier to find, won't they?' I said.

We sat through the morning's classes. June was bouncy with barely concealed excitement and I was twitchy with nerves. As soon as we were let out at noon we made a rush for the lockers and hauled our stuff down to the motorbike park where we wrestled for ten minutes with bungee cords. Phil and Non-Phil appeared just as we seemed to have got everything packed on.

'Where are you going?' asked Non-Phil.

'Scooter rally, of course,' said June. 'Don't worry, you too will one day be old enough to do this.' They watched enviously as we made a slightly jumpy exit and headed out towards the main road. June waved grandly.

'There, that showed them,' she shouted in my ear.

To begin with we made pretty good progress. We'd started early enough and there wasn't too much traffic. We headed through the H's – Harlow, Hertford, Hatfield, Hemel, with its magic roundabout, then down past RAF Halton and on to Oxford.

We stopped just past Oxford for petrol and food. I bought the petrol and June bought the food so I treated myself to jam on my toasted teacake.

'I reckon we're halfway,' I said, stirring my tea.

'And how long did that take us?' asked June.

'Just over three hours.' I stretched my finger muscles out. 'One day I'll get stuck in this position,' I said, making a claw shape.

We watched as a stream of scooters went past the window. 'Looks like we're heading in the right direction at least,' said June.

The second half of the journey was much slower. We hit traffic around Swindon and I got lost negotiating another magic roundabout. June suggested we stop at a welcoming looking pub near Bath that had some scooters parked out in front of it, but I knew if we stopped I'd never get going again. We pressed on, south of Bristol and finally I got a glimpse of the sea ahead of us. The sun was dipping down towards the horizon and the sky was beginning to turn pink and orange and I could feel my spirits lift.

'Nearly there,' I shouted, just as we were overtaken by another gang of scooterists all shouting and bibbing horns.

We followed the scooters through the town to a large sports field somewhere in the middle. As usual there was a big queue to get in so we parked up for a moment.

'My Mum said I had to phone as soon as we got here,' I said to June. 'She's worried cos there's just the two of us.'

I left June in charge of the scooter and walked down the road until I found a phone box. Standing in there, waiting for Mum to answer, I watched more scooters drive past. Just as she answered I saw one that looked like Lance's: green, with an image of what looked like a tree on it. I nearly hung up the phone but Mum was on the other end wondering who the silent caller was.

'Did you see him?' I asked June when I got back.

'See who?'

'Lance. I thought I saw his scooter go past.'

'Oh no, but I wasn't really looking. Anyway if he's here, he'll be with the others won't he?'

'Maybe.'

We spent twenty minutes riding slowly around the site looking for Dave and Sam's scooters.

'It'll be the cleanest spot,' said June, 'if Sam's got anything to do with it. If you see a discarded beer can, you know it's not them.'

We found them eventually up by a hedge spread out as far as they could so there would be room for us all to join them. There was no sign of Lance.

I didn't want to sound too keen, so I didn't mention to Dave that I thought I'd seen him. The more I thought about it, the more uncertain I became that it had actually been his scooter anyway.

I let June put the tent up and I lay out flat on the grass alternately flexing and relaxing my muscles.

'You can walk into town,' said Dave, sitting down beside me. 'We found a couple of good pubs earlier that we thought we'd go back to this evening. Maybe we can leave a note on one of the tents for the others, to let them know where we are.'

June, I knew, was up for a heavy night so I helped her finish putting up the tent and we joined the others on the walk into town. A pint of snakebite later and I found I was up for a heavy night too. There was no music in the first pub we'd gone into so we went in search of somewhere more lively. There were gangs of scooterists also roaming the town and we ended up merging with a group from Birmingham who reckoned they had a good tip for a pub that played soul music. By the time we got there, there were about thirty of us, all piling into the pub at once.

Lost in the middle of the crowd someone handed me a pint I hadn't ordered and I took a sip from it quickly before anyone realised they'd given it to the wrong person. Suddenly arms came around me from behind and closed over my eyes. A voice in my ear said: 'You said you were going to phone me.'

The hands dropped down to my shoulders and turned me around and I found I was looking at Jules' chest.

'Yes, sorry,' I said. I didn't have a good reason as to why I hadn't phoned so I didn't try.

'Who are you with?' he asked. I pointed vaguely over to where the others were still queuing, trying to get drinks.

'We're over here,' he said and I could see his friends sitting around a table by the window.

I shouted to June to join us and followed Jules to his table.

'This is June,' I said, when she arrived. I think you've met, briefly. They all nodded and I saw Fred's eyes light up as he spotted her. 'You can call me Fred,' he said to her.

'That's not his real name,' explained Jules. 'Someone once thought he looked like the guy off the flour packet.'

'Yeah, well,' said Fred. 'It's better than Dennis.' He pulled up a stool and June squashed in between him and Sandy who blushed bright red when she accidently put her hand on his knee.

'Have you brought your camper van this time?' I asked.

'No,' said Jules. 'Unfortunately Billy's Dad found a tiny stain on one of the seats that no one can account for and we're currently banned from using it.'

The Birmingham lot had been wrong about the pub playing soul music. It did have a jukebox so everyone was choosing the most scooter-related tunes. There was some Beatles and a Secret Affair track and both were being played on repeat interspersed with some Wham! and Duran Duran songs presumably chosen by the few disgruntled locals who had been overrun in their own pub.

'We're only here this weekend,' shouted somebody when 'Twist and Shout' came on for the fourth time, 'make the most of us.'

June, at least, wasn't torn between dancing and chatting and she settled down to find about more about Fred. That left me free to talk to Jules.

'So,' he said, 'what books have you been reading recently?'

I don't think anyone had asked me that question before and momentarily I didn't know how to answer.

'I've been reading a book about working abroad,' I said finally, 'if that counts.'

'Yeah? Are you going travelling?'

'Maybe, when I've finished college next summer.'

'I've always fancied touring Europe on my scooter,' he said. 'You know, through France and down to Southern Spain, perhaps. Maybe take a couple of months to do it.'

'That does sound good,' I agreed. 'Though I'm not sure my scooter's very suitable for that.'

'Ah, but you have to think about possibilities, not limitations,' said Jules. 'You've passed your test, haven't you?' I nodded. 'Well, then you could get a bigger scooter. If that was something you wanted to do.'

I was distracted by June who was making wild gestures with her hands to catch my attention.

She was pointing in the direction of the bar and mouthing something.

'What?' I shouted above the noise of the pub.

'L–A–N-C-E,' she spelt out.

I looked over to the bar and saw Lance talking to Dave and Perry. Suddenly the room felt too hot and too crowded. I didn't know what to do. I wanted to speak to him, to find out what he'd been up to and to tell him that I had seen his Mum, but not in the middle of a busy pub.

'Who's that?' aske Jules.

'That's Lance,' I replied. 'The one I told you about.'

'And how are things with you two?'

'No news. I haven't seen him since Isle of Wight, or heard from him.'

Lance looked pretty happy I thought. He was sharing a joke with Dave. I watched him lean in to say something and watched as Dave pointed in my direction. Lance turned around to look and I saw his face change. As if in slow-motion the corners of his mouth dropped and his face took on a scowl. I was in the middle of a wave but dropped my hand. I saw him mouth something and Perry answer, all the while looking in our direction. Perry had a kind of triumphant look on his face.

'Uh oh,' said June, who had been watching too.

'What's that?' asked Jules. I turned back to look at her.

'Well, it looks as though Lance has spotted that Annie's sitting with you and he's not very happy about it. It also looks like Perry's said something to stir it all up.'

I found I was shaking but not from nerves or cold. I took a moment to consider what emotion I was feeling and decided it was anger, an emotion I experienced so rarely I didn't recognise it.

'He doesn't have any right,' I said, almost spitting it out. 'He broke up with me,'

'I don't know about you guys,' said Jules to the table in general, 'but I've had enough of it in here. Shall we go and see if anything's happening down on the front?' He got up and his friends followed suit.

'Are you two coming? He said to June and me. I looked across at June.

'I am,' I said. June hesitated then said 'Me too.'

Jules held the door open and I ducked underneath his arm. I couldn't resist looking back at Lance but he had turned away. I caught Perry's eye though and he seemed to have a self-satisfied look about him that turned slightly to sorrow when he saw me looking. At some point I would need to find out what he had said to Lance, but that wasn't going to happen right now.

June put her arm through mine and we walked down the street together. I had so many conflicting thoughts going round my head I couldn't get them straight.

'He broke up with me,' I said again. 'So I shouldn't care what he thinks. Why do I care what he thinks? And why does he think what he thinks?'

'I expect,' said Jules, coming up behind us, 'it'll come under the heading of 'indecent haste'. His friend was the one who saw us at the Isle of Wight, right?' I nodded. 'Well he'll probably have said that he saw us together on that Sunday night. And your chap . .'

'Lance,' said June.

'Yes, Lance, will have boiled over at the thought that you could move on so quickly,'

'Even if I haven't'

'Yup. The facts aren't very important. The point is he thinks someone is moving in on what he still regards as his territory. It's basic male psychology.'

'Men,' I said. 'They are such arses.'

'Thanks,' said Jules. 'Unfortunately we're not going to change so you're going to have to get used to it.'

'So have I made it better or worse by leaving now?'

'Who knows? It depends on how he feels about you deep down probably. What he thinks about you when he's able to think rationally.'

'If he's able to think rationally,' said June.

'Indeed,' agreed Jules. 'I do know I've made it worse for myself. Well, better and worse.'

'How do you mean?'

'Well, right now, I'm the winner, I'm top dog, if you like. You left with me, didn't you?'

105

'Yes.'

So if I bump into him later, he won't be able to let that pass, he'll have to try and balance it up somehow, probably by giving me a bloody nose.'

I had never seen Lance fight or even threaten someone but I did think he would be capable of it.

'Sorry,' I said to Jules.

'It's alright,' he said. 'You might think though, if we did get into a fight, who would you be rooting for?'

'You, obviously. He's in the wrong.'

'You say that now but you might not feel the same when we're actually throwing punches.'

'I've never had anyone fight over me,' said June.

'Are you sure?' Somehow it seemed as though this ought to be something that happened all the time to June; she changed her partners so often.

'Yes,' she said. 'Maybe they just don't care enough.'

'I don't suppose that's got much to do with it,' said Jules. 'It's mostly about possession. You know, we're all secretly playing 'see who has the best stuff when the music stops'?'

'But girlfriends aren't possessions,' I said.

'You don't think so? Haven't you ever listened to men when they talk about their girl?'

'That doesn't explain why they don't fight over me though,' said June.

'But it could,' argued Jules. 'I don't know you well enough, but maybe you go into a

106

relationship with the main aim of getting what you want out of it and that makes you a bit different. It changes the man's expectations.'

'How about me then?' I asked.

'Well, I'm thinking that you're very different. Quite innocent and maybe a bit vulnerable. Boys probably want to protect you, but to do so they've got to own you in some way. The reason Lance is likely to want to have a go at me is that I've taken away his protection privileges.'

'Wow,' said June, 'That's deep.'

'And also quite depressing,' I added.

'Of course,' Jules continued, 'we don't actually know that's what your guy is feeling. Maybe he's just wondering if I'm worthy of you.' He thought for a moment. 'We could go and look for him and find out.'

'Are you looking for a fight?' asked June.

'No, I can usually talk my way out of them,' he said. 'It does get the adrenaline flowing though.'

We'd arrived at the end of the street and there was a big crowd of people hanging about in front of the pier. We skirted round them and headed left along the seafront. Below us the beach seemed to stretch away for miles. I couldn't even see where the sea began. There were small groups of people dotted about the beach and a larger livelier looking group further ahead of us. As we got closer we could hear music and some people seemed to be dancing.

'I reckon that's the Minehead lot,' said Fred who was just up ahead of us.

'How can you tell?' asked June.

'That's what they do,' said Jules, 'hang out on the beach. They'll have a barbeque going probably.'

'Shall we join them?' asked Fred.

'Can do, if you girls don't mind,' said Jules. 'I reckon they'll have enough to share.'

'Emma will be there though,' said Billy.

'That's okay,' replied Jules. 'I reckon I can handle her.'

I wasn't sure I was ready to meet a whole gang of new people but June looked keen so we followed the others on to the beach.

'If I say I want to go, will you come with me?' I whispered to June. 'I'm not sure I'll find my way back on my own.'

'Of course,' said June. She grabbed my hand and gave it a squeeze.

As we got closer there were shouts of recognition from the group on the beach. There seemed to be more than a dozen of them. One boy came up and jumped on Sandy, wrestling him to the ground.

'We've joined up with this lot on a few rallies,' explained Jules. 'This is how we greet each other. They pick on Sandy because he's the easiest target.'

'I've brought some people to meet you,' he shouted above the noise. 'This is Annie and June, all the way from sunny Essex.' I waved self-consciously. Jules introduced a few of the group who were closest to us. There were three or four girls and one was indeed named Emma. She had a sharp angled haircut and was very blonde and pale. She looked delicate despite being clothed in combat trousers and a flight jacket. Jules bent down to kiss her. He kissed her cheek but in a very familiar rather than a friendly way. We smiled warily at each other. I wanted to tell her that she didn't have anything to be suspicious of, but felt this was assuming too much so I just said 'Hi'.

Jules seemed to have some catching up to do so I followed June who had found a boy attempting to create a dance step diagram on the sand using his footprints and dotted lines to show which foot should go where.

'Try it out,' he suggested. June had a few goes but it just looked as though she was doing a complicated hopscotch.

'No, you need more glide,' the boy said and tried to demonstrate but tripped and kicked sand over all his hard work. 'Now I'm going to have to start over again,' he grumbled.

I was starting to get a bit cold so I edged us over towards the barbeque to see if there was any warmth to be had. Two boys were hunched over it, obsessively turning sausages but they moved over to give us room.

'It's a good job you came,' said one of them. 'Si here seems to think he's feeding a football crowd.' He pointed to the sausages with his tongs. 'We'd never eat all of this lot.'

Si tutted. 'Jon's not got the experience with beach barbeques that I have,' he said. 'The rule is

109

you always cater for three times as many people as are there at the start because everything takes so bloody long to cook that by the time you're done, the people you started off with are starving so they eat twice as much as you think they are going to and the smell has attracted loads of new people.'

'Plus,' he added, 'you've got to feed the stray dog that always shows up.' He did indeed have a dog sat down by his feet waiting for sausages to be fed to him.

Some of the others began crowding round, looking for food. 'Come on, Si,' complained one of them, 'you said this was going to be ready in half an hour over an hour ago.'

'Nearly there,' said Si, clearly under pressure. He put Jon to work tearing rolls in half and began handing out the food.

'There you go, ladies,' he said, handing us the hot dogs, 'as you're guests you can have the first ones.'

'Oh, yeah, kill them off first,' said someone from the back.

June and I went a sat a little way away from the crowd. I looked for Jules but couldn't see him anywhere. June saw me looking.

'He's gone off with that girl he introduced us to,' she said. She pointed in the direction of where I assumed the sea must be. I could just see two people standing very close together.

'Oh.' I felt my stomach knot.

June grinned and kicked the side of my leg with hers. 'Now you're in Salty's position. You've

110

seen Jules with someone else and you've suddenly realised how much you wanted him.'

'Yeah, I suppose. Shouldn't I be looking to fight her then?'

'Good idea,' said June, 'cat fight. That'd get the party going.'

The music had died a bit but someone put new batteries in the ghetto blaster that was supplying it and it began again with renewed vigour. June and I decided to join in with the dancing.

Sandy sidled up. 'Couldn't you girls incorporate some cartwheels into that routine?' he asked.

'Okay' said June, giving him a bit of a shove, 'now you're beginning to get a bit creepy.' He moved away and started dancing on his own, a little sadly. Fred came up and, despite June's dancing being something not easily turned into a paired experience, started dancing close and trying to match her moves. I watched her try to resist him for a bit but then give in and take the lead. I found dancing on the sand to be quite hard so after a couple of tracks I sat down on the edge of the group and just sang along quietly to the songs that I knew.

Chapter Nine

Sitting on the beach watching the dancing, I began to realise how tired I was. College seemed to have happened about three days ago, not that morning. I wondered if I even had enough energy to walk back to the campsite, wherever that was. I could feel myself drifting, my head nodding in time to the distant sound of the waves.

I don't know how long I had been asleep or even if I had been asleep but when someone sat down next to me I jumped, not sure where I was. My head felt thick and my tongue caked in sausage fat.

Blearily I looked to see who had disturbed me. It was Jules, on his own now. The music was still playing and people were still dancing. For a while I couldn't see June but then I spotted her, seemingly entwined with Fred. Either that hadn't taken long or I really had been asleep.

'Sorry,' said Jules, 'did I wake you?'

'Yes,' I said. 'Good thing you did though. The beach is not a good place for falling asleep. Anything could have happened.'

'Ah,' he said, 'I was keeping an eye on you.'

'Where's your friend?' I asked.

'Emma? She's gone off with someone. Gone to get some drinks I think.'

'Is she your girlfriend?'

'Was. But that's all done and dusted a while back. Currently she has only disdain for me. But her brother, who's a good mate of mine, is thinking of joining the army and she sees me as the likeliest person to be able to talk him out of it.'

'Why's that. Did you join yourself?'

'No. No way. It's complicated but basically his argument for joining up is there's no future otherwise and I have to persuade him that there are opportunities and he just has to look harder. I'm sort of the beacon of success.'

'With your paint spraying?'

'It doesn't sound much, but yes.'

We were quiet for a bit, listening to the music and watching the dancers. Fred and June had stopped dancing and were deep in a long and involved kiss.

'They didn't waste any time, did they?' Jules said.

'No,' I agreed. 'June doesn't tend to.'

'Do you mind?'

'Do I mind what?'

'Well, your friend getting off with people as quickly as that. I'm guessing this happens quite regularly.'

'Oh, I don't mind it, it's usually fairly short-lived. It's not like she abandons me completely. I don't quite understand it though.'

'You mean the impulse?'

113

'Sort of. It's like she looks at who is available and picks the most likely. I couldn't do that.' I didn't say that my sexual experience so far had been limited to Lance.

'But it's not like I don't understand the impulse,' I continued. 'When I do feel that pull, I get it. It's like the best feeling ever. But I don't feel it for many people.'

'Drink more,' suggested Jules, 'or take the right sort of drugs. That helps.'

'Or just find someone you could like, who's feeling it for you?'

'Yeah, that's a pretty good turn-on.'

I wasn't sure quite how we'd got into this conversation, or how I was going to get out of it.

Jules looked closely at me. 'Shall we try it?' he asked. He took my silence for agreement and leaned in slowly until his lips touched mine. I felt a tingle move from my lips down into my stomach. Jules moved away.

'That worked,' I said.

'See,' he said. 'The feeling's there. You just have to know how to draw it out. You could think of it as originating with me and I passed it on to you with the kiss.'

'So, what do we do with it now?'

'Well, we could act on it right away, under the pier or on the fourth green of the pitch and putt over there.' He looked at the expression on my face. 'I'm joking, of course.'

'Or,' he continued, 'you could think of it as a promise. Something we've shared between us.

114

Something we've even talked about so you know you're not imagining it. Maybe sometime we'll act on it, but if we don't we'll always have it, that little spark of attraction. Sometimes, you see, if you act on it, you put it out.'

'Are you speaking from experience?'

'Yeah. It's usually good at the time, but I struggle with the thought afterwards that the attraction was better than the act itself.'

'Perhaps it doesn't help if your choice of location is the fourth green of the nearest pitch and putt?'

'That is a bit of a passion killer,' he agreed.

'And, I'm just thinking here, but maybe you should be better at it?'

He laughed. 'Yes, maybe that's the problem.'

We were quiet for a moment.

'Of course,' said Jules, breaking the silence between us, 'now we've shared a kiss, that makes you mine. No getting off with anyone else, no getting back with Lance.' I could tell by the look on his face he wasn't being completely serious.

'Okay,' I said, 'but maybe we should make the agreement binding. With another kiss?'

The second kiss was less tentative. This time I joined in and we got closer, drawing each other in. I held his shoulder then his neck and then his hair. We collapsed back onto the sand and we stretched out together. Finally I pulled away.

'Pitch and putt?' he suggested as I rearranged my clothes.

I could see June heading in our direction.

'Are you done?' she asked.

'For now, maybe,' said Jules.

'Good, cos Fred and I are heading back to the campsite and we wanted to know if you two are going to come with us.'

'I'd better say some goodbyes first,' said Jules and disappeared into the group.

'Where are you sleeping?' asked June urgently.

'My tent,' I said. I looked at her. 'No,' I said, 'I am not going elsewhere so you and Fred can have my tent. Doesn't he have one?'

'He does, but he's sharing with Sandy.'

'Oh, well, you'll have to bribe Sandy somehow then.'

'Aren't you wanting to spend the night with Jules?' she asked.

'No, we're kissing, that's all. I'm not planning on sleeping with him.'

'Really?' said June. 'Madness.' She shook her head as if to suggest she would never understand me.

We weaved our way somewhat uncertainly through town, looking for clues to the location of the campsite. There were a few scooters still about so we followed the direction they were heading in. Finally Jules spotted an alley between some houses that we recognised and we found the site at the other end. We stood for a moment trying to get our bearings.

'I think we're over this way,' I said, pointing to the right.

'So are we,' said Jules.

It turned out that we had pitched within a hundred yards of each other. Fred and June immediately crawled into Fred's tent while Jules walked me back to mine. At our site, no one was about but there were more scooters and more tents, meaning Sarah and Andrea must have arrived. I didn't see Lance's scooter or tent which I was glad about.

'Night, then,' I said.

'Can I have a goodnight kiss?' asked Jules.

Standing up I had to stretch to reach, even as Jules bent down to meet me. His kiss was gentle and thoughtful.

'Will you come and find me in the morning?' he asked. 'You know where we are.'

I nodded and watched him leave, a tall thin figure with a confidence in his walk rather than a swagger.

In the tent I made myself comfortable, leaving room for June should she need it.

I woke in the morning cold and alone. June had obviously managed to sort something out with Sandy. I could hear girls' voices outside so I unzipped the tent and stuck my head out. Sam was there, along with Karen, Andrea and Sarah. I got up and went to join them.

'Where did you get to last night?' asked Sam. 'We all went to the pub together,' she explained to the others, 'but then Lance showed up and at the same time Annie disappeared.'

'So,' she said to me, 'I'm curious about what's going on.'

I tried to recall the sequence of events. 'Well,' I said, 'the boys we met at the Isle of Wight were already in the pub. So we sat with them. And then I saw Lance was there and he saw me. Then Perry said something to him, about Jules I think and Lance got all cross-looking, so we left.' As I explained it, it did sound as though we'd over-reacted slightly although it had made perfect sense at the time.

'You don't actually know what Perry said though?' asked Karen.

'No, but I don't think it was very kind, from his look,' I said. It occurred to me that Perry and the others could be lying in their tents listening to me. 'They're not about are they?'

'No. They've gone out to a café for breakfast. I'm surprised they didn't wake you, they made so much of a racket.'

'So you saw Lance then?' I asked. 'How is he?'

'Well when we first saw him he was quite happy' said Sam, 'but then he came over all grumpy and left early. I suppose your story might explain that.'

'Did you find out what he's been up to?' I asked.

'Yes. He's still in Portsmouth, apparently.'

'With the guy who gave him a lift back? Has he not fixed his scooter yet then?'

'Oh no, he's fixed his scooter. And the guy was so impressed with his mechanical ability he gave him some work on some other vehicles, scooters and stuff, that he had lying around in the garage. So he's been doing that for the past few weeks.'

'Where's he living?'

'Above the garage, I think. It all sounds a bit temporary but he had nothing permanent anyway so I guess that doesn't matter. He's helping out on the stall this weekend so he's staying over with the traders.'

'Oh. Well that's good, I suppose,' I said. 'I never know why he can't pick up the phone and let people know where he is though.'

'Perhaps he doesn't think there's anyone who cares enough to tell,' said Sarah.

'Well then, he underestimates us, doesn't he,' I said.

'Are you going to go and see him?' asked Sam.

'At the stall?'

'Yes. I wouldn't wait for him to come up here.'

'Well, I should, I suppose. Not when it's busy though.'

I thought about how I'd agreed to go and see Jules. The idea of shuttling between them made me feel anxious.

June appeared, looking quite rough.

'Alright?' I said. 'Did you find somewhere to sleep?'

'Yeah, we shunted Sandy out to someone else's tent. I didn't get much sleep though.' She looked longingly at my tent. 'I think I'll just have a bit of a catch-up now,' she said and disappeared inside.

'Oh, Jules is up,' she shouted through the canvas. 'He said for you to go over any time.'

'What's going on there?' Sam asked

'With me and Jules?' I asked. 'I don't know really, something and nothing. I do like him, but it's not simple. I still feel attached to Lance, however stupid that might seem.'

'Jules might be the better bet though,' said Sam.

'He is lovely, really lovely,' I agreed, 'and he's smart. But he lives too far away.'

'He could be your scooter rally boyfriend,' suggested Sarah. 'You'd meet up six times a year and never have sex anywhere but in a tent.'

'You make it sound so attractive,' I said.

I took some time that morning making myself look presentable. I put on as many clean clothes as I had, and, as there were proper washrooms, had a shower and gave my teeth a good brush. By the end I felt almost human and decided I was ready to go and see Jules. He was looking similarly scrubbed up. He was on his own, sitting on a camping chair whilst tending a kettle on a gas burner.

120

'How come you have so much stuff?' I asked. I was curious about the contents of his tent which presumably had proper beds and a light and maybe some heating.

'Oh you should always get someone to come in a support vehicle,' he said. 'A car, or preferably a van. Then you've got a few home comforts and if someone's scooter gives up the ghost you're not stuck by the side of the road for hours.'

'The SeaDogs would never agree to that,' I said, even as I remembered that we'd gone up to Morecambe in a car with Lance and Dave. I wondered why they hadn't taken one since.

'Loads of clubs do it,' said Jules. 'How do you think the Minehead lot got their barbeque and ghetto blaster here?'

'Hmm,' I said, 'I'm beginning to think we are being unnecessarily hard on ourselves.'

Jules made me a cup of tea in a proper mug and I drank it gratefully.

'So have you seen your ex yet?' he asked.

'Lance? No, he's not camped with us. He's down with the traders apparently.'

'He should be easy to find then,'

'Should I want to.'

'Come on,' he said, 'you've got to. You must want to clear the air. I'll come with you, if you like.'

'Do you really think that's going to help?'

'Why not? I reckon we've got quite a bit in common. We both like fiddling about with scooters and we both like you.'

'When you put it like that I think what can possibly go wrong?' I said, then changed the subject: 'So, what are you going to do today?'

'The boys were talking about taking a ride out somewhere. Cheddar maybe, or Wookey Hole.'

'Isn't that where the witch is?'

'Yeah, we like a good tacky tourist spot. Well, you saw us at Alum Bay, so you know. If you time it right you get there with all the other tourists and that's great fun. Half of them are scared you're going to start a fight. Of the other half, the Dads want to talk mechanics or tell you about their days as a mod, the kids are fascinated by the paintwork and the Mums secretly fancy you. Well, they fancy me. Not you.'

'Obviously.'

'And if there's enough of you parked up it seems like an event and everyone gets their cameras out and you get to preen a bit, like film stars. So, are you coming?'

'Won't I cramp your style? What with all the Mums getting the hots for you?'

'No. You can distract the Dads. Plus I think there's a mini-golf course at Wookey Hole, so we have to go.'

We agreed to meet up a bit later and I went back to our tents to rouse June. A scooter passed me on the path and stopped in front of me. It was Perry. He got off and began pushing his scooter along next to me.

'I came looking for you,' he said. 'I hear you've been bad-mouthing me.'

122

'Yeah?' I said, picking up pace so he had to concentrate on manoeuvring his scooter safely over the bumps in the grass. 'Who said that?'

'I can't reveal my sources.'

'Was it Sam?' I asked.

'Yes.'

'What did she say?'

'She said you'd been slagging me off for telling Salty the truth about you.'

I stopped and looked at him. 'Did she actually say that?'

'No, well, something like that. I think she actually said that you were upset because I'd said something to him about you.'

'So she didn't say I'd been bad-mouthing you then?'

'No. No, not as such.'

'So what are you cross about? Why come looking for me? You did say something and that did make him annoyed. It sounds more like it's you who's been bad-mouthing me.'

Perry pulled his scooter on to its stand.

'It's not like we've ever really had a conversation, you and me,' I said. 'We hardly know anything about each other. Why have you got it in for me?'

'Salty is my mate,' he said. 'We've known each other since primary school. I lived round his house for nearly a year when my Dad started getting lairy. For a bit we did everything together, he was better than a brother.'

A couple of scooters came past and their riders shouted out to Perry. He gave them a wave. As he carried on, I could see the colour rising on his cheeks.

'All that time,' he said, 'but I've never seen him as happy was he was with you.'

'So you were jealous?'

'Yeah.'

'But you've had girlfriends, haven't you? So you know what it's like?'

'I've had girls,' he said. 'That's not quite the same thing.'

'So you took the opportunity to make Lance think I'd found someone else. And I'd found him really quickly.'

'Yes, I suppose.'

'But you know Lance broke up with me?'

'Yeah, but that was just Salty being Salty. He didn't mean to do it, he just did and once he had, he had to stick to it. That didn't mean he wouldn't try and get back with you once things had changed.'

'So you saw your chance to put him off me?'

'Yeah. I suppose. I didn't plan it, but you were with that guy.'

'I was. But it doesn't mean there's anything going on. Not that that's any of your business,' I added.

'No.' He looked a bit deflated. 'I thought it would feel good, giving you a bit of a kick and getting my friend back.'

'But it didn't.?'

'No, it just made Salty unhappy and left me feeling like a bastard. When I said earlier that you'd been bad-mouthing me, I knew you hadn't because I knew you weren't capable of it. And you've got all these blokes running around after you but you'd never look at the likes of me. I could fall in love with you,' he said, all in a rush.

'Oh, Perry,' I said. 'That's not me who you could fall in love with, much as I might like it to be. It's an idea of me, but I can't live up to that. I'm just as rubbish as everyone else.' It all suddenly made me feel very sad.

'You could find a girlfriend if you wanted to,' I said. 'There's lots of really lovely girls out there.'

'Maybe I just go about it wrongly?'

'Maybe. I'm not going to give you advice expect for perhaps try to get to know them a bit before you move in on them. Talk to them and let them find out about you.'

'Should we go and find Salty and tell him I was wrong about what I said?'

'No,' I said. 'The damage is done now. And I'm about to go and spend the day with Jules and his mates.' I thought for a moment. 'Perry, you said you lived with Lance for a while?'

'Yes.'

'Did you get on well with his Mum?'

'Yeah, she looked after me really well. I always felt welcome there.'

'And have you been to see her recently?'

'Since Salty left? No.'

'Well, perhaps you should. She could probably do with the company. You only have to drop in for a coffee.'

'Yeah,' he agreed, 'maybe I'll do that.'

Chapter Ten

Perry and I walked back to the tents together. I dived into my tent and prodded June until she woke up. I felt quite happy, although a little disorientated. I'd never had much interest from boys until I'd met Lance but now I seemed to practically have them falling at my feet. I couldn't help thinking it was more to do with being a fairly rare scooter girl in a mass of scooter boys rather than any particular qualities I might possess. Still, I was about to have a day out with Jules and had sorted things out with Perry. That only left Lance to see and clear the air with and all would hopefully be good.

June was bleary-eyed and gasping for water so once I'd got her up we went down to the food stalls and bought some breakfast. I told her something about my conversation with Perry although I left out the last part.

'Boys always get jealous when their mates find a girlfriend,' she said. 'Sounds like you got off lightly. He backtracked pretty quickly.'

'Yeah. Sounds like Lance believed him though.'

'You don't know that. You only know he looked cross and then Perry said he was grumpy.'

'I should probably go and find him,' I said. I could have put this off for most of the weekend, but talking and thinking about his response to seeing me made me nervous and at that moment it just seemed as though I should get I over with.

'We need to get patches anyway,' said June.

I didn't know where I'd find Lance, so I was just looking for a stall selling spare parts. There seemed to be quite a few of these and I didn't see him behind any of them. We found the Paddy Smith stall though and bought our rally patches. I was just about to send June up one side of the stalls and me the other when I saw him coming along towards us, carrying several cups and some wrapped food. He didn't seem to have seen us.

I stood and watched him as he came closer. In the crowds of scooterists milling about the stalls you wouldn't have picked him out as being anybody special and yet I felt myself melt a little at the sight of him. My throat felt a little constricted as if I would have trouble speaking.

Lance was concentrating on balancing the cups he was carrying and there was a moment that I thought about bolting and perhaps would have done if June hadn't been standing right next to me. I called his name, quite quietly, but he didn't hear. June took the cue and bellowed out 'Lance!' whilst pointing manically in my direction. He jumped and juggled the cups for a second, spilling some of the contents. He looked at June and then looked at me and I felt suddenly upset as if I'd broken something that couldn't be fixed.

Lance inclined his head to the right, indicating that we should follow him. He put the drinks and food down at one of the stalls and said something to the guy working there. He came back to us and taking my elbow, led me off towards the sports pavilion. June came with us but I stopped her. 'I'll see you back at the tents,' I said and she nodded, rather reluctantly I felt.

When we'd found a quiet spot, Lance stopped and let go of my arm. He was standing really close to me, looking at me intently. Without warning he moved in closer, pushing me against the wall of the pavilion. With his hands on my shoulders he bounced his lips off mine and then pushed his tongue into my mouth. Our bodies touched all the way down one side and he moved his hand down the other, over my breast and down to my hip.

Much as my body responded to this I was also shocked by the suddenness of his action and after a moment or two I pushed him away. I resisted the urge to wipe my mouth with my sleeve.

'That was a bit much for a Saturday morning, wasn't it?' I said wanting to get to a point where we could talk about what we felt rather than have it hovering unspoken, revealing itself only in surprise sexual approaches. 'I should walk away, you know.'

'Yeah, sorry,' he said. 'I don't know what came over me.'

'No, me either.'

'I've missed you,' he said as if that was an adequate explanation.

'I didn't think you were like that,' I said. 'Remember the time you saved me on Morecambe beach?'

'Yeah. Like I said, I don't know what came over me. It wasn't how I'd planned to greet you.'

'How had you planned to, then?' I asked.

'Well, I was going to tell you what I'd been up to. I thought you'd like to know.'

'I do. You didn't have to leave it until now though.'

'I didn't get a chance last night. Not after you walked out.'

'I didn't mean that. I mean you could have phoned.'

'I did. Twice. But no one answered. I have to use a pay phone so I couldn't keep trying.'

I was still leaning back against the wall and I slid down it until I was sat on the ground. Lance looked down at me for a bit and then joined me.

'I know a bit of what you've been up to,' I said. 'Perry told me. You're still in Portsmouth.'

'Yeah, Gary kept me on. I've never met anyone who's appreciated my work like he does and he thinks I should start a business.'

'Wow. Well that's good news.'

'It's only temporary for now, I'd need to find somewhere to live.'

'So, you're staying down there?'

'For now.'

'I saw your Mum,' I said.

'You did? Why?'

'I saw her in town. She invited me over. She misses you, you know. She'd have you back, you only have to phone.'

'Maybe,' he said. 'How about you? Do you miss me? I thought perhaps not, as you've found this new bloke. Perry said you'd met up at the Isle of Wight.'

''So I didn't waste much time,'' I said, before he could.

'I didn't say that.'

'No, but you thought it. I saw the look on your face.'

'Yeah, alright, I did think it. I know I've got no hold over you, but it did hurt. Is he your boyfriend now?'

'No. We're not together and I've not slept with him. I know that's the sort of information you'd like to know. At the moment he's just a friend.'

'At the moment.'

'Yeah. Everything's a bit confusing right now. I come away on these weekends and everything gets so intense, it's hard to think straight. All of a sudden I seem to be able to attract boys without trying and that's so weird, I can't make sense of it.'

'It shouldn't be.'

'Well it is. I keep thinking they are all going to turn around and shout 'Ha, only joking. Whatever would make you think we'd fancy you?' And then call me all sorts of names.'

'Why would they do that?'

'I don't know. I just don't have any confidence in me, as a person.'

'Well, you should. I know I'm not the right sort of person to be advising you because I feel like a fraud too, most of the time, but you ought to have more confidence in yourself.'

'Yeah, you can't just get it though, can you? You've got to find it from somewhere. You splitting up with me gave me a big knock and now I don't think I've got what it takes to be in a relationship.' I could feel that I was close to tears. I tried to hide my face so Lance wouldn't see.

He put his arm around my shoulders and drew me in to him. I let myself lean against him, drawing in his body warmth.

'I'm all or nothing, you know,' I said, snuffling a bit into his jacket. 'I'm not going to sleep with anyone unless we're properly together. I'm not going to sleep with Jules and I'm not going to sleep with you. No matter how much I might want to. I know that makes me a bit odd.'

'Well, you and me both, I suppose,' he said. 'It's easy, if you want to, to find someone at the time when you need them, but if you feel crap afterwards you probably should avoid it. I don't feel good using people. Already I feel really ashamed that I launched myself on you just then and I'll probably be kicking myself about it for days, weeks, maybe.'

He reached down and lifted my chin so I had to look at him.

'I'm feeling better about myself now,' he said, 'but I'm not looking to get back with you. You should know that.'

My tears really started then. I could feel them escape the corners of my eyes and drip down my cheeks.

'That doesn't mean I'm not in love with you. I think, no, I'm certain, that I am. But nothing's changed. You're probably still looking for some great career in some exotic location and I'm still looking for something that gives my life some meaning. We're not heading in the same direction and I've got to let you go. If I feel jealous, and I did feel jealous yesterday, then that's my problem not yours. If you go and find someone else, I'll have to deal with it.'

I pulled away from him and turned my face, blinking to try and stop the tears.

'I've thought long and hard about this,' he said. 'I know you feel something for me and part of me thinks I should grab that with both hands. But I'm not going to hold you back. I can't. I couldn't live with myself and we'd end up making each other unhappy.'

'Well,' I stood up. 'We can be friends though?'

'Yeah, good friends,' Lance stood up too. 'You tell me when you'll be in and I'll call you. We'll arrange a time and we'll keep in touch.'

'And you'll phone your Mum too?'

'Yes. I'll do that.'

'Okay, well I'm going to go then. I'll see you before the end of the weekend?'

'Be here, same time tomorrow, if I don't see you before.'

I stuck my hands in my pockets and turned away. I walked back through the stalls keeping my head down so no one noticed the redness of my face. There was a cool wind, blowing off the sea probably, and I let it whip my hair and dry my tears.

I ducked into the loos and washed my face with cold water, splashing it over and over until I felt a bit more normal. I supposed I should be happy, I'd seen Lance and we'd cleared the air. We'd agreed to keep in touch. I still felt somewhat lost and alone though, even as I knew that everything he said was reasonable and sensible.

By the time I got back over to Jules' tent I was feeling ready for a ride. June was already there.

'You okay? She asked.

'I'll tell you later,' I said. 'Are we ready to go?'

'I think so. Fred's asked me to go with him, that's okay isn't it?'

'Yes. I think I'd prefer to be on my own anyway at the moment.'

I went and got my scooter, holding it in a low gear across the grass, my crash helmet between my knees. The others were in various states of readiness so I just sat there on the front of the seat, feet on the ground, holding the scooter upright between my legs.

'I'll follow you, if that's okay,' I said to Jules when everyone was ready to go.

'Make sure you can see my mirrors then and I can keep an eye on you.'

'Follow the signs for Wookey if you lose us,' shouted Billy as he led the way out of the site.

I enjoyed the ride. We weren't aiming for speed and I could take the time to enjoy the surroundings: the flat land by the coast which became increasingly craggy and rocky as we headed inland. Villages were no more than a few houses clustered around a church and maybe a pub. Just before we got to Wookey we ducked down into a valley that seemed to be choked with greenery.

There were a couple of scooters already in the car park so we lined our alongside, facing outwards so as to present a good photo opportunity. We hung around casually while Curly took a few photos.

It wasn't long before we'd gained a bit of an audience. A couple of Dads were pointing out the scooters to their kids and one of the ticket sellers had left his booth and was talking exhaust systems with Jules and Billy. Sandy was trying to lean casually against his scooter to impress the Mums, but was failing miserably.

'So', said June to me, 'do you want to tell me about Salty now?'

I tried to get our conversation straight in my head. I wasn't sure what had bothered me most: the kiss and the aggressiveness of it, or his confirmation

135

of the fact that he didn't want to be with me. I decided to give her the edited highlights:

'Well we sort of made it up over whatever Perry said but he says he still doesn't want to be with me.'

'Did you actually ask him that?'

'What? Did I say 'Do you want to be with me?' No.'

'Why did he think you did then?'

'I'm not sure I get you.'

'Well what I mean is, he seems to keep telling you that he doesn't want to be an item, but when have you ever said you did? It ought to be you telling him how things are.'

'So you want me to say 'Look Lance, I'd like you to be my boyfriend, but that's not going to happen until you sort yourself out'?'

'Yeah, that sort of thing. It's like he's got the upper hand. You ought to address the balance a bit.'

I thought about what June had said.
'You've got a point,' I said, 'but it's a bit late to change that now, isn't it?'

'It's never too late,' said June. 'Look at Sandy in Grease.'

'Yeah, I don't think I'm getting dressed up in leather just to make a point.'

'Why not? You'd be able to control all men with the tip of your little finger.'

'Who's getting dressed up in leather?' asked Jules, coming over.'

'No one is,' I said.

'Shame. Anyway we're going in. Brian has negotiated us a discount and we're going to see the witch and then the fairground stuff.'

I enjoyed the tour through the cave but the really fun stuff came afterwards where they had a room of mirrors. June found a spot where she couldn't be seen and jumped out on us as we ran through. Jules and I had a competition to see how many reflections we could make of ourselves at one time. Eventually it became impossible to judge as our images began to repeat themselves infinitely.

'I never knew the back of my head looked like that,' said Jules focusing on a reflection in the mirror behind him.

'Oh, it looks alright,' I said.

'That's what I mean. From the back I look hotter than I do from the front. No wonder so many people stop and stare at me when I go past them.' He preened a bit more, admiring his back view and adjusting his jeans to get the best line over his bottom.

Eventually I got fed up and went to find June. She had discovered the slot machines and was obsessively feeding two pence pieces into a coin slot. Every time coins dropped into the hopper she let out a little cheer and began feeding them back in again.

'This is what I'm going to do when I leave college,' she said to me.

'What, become a professional gambler?'

'No, stupid. Set up an arcade. Once you've bought the machines it's all profit. And look at how much fun people are getting from it.'

It did seem that every machine had someone in front of it although not many of them looked as though they were having much fun. Only the casual players raised a cheer when they got a pay out.

'Yes,' I said, 'I can see you sitting in a little booth, doling out change.'

'Oh, no. I'll be employing some YTS kid for that. I'll be at home counting my money.'

When she'd run out of change we found the café and joined the others who'd already spread across a couple of tables.

'So are you going to Skegness?' asked Jules.

'When's that?' asked June.

'Early October, I think.'

'I thought this was the last rally of the season,' I said. 'Sam said it was.'

'Then Sam was wrong.'

'Where's Skegness?' asked June.

'East Coast, just above the Wash.'

'I think I've run out of money,' I said. I had spent quite a lot over the past two rallies and would need to find some work if I wanted to attend any more.

'And I'm dependent on a lift,' said June.

'I'll come and get you,' said Fred.

'Oh, that's so sweet,' said Jules. Fred punched him on the arm.

'Would you?' asked June.

'Yeah, where do you live?'

138

'Essex.'

Fred made a face. 'Maybe that's a bit far.'

'So I won't see you again,' said Jules. 'Until next year?'

'You could come to our party,' said June.

'What party?'

'The one we haven't organised yet,' I said.

'No, but we will,' said June. 'Give us your address and we'll send the invites when we know where and when.'

'It's going to be a joint 18th,' I explained. 'In December, hopefully.'

'That's still a long time,' said Jules. 'You could come a visit me. Bring the invites in person.'

'I'd like that,' I said. 'Although maybe I'd come by train.' I liked the idea of a trip to see Jules. I needed something to look forward to, something to break up what felt as though it was going to be a long winter.

Chapter Eleven

We'd invited Jules and the others over to our tents and they were getting to know the SeaDogs and the Sessex Girls. June had obviously spent the journey back to Weston thinking about and planning our party.

'We'll have it at the Red Cow,' she told me. 'That way we can invite everyone we know.'

'Including people from college?'

'Yeah, we'll get a soul DJ and educate them a little bit. They'll be instant converts.'

'And Mums and Dads?'

'Well maybe they can come for a bit. We'll tell them they have to leave by ten though so they don't cramp our style.'

'And if you invite Fred and Ben, how's that going to work?'

'Who knows? We've got three months between then and now. Anything could happen.'

'And we'll have to find somewhere for everyone who's coming from a distance to stay over.'

'We'll farm them out to all these lot. Look how well they're getting on.' They did seem to be getting on well. Billy and Fred were examining the modifications Dave had made to his scooter and

Sandy was chatting to Andrea and Sarah. Jules and Perry had eyed each other up suspiciously to begin with but seemed to have decided they had nothing to fight over and were sharing a roll-up of some sort. Everyone had agreed they wanted to go to the all-nighter in the town and Curly had been sent to buy tickets.

'I'm going to have to get some sleep if we're going to be dancing all night,' I said to June. 'I'll never do that and drive home tomorrow.'

I crawled into the tent and was just zipping it up when Jules stuck his head in.

'Can I join you?' he asked.

'If all you want to do is sleep,' I said, 'then yes you can.'

We lay side by side for a bit, but eventually ended up curled up together. 'For body warmth,' explained Jules, and even though the sun was shining through the canvas, I slept deeply and without dreaming.

Jules woke me later. 'I think everyone's making a move' he said. I could have stayed where I was quite happily but once I got going I did feel ready for a night out. June, who'd fallen asleep on the grass led us all in a few exercises, 'to get the blood moving' and Dave handed round some cans of lager 'to fool the blood into thinking it's invincible' and we were ready to go.

We headed into town in a big group, looking for a pub with room for us all to pass the time in until the all-nighter started at eleven.

141

We found one with some room outside and June and I sat on a wall and let the boys go inside for the drinks. There seemed to be a lot of lads on motorbikes roaming around the town.

'I think it's just one gang that keeps coming round,' said June as a second group rode slowly past the pub.

'Do you think they're looking for trouble?' I asked.

'Bound to be. I expect they're locals, pissed off about all their pubs being full.'

'Probably most of them are too young to get in anyway,' I said, forgetting that I wasn't exactly of a legal age to drink myself. 'It looked like they were mostly on mopeds.'

The next time they came round they got a bit bolder. One of them shouted something in our direction. It wasn't clear what he'd said. June cupped her hand to her ear.

'Sorry,' she shouted, 'you're mumbling.'

The motorcyclist had gone past by this point and there was a car coming up behind so he carried on round the corner with his mates. We waited for them to make a reappearance. They took their time and I was just thinking that they'd chickened out of riding past again when they showed up. This time they actually stopped by the kerb. The one who had spoken before lifted his visor and, speaking very clearly, said: 'I said 'Get your tits out'. I'm talking to you,' he pointed to June, 'Not you. You,' he indicated at me, 'haven't got any.'

This was a fair assessment of our relative chest sizes but I was still shocked. June was on her feet and at the same time I saw Fred come out of the pub holding two pints of beer.

It looked as though he'd heard what the boy had said. Without warning he ran at the boy's bike and aimed a kick at the petrol tank. The boy managed to hold the bike upright but wasn't ready for the beer that Fred then threw over him.

'Show some respect,' he shouted at the boy and looked threateningly at the other boys who were grouped by the kerb. Some of the others had come out of the pub by this point and had put their drinks down ready for a fight if it looked as though one was likely. Instead the boys on the bikes decided to scarper.

'What was that all about?' asked Dave who was the last to come out of the pub and had missed the whole thing.

'Just some fizzy boys causing trouble,' said Fred. I lost my pint though.' He wiped down his leg where some of the beer had splashed.

'Here, have mine,' said Dave. 'Sorry I missed it.' He went back inside to queue at the bar again.

'Well that was exciting,' said Jules, 'what did they actually say?'

'Oh, you know, the usual,' said June.

'Well, we'll keep an eye out for them,' he said, 'although I'd be surprised if they came back.'

We settled down a bit although the boys were jumpy, buoyed up by the chance of a bit of aggro. Everyone downed a couple of pints in quick succession and we headed for the all-nighter venue.

June was a bit subdued on the walk there. 'I should have been able to deal with that myself,' she said. 'It only needed words, not violence. I'm not some sort of damsel in distress who needs saving.'

I decided not to remind her that she had been complaining about boys not fighting over her only the day before.

'What would you have said though?' I asked.

'Something about the size of his penis probably,' she said.

'Fighting like with like, then?' I suggested, not sure whether one was any more honourable than the other.

'Don't feel you have to defend me though,' I said. 'I'm used to comments like that. I've never felt as though having big breasts was an asset so it doesn't bother me in the way it might.'

'It does bother me that lads think they can comment on them though,' she argued. 'They're such arses.'

'Well some of them are,' I agreed.

Fred was still talking about his part in the argument. 'I'll definitely have put a dent in his tank,' he said to June as we waited in the queue to get in, seemingly expecting her to be impressed. She shrugged him off crossly.

'You don't have to fight my battles,' she said.

By the time we got into the hall there was a band already playing. We went and bought some drinks and stood at the back, waiting for the soul music from the Northern Soul DJs.

As soon as they came on, June and I hit the floor and Jules came with us. There were tracks familiar to June and I from the Red Cow and others we had never heard before but were clearly well known to some of the others in the room.

Jules took my hand and we danced together for a couple of tracks but mostly we just found our space and lost ourselves in the music. The others came and went but June and I danced for what seemed like hours.

'You know most people need drugs to keep this up,' she said when we stopped for a moment. I had seen a few quiet exchanges of money and goods. I didn't know whether any of our group had taken any but no one had offered me anything and I didn't think I would have taken it if they had. The music was enough of a mood-lifter and once you started dancing it was hard to stop anyway.

I knew I wouldn't make it through to eight in the morning though and when some of the others began to think about heading back to the campsite at about three or four I was happy to go with them.

Six of us decided to go: June and I, Fred, Jules and Dave and Sam. It all seemed quiet when we left the hall but as we turned the corner I noticed that we were being followed and that whoever it was that was following was gaining on us.

145

I looked back and saw a group of boys, most of them wearing crash helmets. I knew then that they were following us with intent.

I tapped Jules' elbow and pointed behind us. He stopped and looked back and the others stopped too. We stood six abreast, facing the boys who were continuing to advance on us.

Fred who was stood in the middle took a step forward and then things happened very quickly. One of the boys produced a bottle which he held by the neck. The end was open and jagged and glinted in the street light.

At the same moment June stepped forward too. 'You won't . . .' she said, putting her arm in front of Fred to stop him. The boy came forward quickly and took a swipe at Fred with the bottle. As if in slow-motion, I saw it cut into June's arm and she pulled away, crying out in pain. I dragged her to the side, out of the firing line.

I could see blood seeping from the cut. I pulled her shirt away from it and tried to push the skin together.

'We're going to have to find a hospital,' I said to June, just as the fight behind us kicked off. I couldn't see who was fighting who. There was a smash of glass and I hoped someone had knocked the bottle out of the boy's hand.

I felt I needed to phone for an ambulance but I couldn't see a phone box and I didn't want to leave June. I settled for taking her back up to the hall where the bouncers would know what to do.

Sam was sitting down on the kerb, ashen-faced. 'I tried to stop it,' she said.

'Come with us,' I suggested. 'I'm going to get June some help.'

'No,' she said. 'I can't leave Dave.'

'I'm going back to the hall,' I said. 'Meet us there if you can.' I led June back up the street. She still hadn't said anything and she was beginning to look very pale. She held her arm close to her, bent up so as to stop the bleeding. I mopped up the blood as well as I could with a tissue as we walked.

'We don't have to go to the hospital do we?' she asked.

'Yes, we do,' I said. From what I could see, the cut was deep and looked as though it would need stitches.

'How many of them were there?' she asked.

'Five, I think.'

'But that's five against three. We should go back. We can't leave them.'

'June,' I said, 'you're not thinking straight. We need to get this bleeding stopped. Fred caused this fight so he can finish it.'

Even as I said this I wondered if June wasn't right. What if June's wound was minor compared to what the boys suffered? I wondered if I would feel eternally guilty if I'd walked away when I could have stopped and helped in some way.

Back at the hall there was one lone bouncer at the door. He immediately took charge. He took us into an office near the entrance and gave me the phone while he tended to June's arm.

'Ah, it's only a small cut,' he said to her, 'you've nothing to worry about.' He set about tying a handkerchief around the top of her arm. 'That'll stop the bleeding.'

'But what about the others?' June asked.

'I expect the police will already be there,' he said. 'There's not much goes on in this town without some concerned citizen ringing the rozzers. All your mates will either be at the hospital or at the nick.'

It seemed as though the ambulance took forever but it was probably only a few minutes.

'How did this happen?' asked one of the ambulance men. I could see June was reluctant to say.

'There was a fight,' she said eventually. 'There might be others who are hurt.'

'Was it round the corner?' he asked. June nodded.

'There's already been a call-out to that one,' he said. 'You're keeping us busy tonight.

'Sorry.' I said.

'We always expect extra work when you lot,' he nodded at my patches, 'come into town. Up until now it's not been too bad, though.'

'See you, Alan,' he said to the bouncer as he helped June to the ambulance. 'Try and keep them out of trouble, yeah?'

They took June to the local hospital and I followed on in a taxi. At the hospital Sam, Dave and Jules were sitting in the corner of the waiting area. I went over to them. Dave and Jules looked as though they had been in a fight but they had no obvious bleeding.

'Have you seen June?' I asked.

'Yeah, they took her through straight away,' said Jules.

'And you're okay?'

'Yes. It was over pretty quickly once Fred got rid of the bottle. The others had nothing, no weapons. So we picked them up by their crash helmets and gave them a good shake.'

'Did you really?'

'No. But we could have. They were only young lads. Full of piss and vinegar as my Dad would say.'

'And how about Fred?'

'He's got some cuts to his hands. I think they'll pick the glass out and leave it at that.'

'So June got off worst?'

'It seems like it.'

I looked over at Sam who appeared to have fallen asleep.

'You know we just stayed to make sure you got here okay,' said Dave. 'Do you mind if I take Sam back to the site?' I shook my head. 'Do you want to come with us?' he asked.

'I'd better wait for June,' I said.

When they'd gone I said to Jules: 'Should I phone her parents?'

'What for?'

'To tell them about her injury. Maybe they should know.'

'I think I'd wait for June to tell them. She might not tell the story in the same way you would.'

We waited for June and Fred to emerge from the treatment area. Neither of us said much, both drifting in and out of consciousness despite the brightness of the lighting. There was a large clock on the wall which seemed to jump from half past five to quarter past seven in the time it took to blink, but then Fred was standing in front of us, showing Jules his bandaged hands.

'I don't know how I'm going to ride home like this,' he said.

'Lucky you don't have to then,' said Jules. 'Curly can take you and your scoot in the van.'

They sat with me a little longer and finally June emerged. She looked pale and very tired and had her arm in a sling.

'It's okay,' she said. 'I haven't damaged any main veins or tendons they said. The sling's just to keep the weight off it. I've had five stitches.'

'Does it hurt?' I asked.

'Not right now, I've had some painkillers. They said not to bash it and they asked how I was getting home. Apparently I should try and find a lift or go by train.'

'Oh,' I said. I wasn't looking forward to the long journey home on so little sleep and it would be doubly hard without June for company.

We took a taxi back to the campsite and left Jules and Fred at their tents. By then it was breakfast time and people were moving about, some beginning to pack up.

'You could go and find Lance,' I suggested. 'He might know if there are any traders who come from our way who could give you a lift.'

'Yeah, good idea,' said June.

'Do you mind if I don't come with you though? I need some sleep before I ride home.'

'No, you go. It was me who kept you up all night,' she said. She gave me a hug with her good arm.

'Tell Lance he could give me a ring on Tuesday evening. If you remember,' I said.

Back at the tent I collapsed onto my sleeping bag. At some point I heard and felt June gently lower herself next to me.

'Got a lift to Brentwood,' she said. 'That's nearly home. I'll phone my Dad and get him to pick me up from there.'

The next thing I knew, Sam had stuck her head into the tent and was urging us to get moving.

'It's already noon,' she said, 'and we need to leave soon if we're going to get back home at a reasonable time.'

June was groggy and her arm was hurting so I found her somewhere to sit and packed up myself. We got stuck in a round of being concerned for each other. I was worried about June accepting a lift from someone she didn't know and she was worried about me travelling on my own.

'I won't be on my own,' I said. 'I'm riding with Sam and Dave.'

'And I'm getting a lift from a scooter trader that Lance knows, he's got to be safe,' said June.

That reminded me about Lance and about Jules. I wondered if I would see either of them before I left.

'Oh, I told Salty to phone you,' said June, reading my thoughts. 'He said Tuesday at seven.

That just left Jules. Some of the scooterists pitched between his tent and ours had already left so I was able to see that his tent was still up. It didn't look as though anyone was about.

Just as I was wondering where he was, he showed up with Fred, carrying teas and bacon rolls.

'We've come as a sideshow,' he said. 'Something to brighten your morning. It turns out Fred can't pick up anything with his hands as they are, so he's reliant on us for assistance. He tore off a piece of bacon roll and held it in front of Fred who grabbed at it with his teeth.

'It's a bit like owning a performing seal,' said Jules.

'Watch it,' said Fred, 'I might not have the use of my hands but I still have the use of my feet.'

'And look what trouble that got you into,' said June.

'How do you go to the loo?' asked Sam who was watching with amusement.

'Trust me, you do not want to know,' said Jules.

'Anyway, once everyone's done laughing at me, I wanted to say that I came to apologise,' said Fred. 'To June mostly. I know I caused that fight last night and I didn't do it so you would get hurt. I feel really bad about it.'

'And so you should,' said Sam. June didn't say anything.

'I know we said you should come and visit,' said Fred, 'so I wondered if you would. Give me a chance to make it up to you. Show you the bright lights of Devon, treat you a little.'

'Annie and me?' asked June.

'Yes. We'll put you up somewhere. Can I phone you to arrange it?'

'I'd like that,' said June. 'I don't think it makes up for causing the fight but I don't think you can make up for that anyway. And maybe it was my fault for getting involved.'

Jules looked at me. 'Would you come?' he asked.

'If June does,' I said. 'When would it be?'

'I don't know. End of October, beginning of November? Bonfire night maybe.'

We swapped addresses and I went to pack my things onto my scooter. June offered to take the tent with her which made the packing a lot easier.

The others had decided not to leave until the afternoon so it was just Sam, Dave and me travelling together. I left June in the care of Andrea and Sarah.

'I'll see you tomorrow,' I said. 'You'll be in college won't you?'

'Probably. I'll see how I get on,' she said.

With a last quick good bye to Jules, we set off. Without June and the tent I found I could keep up with the others much more easily and we had an enjoyable ride back through the towns west and north of London.

I felt a bit of a spare part when we stopped for petrol and food though. Dave and Sam were so clearly happy in their relationship. It was hard to see how they could have split up earlier in the year.

'Do people keep asking when you're going to get married?' I asked when we were sat having coffee in a roadside café.

'Yes,' said Sam. 'Especially Dave's Mum. She's desperate for a wedding.'

'What do you say to her?'

'Oh I'm usually a little vague.'

'And I say that I keep asking Sam and she keeps saying no,' said Dave.

'Even though you don't,' said Sam. 'I think people tend to get married because they're expected to or because they want a big do and to wear a fancy dress. I don't, never have. The whole thing fills me with horror.'

She looked at Dave. 'So he knows not to ask.'

'Yeah,' said Dave, 'cos I'd get married in an instant. But we've agreed that she's got to ask me.'

'That sounds like a solution,' I agreed.

'I think I'll probably want to have children at some point, but not yet,' said Sam. 'I can't bear to see girls I knew at school pregnant, it's such a waste. I need to see something of the world first.'

'You're going to go travelling?' I asked.

'I'd like to. Newark, Yarmouth and the Isle of Wight are fun but they are essentially the same

154

thing in different locations. I want to see what people do for fun in Spain and Germany and Peru.'

'Me too,' I said. I told her about the book I'd bought and the ideas I'd had for jobs once I left college. Sam was very interested and I offered to lend the book to her.

'Thanks,' said Dave sarcastically when she'd gone to the loo.

'What for?'

'Giving my girlfriend ideas. Now she'll go off to South America or wherever and she's not going to want to come back to me.'

'Go with her then.' I wasn't very sympathetic. 'You won't keep her anyway if she's bored at home.'

'I know. Maybe that's why people get married. To contain the dreams of their partner.'

'So essentially it's selfish?'

'Yes.'

'You can see why Sam doesn't want to do it then.'

'Don't worry, I do understand the urge. I think all scooterists do. We wouldn't be scooterists if we preferred to stay at home.'

'True,' I said.

'It's just I've got this job at Crendells,' he said, 'in the office, and that's what office people do. They get a nice steady job with reasonable pay; they get married; they have kids. Then they spend the rest of their lives persuading their colleagues to do the same thing. Really I should get out before they

155

brainwash me and I trade in my scooter for a Ford Escort.'

'So we're all going to drift away,' I said. 'In five years' time we'll all be spread across the globe.'

'We'll have to have a reunion,' said Dave. 'In ten years' time we should all meet up on the Isle of Wight on August Bank Holiday, whether there's a scooter rally on then or not.'

Dave's talk of a reunion unsettled me. I'd already got a case of end-of-season-it-is, with Weston likely to be my last rally until the following Easter. With more than six months in between who knew which of us would still be riding to rallies next year. My college course finished in July and after that I would be hoping t find a full-time job and if I really was lucky enough to find one abroad I might only make it to three or four more rallies. It suddenly dawned on me that my ambitions and my present lifestyle were incompatible, something I hadn't really made sense of before, even with all of Lance's talk about us going in different directions.

I realised that at some point in the future I was going to have to make a decision that would affect the rest of my life.

Chapter Twelve

As usual after a scooter rally, I got home ready to drop and when the alarm went off on Monday morning I turned over and slept on. Mum had to go early for college so she let me be, and the next time I looked at my clock it was half past three.

Deciding it was a bit late to phone in sick, I thought I'd leave it until the next day to deal with the fall out. I made it in on Tuesday but there was no sign of June.

'It was very quiet yesterday without you two,' said Steve. 'I mentioned that it was probably because you were too tired after your weekend shenanigans.'

The course principal asked to see me and I got a talk about responsibilities and the importance of showing dedication to a task.

'I was only off for one day,' I wanted to say but I kept my mouth shut and just nodded.

'Have you seen your friend June?' she asked. 'Her father phoned yesterday and I gather she has had rather a nasty accident. He says she might be off for a week or more. Perhaps you can take some work for her so she can keep up.'

I said that I would and raced round to June's house as soon as the last class was over. I found her lying on the sofa watching kids' telly.

'You can't stay here,' I said. 'You have to come back, you're the only thing that makes college bearable.'

'I would,' she said, 'but I saw the doctor yesterday and he said I should avoid using my arm while the wound heals or it might keep opening up and I'll end up with a weak arm.'

'Sounds like a weak excuse,' I said. June groaned.

I flopped on the sofa next to her. 'So, how was your trip home?' I asked.

'Good.' She grinned. 'Really good, actually. He took me all the way home.' She paused for a moment. 'And he has a son, Alex. He might be coming to the Red Cow this week.'

'Oh. Might he?' I decided not to pursue this any further. I'd get a good sense of where this was going if he showed up at the Soul Night.

'How about your journey?' June asked.

'Slow,' I said, 'and I think I caused an argument between Dave and Sam.' I told her about the conversation we'd had about marriage and working abroad.

'Sam's better off out of that relationship anyway,' said June. 'It might look good on the surface but it would never last. Anyway, talking about the SeaDogs, should you be here now?'

'Why's that?' I asked.

'Well isn't Salty supposed to be phoning tonight? Tuesday at seven, wasn't it?' I looked at the clock, it was almost six.

'Oh, I've got loads of time,' I said. I had forgotten that Lance was due to phone and that felt strange, as if I was drawing away from him.'

June and I chatted a bit longer and then I made a move to leave.

'I hope I'll be back at college next week,' said June. 'But if I'm not, I'll definitely be at the Red Cow. I can't let Alex down.'

'I don't know how you keep track of them all,' I said.

'Me either,' she agreed. 'When I call out the wrong person's name, then I'll know it's time to take a break.'

It took an age to get home. There were emergency traffic lights due to a burst water main and a tractor going at fifteen miles an hour that was impossible to get past. As I opened the front door I could hear the phone ringing. I dumped my crash helmet and picked up the receiver before Mum could get there.

'Hello?' I said, somewhat uncertainly, shooing Mum away. I listened to the sound of coins being fed into the machine. Then we were connected.

'Hello,' said Lance. 'Annie, is that you?'

'It is,' I said. 'I just got in, I'm pleased I didn't miss you.' I sat down on the next to bottom stair which was as far as the phone cord stretched.

'Me too,' he said.

Sorry I didn't see you again at Weston,' I said.

'Me too,' he said. I tried to think of something to say that he couldn't just agree to.

'There was a fight,' I said.

'I know,' he replied. 'June told me about it. I was worried about you.'

'Why didn't you come with us?' I asked. 'To the all-nighter I mean. You are still a SeaDog aren't you?'

'Yes, of course I am,' he said. 'I'll never not be a SeaDog. It's hard work being on the stall, that's all. I wasn't up for being up all night as well.'

'So you're still working there then?'

'Since the weekend? Yes, nothing's changed.'

'Have you phoned your Mum?' As soon as I asked that question I wished I hadn't. It sounded too much like nagging. 'Sorry,' I said quickly. 'Not that it's any of my business.'

'It's okay,' he said. 'I did phone her yesterday actually. We kind of made up. She spent most of the time talking about you. It got a bit boring after a while.'

'Sorry.'

'I'll let you off. You can't help being you.' That comment felt as though it was the closest to a joke that Lance had ever got. It seemed as though the new situation was good for him, maybe he was lightening up. Then I wondered if he'd met someone new and maybe that was the reason.

The pips went and I heard him feed more money in.

160

'So,' he said, 'I've only got another couple of 2ps, so I'll phone again next week, same time, if that's okay. I'll save up my change and you can tell me about your week.'

'And you can tell me about yours too,' I said as the pips went again.

'Bye,' I said and he said something too but I didn't catch what and then we were cut off.

I stood holding the receiver for a moment before hanging up. For a short time I'd felt connected and now I felt very alone. I wandered into the kitchen where Mum was experimenting with a Vesta curry to find out about her day and to take my mind off Lance.

I moped around college for the rest of the week. June and I were such good friends that we tended not to hang out with the others on the course and this made it a bit lonely when she wasn't there.

It wasn't even fun avoiding Phil and non-Phil, so I sat on my own in the common room at lunchtime and became a sitting duck for their attentions. Non-Phil I discovered was really called Colin and had just bought a 50 Special.

'It's in bits at the moment,' he said. 'I reckon I've got the winter to sort it out to be ready for the rallies next year.'

'I know someone who could work on it for you,' I said, 'but he's in Portsmouth at the moment.'

'We also need to join a scooter club,' said Phil. 'Do you know of any?'

'I know of a few,' I said, 'but I'm not sure who'd let you join. Not the Sessex Girls obviously and the SeaDogs aren't really open to new members. Probably the best thing would be to hang out at the Red Cow and see if you can't be part of a group from there.'

'And if no one will have us, we'll start our own,' said Colin. I remembered when Ben and I had talked about starting our own club with just the two of us. It seemed so long ago and yet it was only a matter of a few months. Things had changed very quickly it seemed, for me at least, I didn't think Ben was part of a club yet though so maybe he could join in with Colin and Phil and they could start their own.

'I'll introduce you to Ben,' I said decisively, 'he's your age, he'll know who you should know.' I hadn't actually seen Ben since Isle of Wight which was a bit strange. June hadn't really mentioned him either, she had only talked about him when I asked questions about him. I hoped he was okay.

June was back at college on Monday which was a big relief. She had a tubular bandage on her arm but was quite happily showing her scar to anyone who could see.

Phil and Colin were now of the opinion that we had become best mates. They were delighted to see June and hung on her every word as she described and embellished the story of the fight.

'There were at least eight of them,' she said.
'Five,' I amended.

'And some of them had knives.'

'One of them had a bottle.' I thought about it for a moment. 'Actually that could probably have been worse, cos the glass could have gone anywhere.'

'You were really lucky,' said Phil to June.

'Yeah,' she agreed, 'or stupid.'

On Tuesday I was sat by the phone well before seven, waiting for it to ring. When it rang a few minutes early I answered it expecting it to be Lance but it turned out to be Julia, phoning from Ibiza.

'You can't phone now,' I told her, 'I'm expecting a call from Lance.'

'I won't be long,' she said. 'This is important, put Mum on.'

Reluctantly I did so. 'Lance is supposed to be phoning right now,' I said to Mum. 'Get her to call back later.'

'Who's more important?' Mum asked. 'Your sister or some boy who's not even your boyfriend?'

'I think you know the answer to that one,' I said. 'Clue: it's not Julia.'

Mum was on the phone for twenty minutes while I huffed and puffed close by. She didn't seem to say much except for 'Yes' and 'Hm-mm' and once 'They must think a lot of you', so I got no sense of what was so important about the call.

When she finally hung up she said 'Well-l-l' and wandered off before I could ask what Julia had said. I resumed my wait by the phone, not sure if Lance would persevere through twenty minutes of getting an engaged signal.

After ten minutes I was about to give up when finally the phone rang again. This time it was Lance.

'Sorry,' I said, 'my sister was on the phone from Spain.'

'Not to worry,' he said. 'I'm in a pub so I went and had a drink. I've got a few mates here now.'

'It's going well then?'

'Yeah, you could say that. These lads have got a flat and one's moving out in a couple of weeks so they've offered his room to me.'

'Are you moving down there for good then?'

'Well, not for good. For now. I've got work and a place to live. I'd be daft to miss out on that.'

'Your Mum will miss you,' I said. That reminded me that I hadn't been to see her since Weston although I had promised I would. At least I had got Lance to phone her which I supposed was what she really wanted.

'Just my Mum?'

'And the SeaDogs,' He wasn't going to catch me out like that.

I told him about my week although there wasn't much to tell.

'Are you going to the Red Cow tomorrow?' he asked.

'I am.'

'Say hello to the lads for me then,' he said. 'Tell them I'll have an address and a phone number in a couple of weeks.'

'I will,' I said.

'And Annie,' he continued, 'if you'd like to come and visit after that I'd be pleased to see you.'

'Yes,' I said, 'that would be good.'

'I'll phone you next week then?' he said.

'Yes,' I said, 'I'll be here.'

'Alright?' said Mum when I went to find her, 'he did phone then?'

'Yes,' I said. 'So what's the big news about Julia?'

'Well,' she said, 'you know the job was just for the summer?'

'Yes.' I knew she was due home towards the end of October once the season had ended on the island.

'It seems they can apply for winter work, which she did, although she didn't tell me she was going to. So anyway it seems most of her friends got other Spanish locations, Costa del Sol, Tenerife and such like, but guess where Julia got?'

'I don't know, Australia? Outer Mongolia? Bognor?'

'No, you'll never guess, she got Mexico.'

'Mexico?'

'Yes, Acapulco.'

'Blimey, Acapulco. Wherever that is.'

'It's on the Pacific coast.' Mum drew out a map of Mexico in the air and stabbed at where she thought Acapulco was.

'So she's not coming home?'

'No, well, yes, but no. She has to come home to sort out a visa, but she reckons they'll probably send her home one day, give her a day to go to the embassy and then send her straight out again.'

'So we won't see her?'

'Well if she gets the chance she can come home for a night and if not, we could go up to London while she's there.'

'Queue with her at the embassy you mean?'

'Yes, or take her out for lunch at least.'

I thought for a moment. 'So can we go out to see her in Mexico do you think?'

'Only if we could get cheap tickets. It's ever so expensive to go transatlantic,' said Mum, going into travel agent mode, 'and I can't see us getting Dad on a flight like that, it's probably twelve hours or more, so I wouldn't count on it.'

'Just you and I could go then,' I suggested. 'That would be cheaper, wouldn't it? Just think, Christmas on a beach by the Pacific Ocean?'

'What? And leave your Dad alone here? I wouldn't even think about it.'

On Wednesday I decided to go and see Lance's Mum in between college and going to the Red Cow. I found her sitting on the back step taking in the last of the sun.

166

'I'm pleased you've come round,' she said. 'I had some good news I wanted to thank you for but now I've had some bad news too. Come inside and I'll make you a tea.'

'So,' I said, as she put the kettle on, 'the good news?'

'Oh, yes, well you know that one, I'm sure. Lance rang last week. He told me it was you who had persuaded him to pick up the phone. It was so lovely to hear his voice.'

'Has he rung since?'

'No. But he did say he might come and visit soon. I hear his job's going quite well.'

'Yes, I think so.' I decided not to mention the room he was hoping to move into, it might make his move seem a bit final.

'Well, I hope he makes a go of it,' she said. 'You do worry, you know.'

'Yes, of course.' I wondered about the bad news, it didn't sound as though it had anything to do with Lance.

'So that was all good,' she continued. 'Then I was at work yesterday in the Co-op and when Val from down the road came in. She said there had been a scooter accident out on the roundabout by the ring road. She came in to see me in case it was Lance. I told her I didn't think so, not unless he'd planned a surprise visit. But that's not like him. Have you heard anything about it?'

'No,' I said. 'Not a thing.'

'Well, of course I was fairly sure it wasn't Lance, but it could easily be one of his friends. It might even have been you.'

'It wasn't me.' I held my arms up to show how uninjured I was.

'Well, that's lucky. Val said she heard it was quite a bad one.'

'I'm sure I would have heard if anyone was seriously hurt,' I said, even though I wasn't.

'Could you find out?'

'I'm going to the Red Cow later so if it is anyone from around here, I'll find out then.'

'I've met most of Lance's friends at one time or another,' said Mrs Morales. 'The Sea Monkeys or whatever they call themselves, so if it is one of them would you let me know?'

I said I would.

'Of course,' she said, more to herself than to me, 'if it was on the ring road it could quite easily be someone passing through, someone we don't even know.' She brightened a bit at the thought.

The news of the scooter accident made me anxious to get down to the Red Cow to find out what other people had heard. I was so early I was the only person there so I sat on my scooter on my own in the car park for a bit. A few other people showed up but no one I knew well enough to ask.

Finally I saw June coming up from the direction of the bus station.

'Did you get yours?' she asked, before I could tell her about the accident.

'Did I get my what?' I asked.

'Your invitation,' she said, waving an envelope in front of my face.

'No. I haven't been home,' I reminded her, grabbing the envelope which was addressed very neatly. Inside was a hand drawn invite on thick card. It had a very detailed drawing of a scooter with fireworks going off behind it.

'You are invited,' it said, 'to a bonfire night party on Saturday 3rd November at Maison de Jules' and it gave the address. 'Please come on Friday if you are able' it continued 'and stay the weekend. Accommodation and catering provided.' The writing was very neat but quite masculine with tall, thin letters. I was always interested in boys' writing, often I was surprised they could write at all. I hoped this was Jules' hand rather than Fred's.

'Ooh,' I said. 'I hope I've got one.'

'You will do,' said June. 'Can you go?'

'I think so,' I said. I hoped the weekend wasn't the time that Julia was passing through. Mum would take a dim view of me missing out on a family outing.

My excitement over the invite meant I'd missed who'd arrived in the car park. Behind us I could see Sarah and Suzy parking up. I quickly explained what I knew to June.

'We have to find out if anyone knows who it is,' I said.

Suzy was taking off her crash helmet as I went over.

169

'Have you heard?' she said, shaking out her hair.

'About the accident?' She nodded.

'Do you know who it was? I asked.

'Yes.' She was about to tell me but she was distracted by the arrival of Andrea and Karen. 'Andrea will know about it,' she said, 'she's got a friend who's in the police.'

'Who was it though?' I asked. None of the boys had arrived yet and neither had Sam. I was beginning to get worried that it was someone I was starting to care about.

'Who?' said Sarah, 'oh, it was Perry.'

'Perry.' We hadn't been especially close and we had had that run-in over what he'd said to Lance, but I still felt a knot in my stomach.

'And is he okay?' I asked.

'Well he's alive if that's what you mean. But he's got a broken leg and a broken pelvis apparently. Sam's been in to see him but she says he wasn't very aware that she was there.'

Andrea came over and joined us.

'So,' said Suzy, 'what do you know?'

'According to Mo,' she said, 'he was turning right on the roundabout and a car came round on the left and clipped him on the side panel. That sent him one way and his scooter the other and the car behind couldn't stop in time and ran over both Perry and his scooter.' She described all of this in the air with her hands. 'The first car didn't stop so they've taken the scooter to analyse the paint marks on the panel. It's a mangled mess though, it'll definitely be a write-off.'

'When did it happen?' I asked.

'Sunday evening,' said Andrea.

'And who's been to see him?' asked June.

'Well Sam went yesterday,' said Suzy, 'and Dave's over there now, I think. Bertie's probably gone with him.'

'He's not got much of a family,' said Sarah, 'so we'll have to set up a bit of a rota if he's in there for a long time.'

'Apparently he lived with Lance and his Mum for a bit,' I said, 'we should tell them.'

'Will you do that?' said Andrea. 'I expect you're the person with the most contact with them right now.'

'Yes,' I said. 'I don't know how to get in touch with Lance, he's never given me a work number, but I can tell his Mum.'

I thought about it for a moment. 'Maybe I'll do that now.' I wasn't really in the mood for dancing and I don't think anyone else was either. 'Do you mind?' I said to June.

'No, I'll be fine, you know that,' she said. 'Come back here later maybe.'

'Yeah, or I'll see you tomorrow.' I said. 'I hope Alex shows up.'

It was only 8pm so I decided it wasn't too late to go back and see Mrs Morales. She looked surprised to see me again so soon.

'I just thought I ought to let you know that it was Perry who had the accident,' I said as I stood on the doorstep.

'Oh no,' she said. 'Not Perry. Is he alright do you know?' I told her what I knew about the accident and his injuries.

'Well I must go and see him,' she said. She looked about ready to get her coat on. 'Do you know what ward he's on?'

I didn't know any useful details so I sat in the front room while Lance's Mum phoned the hospital. She seemed to get passed round several departments but finally hung up and came through to show me the scrap of paper she had written on.

'There we go,' she said. 'He's on Ward Seven. Visiting hours are three until eight in the afternoon.' She looked at the clock. 'So we've missed it today. I'll go tomorrow. Will you come with me?'

I hadn't really thought about actually going in to see Perry myself, but I didn't want to let Mrs Morales down so I said I would. We agreed to meet at the hospital the next day after I'd finished at college.

I wasn't in the mood to go back to the Red Cow so I rode home. I was a bit more careful than I been for a while and was extremely aware of other vehicles passing around me. It felt as though every junction was fraught with danger and every driver a self-centred jerk with no thought for any other road users. Nevertheless, or perhaps because of my extra care, I got home safely.

I found my invite letter on the kitchen table. It looked very similar to June's but the scooter looked like mine and had a design of the Needles lighthouse on the leg shield. The invite was signed 'Jules and Fred' and there was an x under Jules' name. I took it upstairs and pinned it to the wall behind my bed.

Chapter Thirteen

I woke up on Thursday feeling a bit nervous about visiting Perry. I wondered what I'd have to say apart from 'How are you?'

'Did anything interesting happen last night?' I asked June when I got to college.

'Not really,' she said. 'Alex didn't come. None of the SeaDogs were there and the girls left quite early. Your boys showed up though.'

'My boys?'

'Yeah, Col'n'Phil, Phil'n'Col, we need a better nickname for them. So did Ben, surprisingly. I haven't seen him for ages.'

'But you live next door to him.'

'I know. I think he's been avoiding me. I haven't seen Tom for even longer. It's like the house next door is empty.'

'I'd heard Tom was shacking up with a girl in Southend,' I said. We had both fancied Ben's brother Tom and June had had a bit of a thing with him, but I hardly thought about him these days.

'I'd heard he was in Rayleigh.'

'Oh well, down that way somewhere, it hardly matters.'

'So, anyway, I palmed your boys off on to Ben and they seemed to be getting on well. Ben was really upset about Perry though.'

'Well, he's only just got over his accident hasn't he? I expect he's thinking about what it was like for him.'

'Yes, probably. He said he would go and visit this afternoon.'

'Oh, I'm going then with Lance's Mum.'

'Poor Perry,' said June. 'I expect he's never been so popular.'

Later, at the hospital I waited for Lance's Mum in the car park. She arrived by bus, laden down with Co-op bags.

'The manager donated all of the nearly out of date and damaged stuff,' she explained. 'The catering in these places is always poor.' She showed me inside one of the bags where I could see a bunch of lightly blackening bananas and a squashed box of shortbread. There was also a car magazine and a puzzle book.

'I haven't brought anything,' I said.

'I'm sure just yourself will be good enough,' she said. Besides, I've brought enough for two.' Or three or four, I thought.

We wandered the corridors together looking for Ward Seven which wasn't logically located between Wards Six and Eight as I'd thought it might have been. We eventually found the ward and Perry who was in a bed near the nurses' station. He appeared to be awake but tired. He gave a weak smile when he saw Mrs Morales.

'Hello Marie,' he said. 'Hi Annie. Is Salty here?' He looked behind us as if expecting him to come through the doors.

'No,' said Lance's Mum. 'We don't think he knows yet,' she paused and looked at me. I shook my head. 'Otherwise I'm sure he'd be straight up here.'

'So', I said, before Mrs Morales could, 'how are you?'

'In pain,' he said. His arms were free but under the blanket he looked quite bulky. He lifted it to show us the plaster cast which started at his chest and covered both legs.

'Wow,' I said. It was quite an impressive sight.

'Yeah,' he said. 'That's what everyone says.'

'Have you had a lot of visitors?' asked Mrs Morales.

'Loads,' he said. 'All the SeaDogs, apart from Salty, came yesterday. The nurse got annoyed and threw half of them out. It's good to see you though.'

'Well, I've missed seeing you,' said Mrs Morales. 'Lance goes and his friends disappear too.' She looked quite weepy for a moment. 'It's just a shame you have to be in hospital for me to get to see you.'

'Anyway,' she said, giving herself a shake. 'I've bought you a few bits.' She piled the contents of the bags on to his bedside table and in the cupboard. When she'd filled those she gave up and left the rest on the floor in a bag. Conversation lulled for a moment. I saw Ben coming through the ward doors clutching a box of Milk Tray so I saw my opportunity to escape for a moment.'

'I'll go and get some teas, shall I?' I asked.

When I came back, juggling four hot paper cups I looked through the glass in the door to see Perry laughing at something. From the back it looked as though Lance's Mum was giggling. Ben was waving his hands in front of him, explaining something. I was a little reluctant to butt in on such a happy scene. I could see Sam coming down the corridor so I waited for her.

'They won't let him have more than three visitors,' I said to her, 'so why don't you go in instead of me.' I gave her the teas. 'Tell Lance's Mum I'll go round and see her next week sometime.' I didn't give Sam a chance to argue. As I escaped down the corridors I felt a bit guilty but also felt quite relieved I'd managed to get away. I'd not had much experience of hospitals but what I had seen didn't make me want to stay there any longer than necessary.

I wondered if I would hear from Lance before Tuesday. If he'd phoned someone else and they'd told him about Perry then he would probably come and visit and I was sure he would let me know if he was going to be in the area. We could meet for a coffee at least. He didn't phone though.

I spent quite a lot of Saturday drawing my invitation acceptance to Jules. I'd tried to draw scooters before but they usually came out slightly twisted so it looked as though the front wheel would be heading in a different direction to the back one. After the third attempt and lots of rubbing out, I got something I was reasonably happy with and spent another hour colouring it in. I had a rainbow going over the side panels and the leg shields started at indigo at the top, going through the colours, down to red at the bottom. I quite liked the finished effect, at least in felt tips on paper and wondered if the same thing would work in paint on metal.

On the back of my finished drawing I wrote, 'See you on the 2nd November, Love Annie.' I added three kisses since I was a girl and could get away with adding that many without it being an obvious declaration of love. I put it in an envelope and cadged a stamp from Dad and took it to the post box. June and I hadn't discussed how we were going to get down to Devon but I guessed we could figure out the details closer to the time.

By Tuesday I was desperate to speak to Lance. I wondered if I would be the one to tell him about Perry. It turned out that he'd already heard as he'd phoned his Mum before me. He was quite upset.

'I can't believe it happened more than a week ago and I'm only just finding out now,' he said. I wanted to say something about him not being easy to contact but decided it wouldn't be worth it.

'So are you able to visit?' I asked.

'I don't know. It's Skegness this weekend. I'm due to go up in the van and work on the stall again, so I don't know if we can take a detour. I'll have to see.'

'It must be sort of on your way,' I said, 'or at least not too far off it. You could see your Mum too.' And me, I thought.

'Yeah, well I'll see what Gary says. If I can, I'll let you know. I expect it will be a short visit though. I might only have time to visit the hospital.'

'So I might not see you then?'

'Maybe not. Not unless you've changed your mind about Skegness?' I'd already said I wasn't going to the rally. Most of the SeaDogs and Sessex Girls were going but they had jobs and I really didn't have the money. It already felt strange that a rally would happen and I wouldn't be at it but there wasn't much I could do about it.

'No,' I said, 'I'm spent out.'

June had decided that she wasn't going to Skegness either.

'If you're not going, I'm not going,' she said loyally, although I wasn't sure if the reason was really because she hadn't been able to find anyone to give her a lift.

'You are going to see Perry, right?' I said, remembering that he'd given her a lift down to Isle of Wight.

'Yes, I will do,' she said. 'I'll come with you the next time you go.'

'Whenever that is.' I hadn't made any plans to go back up there.

I had made plans to go and see Lance's Mum again on Wednesday though. It only took five minutes to get there from college and so it was easy to pop in.

'I've been to see Perry three time since I saw you last,' she said.

'Oh,' I said, 'how is he?'

'He's okay, I suppose,' she said. 'It's still a little early to say that he's healing. I think he's in a lot of discomfort. His Dad's only been to see him once so I go in the afternoons to give him some company and take his mind off it. We do the crosswords. The boys come round at about tea time so I go then.'

'The SeaDogs?'

'Yes. And that young boy. Ben?'

'Yes.'

'He's a lovely boy, isn't he?' she said. 'Very polite. He tells me he's supposed to be studying for his exams but instead he's spending all his time cheering up Perry.'

Before I could agree on how nice Ben was the phone rang. Mrs Morales jumped.

'I suppose I should answer that,' she said. She went into the hall and shut the door behind her. There was muffled conversation for a few minutes, then she opened the door still holding the receiver.

'It's Lance,' she said. 'I told him you were here and he wants a word.' I took the phone and she went into the kitchen.

180

'Hello,' he said, 'Annie?'

'Yes. Hi,'

'It was strange hearing you were at my Mum's,' he said. I couldn't tell how much Mrs Morales could overhear so I was careful with what I said.

'I've been round a few times,' I said. 'Your Mum has been keeping me updated on Perry.'

'Yes, she says she's been up to the hospital a bit,' he said. 'That's what I'm phoning about.'

'Seeing Perry?'

'Yeah, I'm being dropped off there on Sunday afternoon, about four, and I'll stay until Monday morning then catch a train back here. I was going to phone you at home to see if you wanted to meet up.'

'You won't have a lot of time,' I said.

'Does that mean no?'

'No, it doesn't mean no. It's just that you need to see Perry and your Mum and you only have one evening.'

'Well, I was just thinking, since you seem to be round at my Mum's so often, maybe I could meet you there?'

'It's possible,' I said.

'Can you put her back on then, and I'll sort it out with her?'

'Okay.'

'I'll maybe see you on Sunday, then, about seven?'

'Yep,' I said. 'I'll see you then.'

I called Mrs Morales back and gave her the phone. A couple of minutes later she came back into the front room looking happy but flustered.

'Finally,' she said, 'I get to see my boy.'

'Is that okay if I come over too?' I asked. 'Lance invited me, I don't know if he said.'

'Yes, of course, it is,' she said. 'I'll cook us something special, shall I?'

'That would be nice,' I said, 'but only if you let me bring a pudding.'

That weekend I had some work with the outside catering company. As usual it was hard work at a fast pace but it paid quite well and I needed the money. One of the men on one of my tables slipped me a tenner. 'For good service,' he said, pushing it into my skirt pocket and taking the chance to feel me up at the same time. His wife looked on grimly. I wished I had the nerve to make a fuss but ten pounds would go quite a long way towards my upcoming trip to Devon, so I smiled and thanked him.

Running up and down the tables I spent the quiet moments when no one was demanding my attention wondering what the others were up to at Skegness. Maybe they were in a pub gearing up for an all-nighter or just hanging around the campsite drinking and chatting. There was a chill in the air as we packed up the van with the crockery and cutlery at the end of the evening and for a moment I was quite thankful I had a warm bed to go back to.

I spent Sunday morning making my pudding for the meal round at Lance's. I had had a hard time thinking of something that could easily be transported on the back of a scooter and had finally decided to make an apple and blackberry pie. That involved going to pick some blackberries from some bushes near the allotments. Dad said he would come with me.

'So,' he said, as we were examining the bushes for ripe berries, 'it seems like we haven't talked for ages, you and me.'

'I've been here,' I said.

'Yes, I know,' he said, 'but it seems you're either just off somewhere or coming back from somewhere. I can't even remember where you've been this year. You've seen more of the country than me.'

'I have seen quite a bit of it,' I admitted. 'Not the North East though, I should've been in Skegness this weekend.'

'Well, I'm more pleased you're here.'

'Dad,' I said, 'I finish college next summer. After that I could go anywhere.'

'Yes,' he said, 'I do know. I was hoping Julia would come home, that she'd have got her wanderlust under control with a summer in Spain, but it appears as if she's going even farther away. And Mum's busy with her new job.'

'I'd make the most of it, Dad, I said. 'A little bit of peace and quiet.'

'Well a little bit is alright, of course, but I'm finding I don't like too much of it.'

183

'Maybe you need a new hobby,' I said. 'Men your age like Harley Davidsons don't they? Buy one of those and you'll be out more than me and have something to polish when you're at home.'

'Not quite my thing,' he said, 'I'm not having a mid-life crisis. I've just got to adjust with not living in a female-dominated house anymore.'

'Oh, it'll still be female-dominated,' I said. 'You don't think Mum's going to let you have your way do you?'

'No,' he agreed, 'perhaps not.'

Later, on the way to Lance's Mum's house I thought about how I took my parents for granted. So many people I knew seemed to have difficult relations with theirs and some of them had no parental relationship at all. It made me feel grateful that my parents had always been there for me. They'd given me enough space to find out who I wanted to be and didn't impose their own preferences on to me. If I failed they were disappointed, but not cross, and we talked about how I might not fail the next time. Although they never actually said it, I knew they loved me and that helped me feel safe and secure. It made me realise how lucky I was.

Mrs Morales was on her own when I got round to her house.

'I was expecting him about half an hour ago,' she said, 'so I'm hoping he's alright. He'll have to get a cab from the hospital though as there aren't any buses at this time on a Sunday.'

As she was saying this, there was a noise at the back door and Lance came in, looking grubby and tired. His Mum twitched as if she was desperate to hug him but was holding herself back. I also didn't know how to greet him so just stood there in the kitchen grinning a bit stupidly. We all three of us stood there for a moment, no one really sure what to say.

'Well,' said Lance, in the end. 'Hi, Mum, sorry it's been so long.'

Mrs Morales moved in and put her arms around his neck, hugging him close. She was about his height. Her hair covered her face and as Lance put his arms around her and whispered something into her ear for a second I was unsure if I was watching a mother and a son or two lovers. I stood there awkwardly, waiting for them to finish.

When they drew apart, Mrs Morales wiped her nose with a tissue and kept her eyes down on the floor. Lance moved over to me.

'Hi Annie,' he said and gave me a quick peck on the cheek. I held on to his sleeve and breathed in his slightly fuggy breath.

'Sorry,' he said, 'I'm really smelly. Would either of you mind if I had a quick shower?' His Mum fussed about finding fresh towels and non-flowery soap and I sat on my own in the front room for a bit. After a while I thought I should check on the dinner and so went into the kitchen and took the potatoes off the boil and put them into the roasting

185

tray in the oven. I was just basting the chicken when Mrs Morales came back in.

'Oh,' she said, 'have you done all that? You are good.'

We made small talk for a while until Lance reappeared looking much cleaner and in fresh clothes.

'I'll go through my wardrobe in the morning before I go, Mum,' he said. 'I didn't realise I had so much stuff here.'

I could tell Mrs Morales was hoping he would stay more than just a night and she looked a bit deflated at his comments.

'Of course, love,' she said. 'Take anything you like. I've got a bag you can use I'm sure.'

She put the kettle on and we sat around the front room talking about Perry. There seemed to be a lot they wanted to say to each other so I offered to do the vegetables and left them to it. When I went back in they seemed a bit more relaxed and I just listened to Mrs Morales tell Lance about some incident that had happened at work and a run in she'd had with the DHSS.

Over dinner Lance told us about his work and the flat he was planning to move into.

'I should be able to move next weekend,' he said. 'Then I'll feel a bit more settled.'

'Portsmouth, though,' said Mrs Morales. 'It's a long way away.'

'It isn't really though, is it, Mum?' said Lance. 'It only takes a few hours on the train. It's not like I've gone abroad or anything.'

186

'Well you have to come back and visit me,' she said. 'You can't expect me to stay in a flat full of boys. I'm sure they wouldn't want me, anyway.'

'I'll come back for Christmas,' he said. She looked a bit happier.

I hadn't said anything for ages except for accepting their praise for my pie which had only got slightly squashed in transit.

Finally they remembered I was still there. 'Why don't you and Annie go for a walk while I wash up?' said Mrs Morales to Lance.

The air outside was fresh and welcoming after the slightly stale atmosphere in the house. It was dark and cloudy and no stars were visible.

'So,' I said, in order to put off any more serious talk, 'how was Skegness?'

'Good,' he said. 'We were really busy on the stall. Everyone was thinking about what work they're going to do on their scooters over the winter and buying up the parts.'

'Are you doing work on yours?' I asked.

'Yes, in the evenings and at weekends. You won't recognise it when you see it.'

'Did you see the others at the rally?'

'Yeah, I spent Saturday evening with Dave and Bertie. The girls had gone off somewhere. We were talking about having a Portsmouth chapter of the SeaDogs.'

'You mean you'd invite new members?'

'I suppose, otherwise it would just be me. At least being a SeaDog makes sense on the south coast. You see the navy vessels coming in and going out down there, it just makes you want to join up.'

We had walked as far as the local playground and we took a seat on neighbouring swings.

'You're not going to though?' The thought made me feel quite worried.

'No.' He looked at me and laughed. ''See, it's not so much fun when it's me talking about traveling is it?'

I had to agree that it wasn't. It was actually quite unsettling.

'So, anyway,' he said, 'will you come and visit? There's lots I'd like to show you.'

'Yes, if you think that's a good idea. Do you know when would be good?'

'In a couple of weeks, maybe. Sometime before the end of the October?'

'That would be good.' At least he wasn't wanting me to visit the same weekend I had the invite to Devon. I hadn't told Lance about Jules's party, I wasn't sure what his reaction would be.

'I'll phone you after next weekend then. Hopefully I'll have moved in and we can fix a date.'

'A date,' I said.

'Yes, you know what I mean,' he said. 'Fix a date, not 'a date'.'

'Oh.'

'Come on, Annie,' he said. 'You know where we stand.'

'Sorry,' I said quietly. 'It's just that no one else makes me feel like you do.' I couldn't believe that I had actually said this out loud. I could feel myself blush.

Lance came over, took my hands and pulled me upright.

'I could really take advantage of that, you know,' he said. 'I am trying to do the right thing, but it's very hard.' We leaned in towards each other and my breath caught in my throat. He bent down and kissed my neck under my ear and I moved in so my cheek was touching his. He'd had a shave and his face was smooth. I lifted my hand and stroked his other cheek, feeling up to his forehead and across the back of his head, my fingers getting caught in his hair. Our lips met and we kissed deeply. We only broke away when a man in a mac with a dog on a lead walked past and coughed loudly.

When he'd gone, Lance held my face in his hands. 'I could just take you in the bushes now,' he said. Part of me wanted this, but I knew he was joking. I did feel a little triumphant knowing I could still turn him on, that I still had a hold over him. Then I felt ashamed that I'd even thought that without knowing quite why.

'Your Mum will be worried about you,' I said and began to move back towards his house. He came with me and we joined hands.

'An evening's not long enough,' I said.

'Nor for me either,' he agreed. 'I can't say I'll be able to control myself if you come for a weekend. You ought to be ready for that. Know whether you want to fight me off or not.'

189

'You'd better be ready for it, in case I don't,' I said and he squeezed my hand tightly.

On the corner near his house he stopped and kissed me again and then broke away abruptly. 'I ought to look your scooter over before you go,' he said. 'I bet you haven't.'

We spent the last half hour before I left with Lance on his knees examining parts of my scooter, poking around and tightening bolts. I sat on the front door step and Mrs Morales stood in the open doorway.

'You're welcome to stay the night if you'd like, Annie' she said. 'I can make a bed up for you.'

'Thank you,' I said, 'but my parents will be expecting me back soon.' Much as I'd have liked to stay and have longer with Lance, I knew that the right thing to do was to go home. Whatever there was simmering between us could wait.

I rode home feeling dazed and aroused. When I got home I parked up and sat on my scooter for ages until Mum saw me and shouted through the window for me to come in.

Chapter Fourteen

The following week I found it hard to concentrate on college work. At the same time it seemed that every teacher was feeling the need to go on about being prepared for the exams at the end of the year and the importance of knowing what we wanted to do once we had finished the course. I couldn't think further than the end of October when I'd have a chance to see Lance again.

'I've got a place on the Hotel Management HND course at Westminster' boasted Steve. 'I reckon I'll have my own chain within ten years. Keep in touch and I'll let you have a five percent discount on a night's room rental. If you can afford it, that is.

I had a careers meeting with the course principal on Tuesday. I told her about my ideas for working abroad but admitted that I was perhaps casting my net too wide. Out of the four letters I'd written I'd only had one reply. This had come with a lot of interesting information but made it clear that they preferred applicants to be at least twenty one. It was obvious as I spoke that beyond a desire to travel, I didn't really know what I wanted to do.

'It doesn't have to be catering, you know,' she said to me. 'It might help to think of this course as the equivalent of A Levels. People do all sorts of things when they leave sixth form. And you can ignore those people who tell you that the HND is the best route. It is for some, but a good proportion of them won't end up in hotel management. The most important thing is to have a plan but also to be flexible, build in some opportunities to change direction.'

She looked as though she was about to get all confessional and tell me about her route to her current job, so I gave some quick promises to come up with a plan and made my getaway.

'How's your career plan coming along?' I asked June, expecting her to not even have thought about it.

'I'm looking into event planning,' she said, 'or tour management, something like that.'

'Wow.'

'I know. The rallies made me think of it. They must take a huge amount of organisation. You've got all the food vans, all the traders, the entertainment, security, marshals and all that. Loads of negotiating just to get everyone in the right place at the right time doing the right jobs. I reckon I'd be good at that.'

'Yeah, I reckon you would.' I'd never heard June talk so seriously about anything. 'You've got the right sort of people skills. So how do you learn about that sort of thing?'

'Well,' she said, 'it looks as though a couple of the polytechnics have courses, or you could just get a job and get them to train you up.'

'Do you know of anywhere?' I asked.

'I'm looking into it.'

I took June to see Perry before we went to the Red Cow on Wednesday. I wasn't sure if he'd already have visitors but he was alone when we showed up.

'Visitor numbers are down,' he reported. 'I reckon they've all got fed up with me.'

'Well, we're here now,' I said, 'and Lance was here on Sunday wasn't he?'

'Yeah,' he said, 'it was good to see Salty. He looks well doesn't he? Did you see him?'

'I saw him for a bit at his Mum's, after he came here,' I said.

'Annie's in lurve, all over again,' said June.

'Thanks, June,' I said. 'I don't know why I bring you.'

'Cos you love me too?'

'Indeed.'

'So,' said June to Perry, 'when are you getting out?'

'Not for a bit yet,' he said. 'They've got to check and see how everything's healing, but they say it takes at least six weeks. After that they might let me out if I have somewhere to go where there's someone to look after me.'

'And do you?' asked June.

193

'Not really. There's only my Dad at home and he can't take care of himself, let alone me. If I can't find anywhere, I'll have to stay here.' He looked mournful and we were all quiet for a while.

'I don't suppose Mrs Morales knows you could do with somewhere to stay, does she?' I asked.

'I don't think I've said anything about it to her,' said Perry.

'But she'd have you,' I said. 'She's quite lonely now Lance has gone, well she seems it anyway, she's always really pleased when I go round. And you get on well, don't you?'

'Yes but it's a bit much to ask her to look after me, isn't it?'

'I could ask her though, she could say no to me,' I said. 'Not that she will.'

'Let me think about it,' said Perry.

At the Red Cow, the others told us about their weekend at Skegness.

'It was a bit quiet without you two and Perry,' said Sam. 'And I only saw Salty briefly.'

'Yes,' said Andrea, 'when we started out there were only a few of us, and then at Isle of Wight there were loads and now the numbers are dropping again. It makes me wonder what it'll be like next year, whether everyone will have moved on.'

'Not me,' said Dave. 'I'm a scooter boy until I die. When I'm fifty, I'll still be riding my scoot to the seaside at weekends.'

194

'You hope,' said Suzy. 'There seem to be more and more accidents.'

'Yeah,' said June. 'Has anyone thought about doing something for Perry, if his scooter's a write off?'

'It is,' said Dave. 'I'm sorting out the insurance for him. Luckily he went for comprehensive because they never found the car. He'll get a pay-out of some sort.'

'Then what?' June asked.

'Well, Salty and I had a chat over the weekend and he reckons he can get hold of something he can do up for him.'

'Would he want that though?' I asked.

'If we gave it with no preconditions, no expectations, tell him he can sell it if he wants. He's already thinking about how he can be mobile for Easter so we should give him a hand with that if we can.'

'But what if you choose a model he doesn't like?' asked June.

'He'll like it if he knows we made it with love,' said Sam. 'We'll get everyone to contribute a part, then it'll be more than just a scooter.'

'Who's going to organise that though?' asked June.

'You should,' I said. 'It would be a good test of your event management skills.'

'Yeah, maybe,' she said. 'You'll have to be the go-between for Lance and me though, find out what he needs.'

195

It felt good to think we were doing something nice for Perry. I wondered what I could contribute, whether I would go for some performance part, or something more showy on the outside. I wondered briefly if I could get Jules to do the paintwork. I'd have to do some digging to find out what sort of look Perry preferred, it would be easy to get it wrong.

Inside the Red Cow June bought us both a half pint of lager. 'You know,' she said, 'I was thinking about our party. Perhaps I could organise it, test out my management skills? I'd ask for your input of course.'

'Yes, of course,' I said. 'I trust you to do a good job.' We were about to get down to the details of what we wanted when June's attention was distracted by someone standing in the doorway. I turned to see who she was looking at. It was Ben, standing next to a small girl with a shock of curly hair. She looked slightly familiar but I couldn't place her. I looked at June to see her reaction. She looked horrified for a second but then her face relaxed.

'That must be the nurse,' she said and as she said it I remembered where I'd seen the girl: she'd been at the nurse's station the first time I'd gone in to see Perry.

'Ben came round the other day and told me there was someone he wanted to ask out,' June explained. 'He wanted to check that I didn't mind.'

'And do you?'

'It would be mean of me to, wouldn't it? I thought we had something good, but it didn't last long. I'm not even sure what that was all about now.'

'Lust?'

'It usually is, but it wasn't with Ben, it was something else that I couldn't quite put my finger on. Maybe I'll regret it in years to come.'

'Maybe,' I said. 'Should we go over and introduce ourselves?' As I said this I saw I didn't need to, as Ben was coming over.

'Hi, you two,' he said. 'This is Katie. Katie, this is June and Annie. Katie is interested in knowing more about scooters and soul music so I've brought her here to find out.'

Katie smiled, then giggled and gave a little wave. Rather awkwardly we waved back.

'Ben showed me your scooter outside,' she said to me. 'He says you've been everywhere on it.'

'Well, I've been a few places,' I said. 'And no major accidents so far, fingers crossed.' It occurred to me that she must see more than her fair share of road accident victims.

Yes,' she said, 'you've got to be careful. Perry was very lucky you know. He could have had much more internal damage than he did.'

'Really?' asked June.

'Oh yes,' said Katie and launched into a detailed explanation of the problems that often came with pelvic bone injuries. June looked fascinated.

197

'Happy?' I asked Ben as we looked on.

'Oh yes,' he said. 'I couldn't be happier. She's lovely, isn't she?'

'Yes,' I agreed, 'I am sure she is.'

I could see someone hovering on the edge of the conversation, looking between June and Katie. I didn't recognise him. It seemed strange, just as Andrea was worrying about people drifting away, here was a whole set of new people. Finally June noticed someone waiting for her attention.

'Alex,' she shouted loudly.

'Yeah,' he said. 'Sorry I didn't make it last time, something came up, you know? I thought I'd try again this week. See if you were here.'

June grinned. Katie moved back to stand with Ben. I hoped June hadn't interrupted her in full flow. I decided to leave June and Alex to it for a bit.

'Do you dance?' I said to Katie.

'I do,' she said, 'but perhaps not like this?' she pointed to the dancers on the floor.

'Come with me, I'll show you,' I said. She looked at Ben as if for approval and he nodded. We found a corner of the dance floor and I showed her some of my moves. It didn't take her long to get into the rhythm and she began to look like she was enjoying herself.

'Thanks,' she said over the noise of the music, 'you're a good teacher.'

'Anytime,' I said. 'It wasn't that long ago that I was standing there wondering how I should dance myself.'

'I didn't know what to wear to come here,' she said. She had a denim skirt and a stripy t shirt on.

'You look fine,' I said. 'The thing to remember is most people come by scooter so they have to wear clothes that are suitable for riding in. You can dress up if you want, some people do the sixties mod thing, and it's nice to do your eyes, but I'd say wear whatever you're comfortable in.'

'Thanks,' she said. 'I might come again. If Ben asks me that is.' I could see the way he was watching her every move from the edge of the floor, clutching the drinks he'd bought for them.

'Oh, he will, I am sure,' I said.

After another couple of tracks Katie said she was getting off the floor and I was left alone in my little corner. June and Alex looked to be deep in conversation so I just carried on dancing.

Sometimes when I danced I listened hard to the music, finding the beat and listening for all the different instruments. Other times I just danced instinctively and my mind wandered elsewhere. This was one of those evenings. I thought about June and her career plans already being put into practice and Lance and Jules with their skills and knowledge. I even thought about Katie and her profession, one that was highly valued and appreciated by the public if not well paid. I thought about Dave with his safe office job that even a couple of years in wasn't satisfying him. I didn't feel as if I had any particular skills or talents I could draw on and wondered what would happen to me,

199

where I'd be in five or ten years' time. Maybe, I thought, I should opt out and find a man who wanted children and was prepared to keep me at home to look after them. The thought filled me with horror and I realised I was going to have to put a bit more effort into thinking about what I was going to do once I was done with college. I was going to have to be a little bit more realistic than just talking vaguely about traveling without any sense of whether such a thing was achievable for someone like me.

After a few more tracks my thoughts started to go round in circles. I decided that June had had enough time on her own with Alex and went over to interrupt their cosy chat. June introduced me.

'Hi Annie,' said Alex, standing up. He put his hand on my shoulder and gave me a kiss on the cheek. He was tall with short blond hair and a wide smile. He wore a cut off jacket covered in rally patches.

'I've heard a lot about you,' he said. 'You're June's driver, I hear.'

'Yes, sometimes. I expect she was more comfortable coming back from Weston in your van though.'

'Probably,' he said, 'although we did have to squeeze her in.'

'So what do you do, exactly?'

'My Dad and I have a shop. We sell new scooters and accessories mostly. Front racks, back racks, florida bars, that sort of thing.'

'So you could help with Perry's scooter maybe?' I wondered if that was a bit cheeky especially as we'd only just met.

'Well June did mention it. I am sure we can do some discounts. You'll have to let me know what you need.'

'Oh, we will do,' said June.

June spent the rest of the week in higher spirits than usual. We settled on a date for the party towards the beginning of December and she went to meet the manager of the Red Cow to see what she could book for that date.

'He said we were lucky,' she said when I saw her the next day. 'He reckons he's usually booked right through December by now, but he had a few dates available and ours was one of them. We've got the upstairs room and buffet food. I said there'd be about fifty of us.' I'd never invited more than about eight people to a party before so the thought of inviting fifty made me feel quite nervous. I was glad that June was in charge. We'd decided to make each other birthday cakes.

'Not as a competition,' said June although we both knew that we would be trying our best to out-do each other. I had already sketched out a few ideas.

We'd thought about booking a band but decided to go with a DJ and June was planning to ask the regular soul night guy. 'I just need to make sure he can do a few requests for the non-scooterists amongst us, like my Nan,' she said.

201

According to June this just left us to decide on the guest list, do the invites and plan some decorations. 'You make it all sound so easy,' I said.

We spent one lunch-time writing out a list of who we wanted to invite. This attracted a lot of attention and a lot of requests for invitations.

Phil'n'Col were the first to make a claim. June was open to their pleas but heartless in her response. 'Well, we'll see if we have any room left once we've invited the people we want to invite,' she told them. 'Sit by your letterbox but don't hold your breath.'

Steve was the next to sidle up. 'So,' he said, 'Revelations not good enough for you, is it?'

'Well quite apart from the fact that Annie won't actually be eighteen when we hold this party,' said June, 'we'd rather choose our guests rather than take our chances with whoever's on the pull in town that night.'

'I'll be on the pull,' he said, 'I'm specifically looking for any smoky-eyed modettes you might be able to send my way. Scruffily dressed scooterists won't be welcome.' He looked me up and down pointedly.

''You'll have to take your chances at the smoky-eyed mod and modette night on the other side of town then,' said June, 'cos, guess what? You're not getting an invite.'

'Oh well,' he said huffily, 'I expect I'll be up in London anyway.'

'Are we going to invite anyone from college?' I asked June as Steve wandered off. She counted up the names we had written down so far. 'Well we have a few spaces,' she said. 'We could invite a couple of the girls.'

'And Phil'n'Col?'

'Yeah, why not? I expect they'll bring good presents.'

I said I'd design the invites and spent a happy weekend with a new pack of felt pens. I wanted something that related to scooters but didn't put off those who couldn't tell a Vespa from a Lambretta without reading the badge. I ended up with a card made in the shape of a Vespa Speedometer with the speed and the miles both showing eighteen. Some people might be confused by the reference, I thought but at least they would understand the meaning.

I was keeping half an ear out for the phone as I was hoping Lance might find the time to call. He kept me waiting until after eight on the Sunday. He sounded happy and possibly slightly drunk.

'Number and address,' he shouted down the line and rattled them off so quickly I had to make him repeat them three times.

'So can I call you next time?' I asked.

'You can,' he said. 'Call anytime. If I'm not in, you can leave a message with Ed or with Stuart. If you have a choice, choose Stuart as he's more likely to write it down.' There was some friendly abuse in background and I realised I might have to get used to calls that were being taken part in by more than just Lance and myself.

'I'll probably still be in the garage most evenings,' he said. 'So try later on, after nine or something. Or I'll call you.' That seemed to be the end of the conversation and I wasn't sure if he was going to repeat his offer of a visit. There was a bit of silence before he remembered.

'Can you make it down then?' he said.

'When?' I asked.

'The last weekend in October? Not next weekend, the weekend after. Come down on Friday if you can.'

'Should I come on my scooter?' I asked.

'It doesn't matter,' he said. 'Mine's on the road, or it will be by then. Come by train, it might be safer if you're traveling on your own. I'll pick you up from the station. Bring your crash helmet though.'

'Okay,' I said. 'Should I bring anything else?'

'No. Just yourself. The boys are looking forward to meeting you.'

There was a muffled sound that I couldn't make out.

'Sorry,' Lance said. 'I was just seeing how far the phone would stretch. Turns out does make it into my room. Look, I won't keep you. I just wanted you to know I'm trying to make it nice for you here, so you'll have a good weekend. And, well, you know, I'm really looking forward to it.'

'Me too,' I said.

204

Chapter Fifteen

There were two more weeks of college before half term. Then I was due to visit Lance over the first weekend of the holiday and Jules over the second. I was desperate to hear news from Julia so I could find out how her flying visit would fit in with all of this. I came home late from an evening working for the outside caterers and found a note on the kitchen table.

'Annie, Julia visiting 31 Oct. Meet at Gatwick, 11am. Mum xxx'

I checked on the calendar and saw that the thirty first was the Wednesday in the middle of the half term so it would all presumably work out nicely with no one getting annoyed because I wasn't able to be where I was expected to be. I didn't keep a diary but I did think I should write it all down so I could keep a track of it.

I asked Mum if she could sort out my train tickets.

'Come in with me on Saturday morning,' she said. 'It's quite quiet early on so we can go through the timetables and decide what you want to book.'

'Won't I be in the way?' I asked.

'No, you'll be a legitimate customer. Anyway it's about time you came in to see what I do. This sort of thing might suit you, you know.'

On Saturday, Mum and I were first at the travel agents. She showed me her desk and made me sit on the customer side.

'Now,' she said, 'where do you want to travel to and when do you want to go?'

'You know all this, Mum,' I said, 'I told you on the way in.'

'Just behave like a proper customer, please Annie.'

I pulled out my list of dates and together we consulted a very thick book with all the train timetables in it. As we were doing so, the manager Paul and Monica, one of the other travel agents came in.

'Good morning,' said Paul to my Mum, 'is this your daughter?'

'No,' I said, 'I am a proper customer.'

'Good, good,' he said. 'I do like it if we do a bit of business this early in the morning. It makes me feel as though we're set up for the day. Now, who wants a cup of tea?'

Mum and I sorted out all the trains and she got on the phone to British Rail to book them. By the time she was done, an elderly couple had come in and were discussing cruises with Monica. I listened, fascinated as she spoke about ports of call and evening entertainment.

'Do you know,' said Mum, 'it can be cheaper to take a round the world cruise than stay at home over winter when you've got all the heating bills. We do quite a lot of this sort of thing.'

'That must be fun,' I said.

'It is,' she said. 'One of my first customers was a man booking a sixtieth birthday surprise cruise for his wife. They'll be on it now. I told him to come back in after they return and show me the photos.'

'I hope I have someone who'll book me a surprise cruise when I'm sixty.' I said.

'Well, I think they only met a couple of years ago, so there's no rush.'

'Just be picky,' said Paul, overhearing our conversation. 'Choose the one who's devoted to you, not the one who is just attracted by your figure.' I looked down at myself. I didn't think he could tell anything about my figure from what I was wearing. He realised what he'd said. 'Just talking generally, of course. That wasn't meant to be taken personally. Not that I don't think you don't have a nice figure, though. I am sure you do.'

'I'd stop there,' said Mum, 'before you dig yourself any deeper. I'm sure Annie knows what you mean, don't you Annie?'

I nodded. ''Find the right guy,' is what you said,'

'Indeed. Not that you need my advice I'm sure.' He busied himself with tidying the brochures on display. I saw Mum stifle a giggle which nearly set me off.

'Well, I'm done,' I said.

'You can stay if you like,' offered Paul. 'You could see what goes on here, do a bit of tidying maybe,' he waved his hands to indicate the already spotless desks and floor.

'As long as you keep out of the way,' said Mum.

I spent an interesting morning in the travel agency. I never knew that the people round our way were so adventurous. Mum sold one flight to Australia to a boy on a year out from university and helped another couple book bed and breakfasts along the Pennine Way.

'You never know who's going to come in,' said Paul to me when it was quiet. 'That's what's so good about this job. That and having people come back year after year because they know they'll get good service.'

I left at lunchtime as I had some work waitressing at a wedding in a hall down near the river. I recognised the bride as someone Julia had been to primary school with. Her dress had been made to accommodate her very obvious pregnancy. The groom, who I didn't recognise, downed several drinks in a very short period of time and became red faced and quite aggressive. While I wished them well, I didn't hold out much hope of their marriage lasting very long and I overheard one of the guests mumble to another: 'I'll give it six months.' I'd waitressed at a number of weddings now and there had been very few that looked like the fantasy wedding that girls talked about. The reality was

always very different from the daydreams it
seemed.

On Sunday I met June for party planning. I
gave her the invitation so she could get it copied
and the train times down to Devon so she could buy
a ticket for the same train.

'You're not going to be planning weddings,
are you?' I asked. 'You know, when you start
working.'

'I'll try and avoid it,' she said. 'I'd probably
end up talking them out of it and never make any
money. Anyway I've found a company that does
big shows up at places like Olympia so I'm putting
together my CV to send to them.'

'Good luck,' I said.

It seemed like a very long week, waiting for
Friday and my trip down to Portsmouth. I had to
take the bus into college so that I could catch the
train as soon as the last lesson finished.

'Give him one for me,' June said.

'I'm not giving anyone anything,' I shouted
over my shoulder as I hurried across the road
clutching my bag and crash helmet.

To get to Portsmouth I had to get across
London. At 4pm on a Friday afternoon this was
somewhat challenging and I ended up with my face
in someone's armpit.

'Lost your horse, have you?' asked a
middle-aged man in a cheap suit next to me,
pointing to the crash helmet.

'No,' I said, 'this is just in case I need to protect myself from my fellow passengers.'

The train out of London was equally packed but I managed to get a seat by a window and spent a happy hour looking into people's back gardens. After we got past Guildford the train had emptied out and I was able to spread out a bit. By the time we got to Hilsea where Lance was supposed to be meeting me, I was the only person left in the carriage.

As we pulled into the station I could see a scooter parked outside under the street lights and Lance was there waiting for me, chewing his nails. I was in the last carriage and he didn't see me at first. When he did, his face broke into a big smile.

'You made it then,' he said as we stood together awkwardly, not knowing how to greet each other. He took my bag from me and we walked out to the scooter. I hadn't seen it since he'd left it at the ferry terminal before Isle of Wight. The paintwork was still the same: green with images of trees on the leg shield and side panels, but most of the chromework looked newer and shinier and the tyres looked as though they'd been barely worn in.

'You can show me what you've done to it later,' I said, 'in as much detail as you like.'

'Really?' he said.

'Yes, perhaps I'll learn something.'

Lance strapped my bag onto the back rack.

'Just listen to the engine a moment,' he said, 'before you put your crash helmet on.' He kicked the engine over and revved it slowly.

'Sounds good, doesn't it,' he said.

'Not 'she'?' I asked.

'Yeah, alright, 'she'. I was trying to avoid giving her a sex,' he said 'but 'it' does sound wrong somehow.'

'It's not far,' he said as we got on. We rode through an industrial area and then into a residential one where we pulled up next to a three storey block of flats.

'We're on the top floor,' said Lance, pointing to one of the corners of the block. It looks south so you can see over the town and out over the water if it's clear enough.

'I bet you never thought that when your scooter broke down in Portsmouth, you'd end up living here,' I said. 'I suppose it all worked out.'

'Yeah,' he agreed. 'It seems to be. So far.'

I was a bit nervous of meeting Lance's flatmates and I hung back a bit as we climbed the stairs. Lance noticed.

'It's okay.' He said. 'Ed and Stuart are out tonight. There's a comedy night in Southampton they go to. You can meet them tomorrow.'

The flat was very blokey. The living room had brown carpet and old black leather sofas. Someone, presumably Lance, had obviously done some cleaning as the vacuum cleaner was in the middle of the room, still plugged in, and the ashtrays were empty. There was an ancient tv in one corner and shelves of albums next to a newer-looking record player.

211

Lance wound up the lead of the vacuum cleaner. 'I ran out of time,' he said. 'I've cleaned most rooms. I just suggest you don't open any cupboard doors.'

In the kitchen he put the kettle on. He looked a bit nervous.

'I've got some food in,' he said, opening the fridge to show its contents, or we can go out to eat. I know last time we did that it ended up badly, so I wasn't sure . . .'. He tailed off.

'Well,' I said. I'd seen in the fridge he had some chicken and some vegetables as well as a bottle of wine. 'I'd like to see you cook.'

'I'm a great cook,' he boasted.

'You can show me then,' I replied.

'There's also the issue of where you're going to sleep,' he said taking a deep breath. 'Let's sort that out now so we know where we stand.' He showed me his room which was empty except for a double bed, some shaped pieces of metal in one corner and a pile of clothes in another. The duvet cover had clearly just come out of the packet as the fold lines were still visible.

'You can have my bed,' he said.

'Well I'm not kicking you out,' I said, not looking at him.

'You're not?'

'No.'

'Okay.' I glanced up at him. He looked relieved.

'It would be a shame to waste the weekend, wouldn't it?' I said boldly.

212

'Yeah,' he said. 'That's what I was thinking. I'll get the dinner on, shall I?'

'Yes,' I said. 'Shall I leave you to it? I'll only be telling you how you should be doing it otherwise,'

Lance left me in the living room with a glass of wine.

'Put some music on if you like,' he said. 'None of the records are mine though so don't blame me for the appalling choice.'

I flicked through the albums. They were ordered alphabetically and began at AC/DC and ended at ZZ Top. There were a few pop albums hidden in there so I chose Altered Images and put that on. They were songs for dancing round your bedroom to but I was too anxious so I just sat and listened. I could hear clattering and frying sounds coming from the kitchen. A while later Lance stuck his head round the door.

'All ready,' he said. I followed him through. There was a small table that he'd pulled into the middle of the room and had set up with cutlery and glasses. There was a plastic flower in a beer mug in the middle.

'I just found that in the cupboard,' he said.

I sat down and Lance dished up. 'It's chicken cordon bleu,' he said, 'with sauté potatoes and carrots and peas.' The chicken was covered in breadcrumbs and looked to be cooked perfectly.

'You were right,' I said as I cut into the chicken and watched the cheese ooze out from the middle, 'you can cook.' He blushed slightly from the compliment.

'I've made pudding too,' he said, when we'd cleared our plates. He brought out a massive trifle from the back of the fridge.

'Blimey,' I said, 'is that meant to last all week?'

'Well, it won't,' he said, 'when Ed gets his hands on it. I've never made one before so I guessed the quantities. The custard's a bit lumpy.'

I worked around the lumps and then got up to help with the washing up. Lance washed and I dried. It all felt very domestic.

'There's some drinks in the other room,' Lance said. 'Spirits, I mean. They're Ed's but he won't mind.'

I went for a Southern Comfort and Lance poured himself a brandy.

'Very grown up,' I said.

We sat side by side on the sofa, not touching. I read and reread the cover of a motorbike magazine that had been left on the table, as our conversation stalled. The nerves were beginning to get to me.

'So . .' I said, just as Lance said 'What . .'. We both stopped. 'You first,' he said.

'I just wondered what we would do tomorrow,' I said. 'Do you have plans?'

'I thought we could go down into Portsmouth,' he said. 'We could walk along the front at Southsea, or take a tour round HMS Victory.'

'Can you do that?'

'You can. I haven't done it yet. It's down in the dockyard, where the ships left from to go to the Falklands.'

'Oh.' I hadn't known anybody involved in that war, but it was quite possible that Lance did.

'We could do that then,' I said.

'But now. .' I took a deep breath, put my drink down, brought my feet up so I was kneeling on the sofa and leaned over and kissed Lance on the mouth. He hurriedly put his drink down too and put both arms round my back, holding my shoulder blades and then moving slowly down. We shifted position until we were lying side by side full out on the sofa. His hands moved back up under my top, exploring my skin, feeling where my body changed direction.

'I hope your flatmates don't come home unexpectedly,' I said, as we broke for breath. 'Don't worry, I've put the lock on,' he said. 'Although we could go through to the bedroom. For safety?'

In the bedroom Lance turned on the light but there was no lampshade and the light was harsh so he quickly turned it off again. I shut the door and we were left with the light from the street lights below the window which cast shadows on to the ceiling.

We fell onto the bed, belt buckles and teeth clashing. Lance was above me, casting monster-like shadows. I decided to take the initiative and manoeuvred us round until I was on top, my legs either side of his hips. I lifted myself to undo the buttons on his shirt and then lay back down onto his bare chest. Hurriedly we removed the rest of our clothes. Lance grabbed the duvet cover and pulled it over us. His excitement took over and he took charge, shaping my body so he could enter me as deeply as possible. I heard sounds as though they were coming from someone and somewhere else other than me, in that room. I gave in to the sensations, working up towards the peak, the warmth spreading through me and I felt the flush up my neck and into my face and scalp. Lance stretched away from me, arching his back. He let out a deep cry and then fell onto me, waiting for his breathing to return to normal. A while later he shifted off me and we moved on to our sides, his legs bent up under mine. I held onto his arm and lay quietly, listening as his breathing slowed, trying to match his rhythm and enter unconsciousness myself. Much later I woke as the front door opened and voices whispered down the hallway. Lance was disturbed too and slowly we began to make love again.

Chapter Sixteen

I woke the next morning with the sun streaming in the window. There was a warm space behind me but no Lance. I heard sounds from the bathroom and then some clattering in the kitchen. He came back in the room dressed in boxer shorts and a t shirt carrying two mugs with plates of toast balanced on top. I dived under the covers looking for my clothes and resurfaced once I was more suitably dressed. Lance got back in next to me.

'Morning,' he said. 'Sleep well?'

'In places,' I said.

Lance placed a jammy kiss on my cheek. 'You look beautiful when you're asleep, especially when you're asleep in my bed.'

'Have you been awake long?' I asked.

'Ages. I'd be in the garage by now if you weren't here.'

'Just itching to get your hands on some metal?'

'Usually'' he said. 'This weekend I'm just itching to get my hands on something else.'

'Oh well,' I said, between slurps of tea. 'Make the most of me. Here for one weekend only.'

'Yeah,' he said. 'We should sort that out. See where we are. I know I broke up with you and you know the reason for that.'

'Yes.'

'Well, maybe I was too inflexible about that. I didn't realise how much you meant to me. I tried to stick to my decision, thinking it was best for you and maybe best for me in the long run. But maybe I shouldn't be too concerned about the long run. Maybe we should just see how things go. If you do decide to travel, then that's the time to decide whether we have a future.'

'Yes.'

'See, I get caught up in my principles,' he continued. 'I can't ask you down here and sleep with you without some sort of commitment. I know plenty of other people who could but that doesn't work for me.'

'So,' I said slowly, 'are you asking me to get back together with you?'

'Yes, I am. And just to make it clear I'll ask you properly. Annie, will you be my girlfriend? You can come down here whenever you like and I'll come up and see you and we'll make it work somehow.'

'Yes,' I said. 'Yes, I will.' I stuck out my hand and we shook on it.

I finished my toast and licked my fingers. A thought occurred to me.

'It's not just the sex is it?'

'What?'

'I mean, you asked me this morning, not last night. You waited until . .'

Lance laughed. 'It's more likely to work the other way on, isn't it? I ask you so you can be sure you'll sleep with me?'

'I suppose.'

'Anyway, to answer your question, I do fancy you rotten and I did feel jealous when I saw you with that lad at Weston but actually I like you beyond all that. I like who you are, how you think and the way you behave. I've said it before, I don't feel that way about anyone else.'

I only half heard this. My heart had stopped at his mention of Jules. I wondered how Lance was going to react when he knew I was planning to visit him the following weekend. For a second I thought about not mentioning it but I knew he would find out somehow.

I sat up and drew my knees up to my chest. 'You should probably know,' I said, 'that I've been invited to a party at Jules's next weekend?'

'The lad from Weston? Are you going?'

'I've said I would,' I said in a rush. 'There's nothing in it. June's going too. You could come over as well if you wanted.'

'Don't be daft. I can't invite myself to a party.' He thought for a moment. 'I suppose I ought to trust you.'

'Well you'll have to,' I said, 'and I you, since we're living so far apart. It'll be a good test.'

'I'll expect a full report,' he said.

Lance checked his watch. 'Now,' he said, 'we could stay here all day, but if you'd like to go out you might want to get in the bathroom before the boys get up.'

I had a quick shower and came out to find Lance sitting in the kitchen with a boy in a Motorhead t shirt. He said something that sounded like the punchline of a joke and Lance laughed out loud.

I stood in the doorway, waiting to be introduced.

'Ed, this is Annie,' said Lance. 'Annie, this is Ed. He's a Pompey boy.'

'Born and bred,' said Ed, holding out his hand. 'Hello Annie. I haven't heard much about you, partly because Lance seems to play his cards close to his chest and partly because I don't listen. But nice to meet you anyway. Have a seat and I'll make some tea.'

I sat down. 'I see you're not a scooterists then?' I said.

'Or I could be in deep disguise,' he suggested. 'No, I've never ridden one, Lance has yet to let me near his, so the scooter's charms are unknown to me. I'm more of a Kawasaki man myself.'

'So how did you meet?' I asked.

'I work in the unit next door to the scooter place. We met over a bacon roll from the sandwich van, I think.'

'How romantic,' I said.

'Yeah, well it was love at first sight. You know what they say about opposites attract.' Lance had stood up and Ed made a grab for him. Being quite a bit heavier he unbalanced Lance who nearly hit his head on the corner of the fridge.

In the middle of the commotion, the door to one of the bedrooms opened and Lance's other flatmate came into the kitchen wearing just his pants. He saw me and scuttled back to his room, coming back a few minutes later, fully dressed. He had a polo shirt and neatly pressed dark blue jeans on. He was small and thin with a vaguely Paul Weller-ish shaped haircut, and wore black framed glasses. He looked like he might be an estate agent or a bank clerk.

'Hello,' he said, 'you must be Annie. Sorry about just then, I forgot you were here. Although I might have realised it from the fact that Ed was showing off.'

'I was not showing off,' said Ed.

'You were,' said both Lance and Stuart.

'So, Annie, are you a scooterist too?' asked Stuart, putting some bread into the toaster. It had got a bit crowded in the kitchen now and both Ed and Stuart were leaning on the counters as there was nowhere to sit.

'I am,' I said. 'Although I came down by train this weekend.'

'I went through a mod phase,' said Stuart, 'although I never had a scooter. I just liked the clothes really.'

The three of them didn't look as though they had much in common apart from their age and gender. I wondered how Stuart had ended up flat-sharing with Ed.

'Well,' said Lance. 'Now you've met Annie, we ought to get going.'

'Seeing the sights, are you?' asked Ed.

'That's the plan.'

'Well we'll be at The Duck later, if you want to join us,' said Ed.

'Is there a band on?' asked Lance.

'Of some description,' said Stuart.

'Well, maybe then. We'll see,' said Lance.

'They seem nice,' I said as we walked down the stairs.

'Yeah, they're alright,' Lance agreed. 'They're cousins, those two. You wouldn't guess, would you?'

'Have they got girlfriends?'

'Well Ed keeps talking about some girl called Jackie but I haven't met her yet.'

'So the flat's not full of women at weekends then?'

'No. You're the first to cross the threshold since I moved in, although that was only two weeks ago.'

'No parties yet? I asked.

'No. The neighbours underneath bang on their ceiling with a broom handle if we get too rowdy so if we had a party they would probably call the police.'

Lance drove us into Portsmouth. It was much like any other big town in the middle with its red brick buildings and roundabouts but there was the sense of the sea even when it wasn't visible. We parked up near the docks and walked past old naval buildings to get to the Victory. It sat in its dry dock, with the grey of the modern navy vessels behind it and I could feel the importance and romance of its history. Even the tour guide's explanations of the number of men squashed onto each deck and the tiny space they had for eating and for sleeping couldn't dampen my thoughts of setting sail for the open sea. I wouldn't be a mere deck hand of course. I'd be the bosun's wife with my own wooden bed and a place at the officers' table. I'd probably be the only woman on board.

'It's weird, isn't it,' I said to Lance, 'how it's all men's history? There's me thinking I can go and be anything I want, but I only can if men allow me to do it. Even now if I wanted to join the navy I could only be a Wren and I couldn't go to sea.'

'Men can't have women around if they have to go to war,' Lance argued. 'They wouldn't be able to concentrate on the job in hand.'

'That's such a rubbish argument,' I said. 'They shouldn't be allowed to make important decisions if they are as weak as that.'

'Oh well, I'm not getting into a fight about it,' he said. 'I don't know much about women's rights.'

'And that's why it is so hard to change things,' I said. 'Men are in charge and they are quite happy with the way things are.'

'I'm not in charge,' said Lance.

'You are,' I argued. 'You decided whether we should be boyfriend and girlfriend or not.'

'Ah, but you could have said no. And you could have asked. But you didn't.'

I stomped down the gangplank. 'No, you're right, I didn't. Because I didn't think I could. I'm just as bad as everyone else, accepting what people expect me to be.'

'You don't accept it though, do you?' said Lance. 'You're out there on your scooter. That's quite unusual. And you're not looking for some safe job in an office in your home town, are you? You can't fight every battle.'

'No,' I said. 'I suppose you can't change everything all at once. Maybe you can do it bit by bit. It does make me mad though.'

We leant up against a railing looking out across the water. Lance reached over, ruffled my hair and grabbed me round the back of my neck. I rested my head on his shoulder for a moment.

'If you've got a fight you want to fight, let me know,' he said, 'we'll fight it together. We're on the same side, you know.'

'Yes, maybe,' I said. 'It's too big a thing though.'

Later we rode through the old part of Portsmouth and on to Southsea. The amusements

224

were open for the half term holiday and we changed up money into 2ps to lose in the slot machines.

'You do a lot of this at rallies,' said Lance. 'Hiding from the rain in arcades.'

'Do you miss them in the winter?' I asked.

'Yeah, you have to find something else to do. Do up your scoot, or get a girlfriend, you know, just something to pass the time until Easter comes around again.'

'Thanks, it's nice to be useful,' I said.

I wondered about whether he would be coming up to Essex and that reminded me about Perry.

'You know Perry might only be able to get out of hospital if he has someone to look after him?'

'I don't think he knew when he was getting out when I saw him,' Lance replied.

'Well I wondered about whether he could move in with your Mum? He didn't want to ask, but I know she liked having him to stay before and I'm sure she'd be pleased to have him.'

'I don't know,' Lance said, 'it might be odd if I wasn't there, if it was just Perry and my Mum. Still it's not up to me, is it? I don't mind, if Mum doesn't. Is anyone going to ask her?'

'I said I would,' I replied, 'but I haven't done yet. I'll go and see her this week perhaps.'

'I can't persuade you to stay on, then? You've got the week off haven't you?'

'I do, but I also have a train ticket for tomorrow evening.'

'Shame,' he said. 'But we've still got tonight.'

'And this afternoon,' I said.

'What do you want to do?' he asked.

'Go back to bed?' I suggested boldly. A grin spread across his face.

'Well,' he said, 'if we must.' We hurried back to where we'd parked the scooter.

'This was your idea, not mine,' said Lance. 'So who's in charge now?'

'I was only saying what you were thinking,' I said.

'True.'

Back at the flat, Ed was in on his own. He was shouting at Grandstand on the tv so we let ourselves quietly into Lance's room and lost ourselves for a couple of hours. As the daylight started to fade, we heard Stuart come in and start clattering about in the kitchen.

'We've eaten all the food,' said Lance. 'Apart from the trifle that is. Are you hungry? There's a fish and chip shop not far, I could go and get something.'

We ended up eating cod and chips with our fingers, in bed.

'So,' I said, 'do you know many scooterists in Portsmouth?'

'Quite a few,' Lance said, 'They come into the garage. There's more about than you see back at home.'

226

'And do they go to the pub, the one that Stuart and Ed are going to?'

'No. That's definitely not a scooterists' pub. I don't wear my rally jacket in there. There's a soul night in a hotel on the front and a pub out along the A3 that people go to.'

'Should we go to one of those then?' I suggested.

'We could take a ride out of town, I suppose,' said Lance.

The pub was in a tiny village, surrounded by woods. There were a couple of scooters parked up.

'Why do they go to this pub?' I asked Lance.

'It's a nice ride out, I think. Sometimes these things just become a habit. That and the fact that the landlord doesn't throw us out.'

The scooter owners were sat in the far corner. They were clearly identifiable by their khaki clothing. They shouted hello to Lance as we came in.

'Do you want to go and join them?' he asked.

'Yes,' I said, 'why not?'

They introduced themselves as Mark and Linda. 'From Chichester,' said Linda. 'Lance did some work on my timing.'

'And it's running well?' he asked.

'Yes,' it's great, thanks,' she said.

'I've not seen you around here before,' said Mark.

227

'No. I'm from Essex,' I said.

Annie's my girlfriend. From back home,' Lance explained. It seemed strange but nice to hear him describe me as his girlfriend.

'Do you have a scooter?' asked Linda.

'Yes, I've got a Vespa 100.'

'She transported me round the island when my scooter broke down before Isle of Wight,' Lance said.

'You've passed your test then?' asked Mark.

'Yes, in August.'

'Linda's about to take hers,' said Mark.

'And then I'm planning to trade up,' she said.

'I've thought about it,' I said. 'But I'm quite attached to the scooter I've got. Luigi, he's called.'

'Yeah, it makes it hard to part with them once you've named them, doesn't it?' said Mark. 'I expect we'll all end up with old scooters in our garages cos we can't bear to sell them on.'

'Like dead pets,' said Linda.

'Well only if you bury them,' said Mark.

'If it wasn't for the scooters,' said Lance later after Linda and Mark had left, 'that would have been how I imagine an old married couple to be. Sitting in the pub talking nonsense with another old married couple.' He thought for a moment. 'That's probably what you're trying to get away from, isn't it? All that sort of predictability?'

'Well, no, I don't think so,' I said. 'I enjoyed that. I'm not sure I'm trying to get away

228

from anything. I'm not trying to escape. I'm just attracted by things I find different and strange.' I told him about my morning in the travel agents. 'That was quite novel. I think maybe I could get satisfaction from just imagining other places and other ways of living without actually needing to live them myself.'

'I always thought you lived a lot in your head,' said Lance. 'That's not a bad thing necessarily, you've just got to learn what you can do with it.'

On Sunday morning I woke first. I borrowed one of Lance's jumpers and went into the kitchen to make some tea. Whilst waiting for it to brew I collected all the dirty mugs I could find and washed them up. I was just finishing the last one when Ed came in.

'Well, you can stay,' he said.

'Why? Because I have good domestic skills?'

'There is that,' he admitted. 'I've only met you briefly, so I can't really comment, but you seem like a good person to have around. Not in your face, like some people.'

'Well, thank you,' I said, attempting a little curtsey.

Lance came in behind Ed. 'Not bothering you, is he?' he said to me.

'On the contrary,' Ed said, 'I was bestowing compliments. If you're ever stupid enough to let her go, beware, I'll be planning how to woo her.'

229

'I like the sound of that,' I said. 'I don't think I've ever been wooed.'

Lance glowered briefly. 'I don't think that's normal these days,' he said, 'what with women's rights and all that.'

'And more's the pity,' said Ed. 'I don't know, men today. Has he ever bought you chocolates? Flowers?' I shook my head. 'Well I would. I'd be composing poetry and reading it under your bedroom window.'

'Isn't that a bit creepy?' I asked.

'Depends on the quality of the poetry, I expect.'

'Anyway,' he continued, 'what are you two up to today?' Lance and I looked at each other.

'I thought you could show me the garage maybe?' I said. 'You've got the scooter for Perry and I need to know what you need for it, so I can let the others know.'

'Ah, the garage,' said Ed. 'You see, this is why I am so enamoured of you, Annie. I can't think of a single other woman of my acquaintance who would ask to see inside a garage.'

'Maybe you just know the wrong sort of women?' I suggested.

'Do you really want to see the garage?' asked Lance later.

'Yes, I told you about the others wanting to help out with Perry's new scooter, didn't I? June's going to organise the list of parts and everyone's going to pick what they want to pay for. She can get accessories from Alex and we can bring those down when you need them.'

'You don't have to go to the garage to find out what we need,' he said. 'I can just tell you.'

'I'd like to see it though.'

'And there was me thinking we could stay in bed all day.'

We rode to the garage which was a mile or so away. Lance had a key for the side door. We went through an office and a parts store and into the main garage where there were various pieces of machinery, two complete scooters and several others in various stages of repair. Lance led me over to the corner where he removed a tarpaulin to reveal an old Vespa frame.

'I've not got very far yet,' Lance said. 'I'm just thinking through my approach to it.'

'What model is it?' I asked.

'It's a 180 Rally, sixteen years old, so there's a lot of work to do. 'I've got most of an engine, but I need to decide what parts need replacing and what performance parts I should use. I'm not rushing it, he's not in any hurry for it, I'm thinking.'

'But you can give me a list for now?'

'Oh, yes, I've got a long list in my head.'

'And what about the paintwork?'

'Well, I need to deal with the rust patches first and then put a primer on it. After that, I don't know.'

'I could ask Jules?'

'Your friend from Devon?'

'Yes, you'd have to get it there somehow, but he could do what you wanted, something classic or a mural of some sort.'

'Well,' said Lance thoughtfully, 'it does need to be a good job.'

'I'll ask him, shall I?' I suggested.

'Okay,' he said. 'You've seen the garage, you've seen the scooter, I'll write you out a list of parts. Can we go back to bed now?'

My train back up to London was at half past four. Having told Lance several times that I did indeed have to catch it and I couldn't stay over longer, I packed my bag and got ready to leave. I went into the living room to say goodbye to Stuart and Ed.

'I'll say 'Au Revoir'' said Ed, 'since I expect we'll be meeting again very soon.'

At the station, Lance and I stood very close together, holding hands. He wasn't the sort to be going in for heavy kissing in a public place so when the train pulled in he lifted my chin, gave me a quick kiss on the lips and a shove towards the carriage door.

'I'll give you a call tomorrow evening, okay?' he said. 'Make sure you got back alright.'

'Okay,'

'And you'll think about when you can come down next?'

'Yes,' I said, 'and you have to come up to Essex, to our party at least, if not before.'

232

I went home happy, but feeling as if I'd left part of myself behind in Portsmouth. Later when I unpacked my bag, I found the plastic flower from the kitchen table stuffed in the middle of my clothes.

Chapter Seventeen

I had the next couple of days to myself. I wasn't planning on doing anything much apart from going to see Lance's Mum, but the phone rang early and kept on ringing so eventually I got up to answer it. It was June.

'Sorry,' she said, 'I couldn't wait any longer. I thought you might be up by now. Just phoning to see how you got on over the weekend.'

'Good, thanks,' I said.

'Good. That's no explanation. I want details.'

'What sort of details?'

'The juicy ones of course, what else? Not how long the journey took, or what you had for tea. Although, what did you have for tea?'

'Chicken cordon bleu that he made himself.'

'Now that sounds promising.'

'Yes, well there you go then. The chicken cordon bleu that he made himself can be used to explain the rest of the weekend.

'Good, then?'

'Yes, that's what I said at the beginning of the conversation. Weren't you listening?'

'Ooh,' she said, 'are you being annoying on purpose?'

'Yes, I am,' I said. 'You're being too nosy. I'm coming in to town today though. I'll tell you all if you buy me a coffee and a teacake.'

We met in Debenham's Coffee Shop as June was trying to score both some extra work and a discount. She got a couple of days work over the rest of the week but had to pay full price for our cakes.

'They're so ungrateful,' she grumbled as she attacked her chocolate fudge cake. 'But now I've paid an arm and a leg for yours you have to tell all. Are you and Lance back together and if you are, and even if you aren't, how many times did you do it?'

'I didn't keep count,' I exclaimed.

'Ah, now that means you must have done it a lot because otherwise you'd remember how many times. It must have been at least four because you'd remember if it was three.' I could feel myself blushing.

'Okay, yes, it was a number of times and yes, we are back together, officially boyfriend and girlfriend.'

'Ah, I knew it,' she said. She wiped her eyes dramatically. 'I do love a happy ending.'

'I'm going up to see his Mum later,' I said, 'to ask her if she'll have Perry to stay.'

'Will you tell her, about you and Lance being an item again?'

'Maybe, if it comes up,' I said. 'Now let's change the subject, how is the party planning going?'

June and I arranged to meet up on Friday for our trip to Devon and I rode over to see Mrs Morales.

'I just thought I would report back,' I said, as she made the tea. 'Let you know how Lance is getting on.'

'Yes,' she said. 'I'd like to know. He sounds happy on the phone, but you can't really tell, can you?'

'No. But he's fine,' I said. 'His flat is clean and tidy and his flatmates seem nice.'

'Oh yes,' she said, 'I've spoken to that Ed. He seems very respectful. Been brought up properly, I'd say.'

'And Lance showed me the garage. It looks like there's plenty of work.'

'And you two?' she asked. I didn't know why I had thought I would ever be able to get away with not answering that question.

'Good,' I said, 'we're back together.'

'Oh, love,' she said, 'that's the best news.' She reached over and hugged me. 'I could tell just by the way you come round and see me that you really like him. I hope you can make it work this time.'

'I hope so too,' I said. I decided that now was as good a time as any to bring up the subject of Perry.

'Anyway,' I said, 'I did have a reason for coming to see you today.'

'That sounds serious,' she said, 'you're not trying to save me for Jesus are you?'

'What? No. No, it's about Perry.'

'Perry? He seems to be getting better don't you think?'

'Yes, well, that was my point. He's getting to the stage where they could let him out of hospital. But he needs to be where there's someone to look after him.'

'Right. So he can't go back to his Dad's.' This was a statement rather than a question.

'No. So we were wondering whether he could come here. Perry would ask you himself but he didn't want to put you in a position where you'd feel you would have to say yes.'

'He should know I wouldn't do that. He's like a second son to me.'

'He would probably have to sleep downstairs for a bit,' I said.

Mrs Morales looked around the room. I could see she was mentally rearranging the furniture.

I rode home feeling quite pleased with myself. Even the persistent rain couldn't get me down. To celebrate, when I got home, I made myself a hot chocolate with squirty cream on top and talked nonsense on the phone with Lance for an hour.

Mum had been spending the past couple of weeks planning for Julia's visit. She had used her travel agent's insider knowledge to book two rooms at a discount in a fancy hotel near Regent's Park. Dad was being sent down to Gatwick to collect Julia off her plane from Ibiza and then we were all meeting up in central London.

'Underneath the clock at Victoria Station,' said Dad, 'it's traditional.'

Then we were going with her to the Mexican Embassy where we hoped she wouldn't have to queue for hours to get her visa.

'There can't be many people wanting to go and work in Mexico, can there?' asked Mum hopefully.

After that, it was Julia's choice of where she wanted to go and what she wanted to do, until Dad had to take her back to the airport.

'It's all a bit of an expense,' said Dad doubtfully. 'But cheaper than flying the three of us out to Acapulco, I suppose.'

Mum and I actually had a lie-in since we weren't meeting Dad and Julia until lunchtime.

'We'll have to make sure we make the most of this,' she said as we waited for the train, 'who knows when the four of us will get together again?'

'When Julia comes back from Mexico maybe,' I said.

'Yes, but we don't know when that will be. She says there's talk of her staying on. After all, they don't want to go through all this visa business just to have her stay three months.'

'Oh,' I said. 'She might end up marrying a Mexican and we'd never see her again.'

238

'You always have to come up with the most dramatic outcome, don't you?' said Mum.

I didn't recognise Julia when I saw her at first. She seemed to have changed in the two months since I'd seen her last. She looked taller somehow, perhaps because she had let her hair grow long and she was definitely thinner. She looked like a grown-up rather than just my older sister. They'd left her suitcase in a locker at the airport so she just had an overnight bag. She was carrying a folder with a sheaf of paper inside. We all hugged. Mum looked a bit weepy.

'Oh, Julia, you don't have to go, do you?' she said.

'Well I do, if I want to keep working,' Julia replied.

'But it's such a long way away.'

'I know,' said Julia, 'but it's not quite on the other side of the world. It just feels like it.' She only had a thin jumper on and no jacket and was shivering. 'It's so cold here.' Mum gave her her jacket and we headed down to the underground.

The Mexican Embassy was confusing and unfriendly. Julia spoke Spanish to the guards and they melted a little. They showed us the right way to go and we joined the end of a queue.

'Do you know what you have to do?' asked Dad.

'Yes, I have to give them this, and this, and this,' she handed him a pile of forms, 'and my passport and then they'll look me up and down, decide I am a suitable sort of person to work in the country, hopefully, and put a stamp in my passport. Then I have to phone the office and give them the visa number.'

'Sounds simple,' I said. 'If only there was more than one person serving this queue, it would be a breeze.'

It took us an hour and half to reach the front of the queue. Julia talked non-stop about her experiences in Ibiza. 'It already seems weird that I woke up there this morning and that I'm not going back this evening.'

'Do you know anyone else going to Mexico?' Mum asked.

'No,' said Julia, 'there's no one from Ibiza and I don't think there's many reps there at all. It's quite a small programme.'

'I did look at the brochure,' said Mum. 'There's four hotels isn't there?'

'Yes, so there will only be a handful of us'

'Oh, well. That will be alright if you're all living together,' said Dad.

'I suppose,' said Julia. She didn't look convinced. 'I still don't understand why they picked me. Either they just picked names out of a hat or they think I'm someone else. I'll expect I'll get there and they'll say 'Oh you're not the Julia Morrish we wanted,' and send me straight back home again.'

'It would be weird if there were two of you,' I said. 'Anyway you're thinking of it as if Mexico is some destination that only the best reps get and maybe they don't think of it like that.'

Julia looked at me crossly. 'I think that was an insult, wasn't it?'

'Only if you want to take it as one,' I said.

'Now, now,' said Dad, 'Julia's only here for a day, don't fight.'

'Yeah, you have to be nice to me,' she said as her turn came at the window.

We emerged later and headed, at Julia's request straight for Top Shop and then Miss Selfridge.

'This is heaven,' she said, as she browsed the rails. 'I haven't had a chance to buy anything apart from flip flops and t shirts for months.'

In Miss Selfridge, Dad and I sat next to a dummy on a display stand, both of us bored.

'Don't you want to look at the clothes?' he asked.

'What this stuff? Floaty dresses aren't really my style,' I said.

'You should try them on though,' he said. 'You might find you like them once you've got one on.'

'Dad,' I said, 'I'm a scooterist, not a milk maid. In case you hadn't noticed.' We smiled and nodded as Julia emerged from the changing rooms in yet another maxi skirt.

'Looks lovely,' I shouted at her insincerely.

'Besides any job I get will probably come with a uniform so it's not like I need this sort of thing,' I said to Dad. 'I don't need to look normal.' Actually I had spotted quite a nice top on one of the racks nearby but I wasn't going to back down on my principles quite so obviously. I could always get it later from the shop in town and cut out the label.

Much later, after we'd eaten a full three course meal in the hotel restaurant, Julia and I collapsed onto the beds in our room.

'I'm tired and not tired,' she said. 'Tomorrow I'm crossing eight time zones so I'm going to be all over the place anyway.' She got up and opened the mini bar.

'Hmm,' she said. 'Brandy and Toblerone?'

'I'm fine,' I said. 'You go ahead.'

Julia opened the tiny bottle and poured it into a glass. 'So, little sister,' she said, 'how are things with you?'

'Yes, good,' I said. 'Quite boring really, compared to you.'

'Got a boyfriend?'

'Yes.'

'The one from before? The scooter boy?'

'Lance. He's in Portsmouth now but I saw him last weekend.' I didn't feel the need to tell her that we'd broken up and got back together in the time since I last saw her. 'How about you?'

'Well, there has been a couple. Boys who've come out on holiday, you know, but that's never going to last. I'm not going to keep in touch once they've gone home.' She thought for a moment. 'I'm not sleeping around.'

'I didn't think you were,' I said. 'I think you are the kind of person who does that or you're not. And I think you're a not.'

'I agree,' she said. 'I don't feel comfortable with that. But that doesn't mean you have to give yourself totally to one person. I guess what I'm saying is, don't think you have to get too serious with this Lance. I thought I was settled with Barry, but as soon as I got out of that little situation I saw how short-sighted it was. You'd be lucky to make it last a lifetime, or even half a lifetime.'

'So, what then?' I asked. 'How do you think we should live if it's not finding a partner and settling down?'

Having finished the brandy, Julia lay down on her bed and broke into the Toblerone. 'Ugh,' she said, chocolate and brandy don't mix.' She went into the bathroom and got a glass of water. 'I suppose I think we should make sure we can still take opportunities if they are made available to us. If you're part of a couple that's hard to do, isn't it. I mean I can go to Mexico if they ask me. Mum and Dad might not be keen, but otherwise there's no one else to tell me it's a bad decision.'

'And is it? A bad decision, I mean?'

'I don't know. Right now, I feel really scared. Don't tell Mum and Dad that, by the way. But that's mostly because Mexico is so far away. Ibiza can be a bit like Southend-on-Sea at times. The weather's better but otherwise there's lots of

Brits and if I want beer and chips for tea, I can find it. In fact, sometimes that's all I can find. But Mexico isn't going to be like that, I don't think. That might be a good thing but I also might feel more like I don't belong.'

'It's still only for a short while, though, isn't it,' I said. 'You're not signing up for life like you are when you get married.'

'True. But that's another scary thing. No one does my job for ever. The longest serving rep has been doing it for three years and she's had enough. But it's not easy to know what you could do next.'

'Does she want to go home and get married?'

Julia laughed. 'You know what, she does. She's always on the look-out for 'the one', expecting to recognise him when he comes through the arrivals hall at the airport.'

'Maybe,' I said, 'what we get wrong is thinking we can plan our life out. Some people at college do that, they talk about where they'll be in five or ten years' time. One person's even planned out when he's going to retire.'

'So maybe if we sign up to something we should only do it for two years or so,' Julia suggested. 'I like the idea. If we all did that then there would be lots of opportunity for change wouldn't there?'

'So the marriage vow could change from 'until death us do part' to 'until October 1986 and then we'll have another think about it,' I suggested.

'Yeah, that sounds about right,' Julia agreed. 'Then people would have to think more about what they're doing. Someone might be less likely to take their partner for granted if they knew they'd only signed up to be with them for two years.'

'Maybe what should happen is every two years we should be matched up with someone of a similar age to us and then on a given day we swap lives and we'd have to try and improve it as much as we could before we got moved on again.'

'Like get rid of the bloke you'd get as part of the deal?'

'Ah, but you couldn't do that, you'd have to take on everything: house, job, bloke, pets, kids, the lot. There could be a prize for most improved life, like you get to escape the next one if you didn't like it.'

'It's beginning to sound a bit complicated,' said Julia. 'Maybe we should leave things how they are. Just don't make any hasty decisions. Keep your options open.'

Julia turned on the television and began flicking up and down through the four channels.

'So who do you think is going to be the first to get married out of us two then?' I asked. 'I always thought it would be you, but now I am not so sure.'

'Neither of us,' said Julia. 'If Lance asked you right now, suppose he had the phone number here and the phone rang and it was him and he said 'Annie, I've been thinking, I can't live without you, you have to marry me,' what would you say?'

245

'I'd say no, it's too soon.'

'Ah, but when won't it be too soon? When you've got a job? When all your friends are married? When you've accidently got pregnant?'

'I don't know. I won't know until I know will I?'

'But suppose you think you know but it's all due to a knock on the head or something and you wake up the next day to find out you've already said yes?'

'Hmm. Well you'd better stay in Mexico so I have somewhere to run away to.' I said.

I woke the next morning to the sound of the shower running. It seemed to go on for hours. Dad knocked in the middle of it to say that they were going down for breakfast. As I was part dressed I pulled on a jumper and went down with him. Julia joined us just as our bacon and eggs was being served. She looked a bit red around the eyes.

'Are you okay?' asked Mum.

'Yes, fine,' she said. 'I've just come out of the shower and the water was a bit hot.' Just the fact that she knew we were referring to her red face made me think she had been crying.

'Who knows,' she said, taking out a tissue to blow her nose, 'when I'll get the chance to have a shower again?'

Mum understood her immediately. 'You don't have to go, love,' she said, 'they can't make you.'

'No, I know,' Julia replied, 'but I can't let people down, can I? I've said I'll do it and I will.'

'It will be alright,' said Dad. 'And if it isn't, you can hand your notice in and they'll have to fly you home, won't they?'

'We don't want you to go,' said Mum.

'I know you don't,' said Julia, 'and that makes it harder. I won't be able to phone you know. It was hard enough from Spain.'

'I'll write once a week,' said Mum, 'without fail. Will that help?'

'It might, a bit.' Julia took a deep breath.

'And you'll make some friends really quickly won't you? You always do.'

'It's a great adventure,' said Dad. 'I tell them at work that you're off to Mexico and they're all really impressed. No one I know has been that far away, some of them have never left England.'

'Yeah,' I said, 'make the most of it. Not many people have the chance.'

Julia blew her nose loudly and managed a smile.

'Now,' said Dad, 'have some breakfast and we'll go and do something fun this morning. I've picked up all the brochures from reception.'

'You can do anything you like as long as it's not shopping,' I said.

We ended up taking a boat trip along the Thames. Julia took lots of photos both of us and of London. 'I'll put them on the wall of my room so it feels like home,' she said. 'As long as I can find somewhere to get them developed.'

247

'It's not the back of beyond,' said Dad. 'You'll find everything you need there, if you look.'

Mum and I said goodbye to Julia at Victoria Station where we'd met her the day before. I could tell Mum was desperate to go with her to the airport. She gave Julia the longest hug and then stood there with tears running down her cheeks as they went through the barrier.

'Tell her,' she said to Dad as they left. I put my arm through hers as we headed back to the tube station.

'Tell her what?' I asked.

'Oh, nothing important,' she replied.

We passed a souvenir stand and I had an idea. 'Hold on a minute,' I said to Mum. I chose a postcard from the rack, a silly one with Big Ben with a smiley face on the front. Mum and I wrote our messages to Julia on the back along with the Mexican office address that Julia had given us. We stuck loads of stamps on it so it would have enough postage and put it in the nearest postbox.

'There you go,' I said. 'That will probably get there by Christmas'.

Chapter Eighteen

Mum and I got back home late on Thursday. June and I were meeting early on Friday to travel down to Devon and I almost wished I'd stayed with June overnight to at least cut out some of the journey. Still it gave me a chance to think about what I wanted to take with me. As with visiting Lance, I needed my crash helmet and a bag small enough to fit on a scooter. I could write a book on the art of travelling lightly I thought, as I discarded items that were too bulky or unnecessary.

I decided to ride my scooter to June's and leave it there. She emerged from her house still in her pyjamas, at which point I realised I had forgotten to pack mine. I hadn't needed them at Lance's but probably would do at Jules's. Still, I thought, I was getting used to sleeping fully dressed since I never changed to sleep at rallies.

'Hurry up,' I said, 'or we'll miss the train.'

'Sorry,' she said. 'I was up late last night with Alex. He didn't leave until nearly two and he only went cos my Dad made a fuss.'

'Would he still be here otherwise?' I asked.

'Probably.'

'He does know you're going to Devon to meet another bloke, doesn't he?'

'Oh yes.'

'That's okay then.'

'Well,' she said, 'the situation's changed for both of us since we saw them last. Maybe it has for them too and we'll have to spend the weekend watching them snog their new girlfriends.'

'You couldn't blame them,' I said. 'But it would be weird.'

June packed her bag hurriedly and we went to wait for the bus into town. I began to get a bit anxious when it didn't show up on time, even though there were plenty of trains into London and we had ages to get across to Paddington.

'You know,' I said, 'going by scooter can be cold and wet and dangerous but at least you can go when you want.'

'Your scooter's at my house,' June said. 'We could still use it.'

'No,' I said. 'Luckily, the bus is here.'

We'd started early so the train out of Paddington was fairly quiet. We found window seats with a table and spread out.

'If you put your helmet on the seat next to you, everyone will think that's your boyfriend's seat and won't try to take it.' June reasoned. It seemed to work as everyone walked past us.

'So what do you hope to get out of this weekend?' June asked.

'I don't know really,' I said. 'A fun time?'

'Yeah,' she said, 'that's enough, isn't it.'

She rummaged in her bag. 'I've brought the invites

for Jules and Fred. I sent one out to Lance yesterday and gave them out at the Red Cow on Wednesday night.'

'Are we asking for replies?'

'Yes. I gave my number so probably my Mum will be answering the phone all weekend. I gave her a list so she can tick them off.'

'So it's all sorted then?'

'Pretty much. We've just got to agree the playlist. For the first hour at least, just to get the party going.'

At Exeter we had to change for the North Devon line. I started to feel a bit nervous.

'Relax,' said June, as she noticed me stuffing one Opal Fruit after another in my mouth.

'I don't even know what I'm nervous about,' I said, 'although I don't think I'd be going if you weren't coming too.'

When we finally pulled into the station I let June get off the train first. There was no one there to meet us though and part of me felt relieved, as if I had been let off something. We loitered on the station steps for a bit.

'I've got a phone number somewhere,' said June. 'I could ring.'

'I don't think you need to bother,' I said, as two scooters turned the corner into the car park and pulled up in front of us.

'Did you think we'd forgotten?' asked Jules cheerfully.

'We were almost on our way back,' June said. 'You nearly missed out on the pleasure of our company.'

'We'd have been chasing you up the line,' said Jules. 'We didn't forget, it's just that neither of us had a watch on. Fred reckons he can tell the time by the angle of the sun, but that only works if it's not cloudy.'

'Anyway, you're here now,' I said. Jules had taken his helmet off and he bent down to kiss me on the cheek.

'Hello Annie,' he said, 'you're looking ravishing as ever.'

'And me?' asked June.

'Yes, June, you look ravishing too, doesn't she Fred?' Fred grunted something unintelligible.

'Well,' said Jules, 'the evening's yours. What do you want to do?'

'Eat?' suggested June. 'Drink? Dance?'

'We can do all of those things,' said Jules, 'but perhaps not in the same place.'

'Let's eat first then,' I said decisively.

'Well we have a choice of cuisines. You can have pie and chips, sausage and chips or everyone's favourite: fish and chips.'

'Pie,' said June and I said 'fish, please.'

'In which case,' said Jules, 'we'll go to Paul's fish, pie and sausage shop.'

'Sometimes he also does pasties,' said Fred, 'but he deep fries them so I wouldn't recommend them.'

'Just a second,' I said to Jules, 'you're not planning on letting me sit on your scooter are you? I thought no one was allowed to sit on Flo except for you?'

'I've decided to make an exception in your case,' said Jules. 'I think I can trust you. Plus, she got a bit of a dink the other day,' he pointed to a miniscule scratch on the front mudguard, 'so she's not perfect anymore.'

June and I climbed on the backs of their scooters and we rode out of town, heading west. In a small village somewhere along what felt like a coast road, even though you couldn't see the sea, we pulled up in front of a large busy chip shop. June and I ordered and went to find a table. The boys joined us carrying large polystyrene containers and cans of coke.

'So,' said June, attacking her chips as though she hadn't eaten for a week, 'where do you actually live?'

'Well, Fred's in town, Jules indicated vaguely north-west with his plastic knife, 'and I live in the woods.'

'What, like some sort of hobo?'

'No,' said Fred, 'like some sort of person with rich parents.'

'Yes,' said Jules, 'you can see my estate shortly. That's where we're staying. And we can fulfil your other two requirements there.'

'What? The drinking and the dancing?' asked June.

'Yes, I have drink and I have music. I just don't have much in the way of food.'

'Apart from the eggs from the chickens,' said Fred.

'Apart from those,' agreed Jules, 'but I thought you girls might appreciate more choice than omelettes.'

'So what about the fireworks?' I asked.

'That's tomorrow night, down on the beach.' Jules said. 'It has turned into quite a big thing, somehow. We've got people coming from Minehead and all points in between.'

'The club who were on the beach at Weston?' I asked.

'The same,' said Jules, 'they're good people to have around. They can do the barbeque and we'll do the fireworks.'

'Curly'll do the fireworks,' Fred corrected.

'Yes, when I said 'us' what I meant was 'Curly', I am just directing operations.'

'I'm good at that,' June said. 'Which reminds me . .'. She dug the now slightly bent and dog-eared invitations out of her bag and handed them to Jules and Fred.

'We can put you up somewhere or find you a hotel,' she waved her hand vaguely.

'Can you come?' I asked.

'I expect so,' said Jules. 'I've never been to Essex.'

'Oh well, you have to come then,' June said.

It was dark by the time we left for Jules'
house. We turned off the main road and negotiated
a few twisty narrow roads. After turning down into
what seemed to be a small valley, Jules braked in
front of a wooden three bar gate.

'We're here,' he said. 'I have to open and
close this gate so you might as well walk in.'

June and I walked down the drive.

'I've never know anyone who's had a drive
like this,' June whispered.

'You mean one that wasn't just for parking
your car on?' I whispered back.

There was a house in a hollow at the bottom
of the valley. It looked like a fancy wooden chalet
that you might expect to find in Switzerland. We
stood in front of it a bit nervously.

'There's just my brother in,' said Jules when
he'd parked up. My parents' are away. Fab's in
charge. Well he thinks he's in charge and if
anything goes wrong he's responsible, so we're in
the clear.'

'Fab?' whispered June to me. I giggled.

'I'll show you round the house later, but
we're in here.' Jules said. He led us through a large
garage which contained some sort of jeep, loads of
bikes and several surfboards.

'Ooh, do you surf?' asked June.

'I can, but Fab's the surfer in the family.'
Jules said. He led us up a narrow metal spiral
staircase in the corner up to a room that had been
made out of the loft space above the garage. The
wooden roof came to a point high above us.

255

'Wow,' said June and stood there with her mouth open. Over in the corner there was a wooden table and chairs in front of a kitchenette and the rest of the room was filled up with sofas, and shelves of books and records. Behind us was a window that started at the floor and stretched above our heads. I guessed that this looked out over the rest of the valley.

'There's a loo and a shower in that cupboard over there,' said Jules pointing to the far corner.

'Are we sleeping here?' asked June.

'Yes,' if that's okay. These sofas flatten out and I've got loads of quilts and stuff so we should be quite comfortable.'

I looked around and relaxed a little. I didn't feel as if I would be in a position where I would have to fend Jules off if we were all in the same room.

'Anyway,' said Jules, 'dump your bags and I'll show you round the house and you can meet Fab.'

'I'll get the fire started,' said Fred and got to work with some logs and a burner in the fireplace.

June and I trooped back down the staircase behind Jules.

'His family's seriously loaded,' she muttered to me. 'Did you know?'

'No, I had no idea,' I muttered back.

'The house was big but cosy somehow. There were lots of rugs and cushions and large paintings of wild seas on the wall.

256

'That's beautiful,' I said, stopping in front of one. 'That's one of my Mum's.' said Jules. 'It's how she ended up here. She came to Devon for the seascapes and never left.'

'Does she sell them?' I asked.

'She does, and she also gives them away. You're lucky she's not here or you'd both end up going home with massive canvases under your arms.'

'That would be nice,' I said. 'I think I could be very happy waking up in front of this picture every morning.'

'Play your cards right. .' said June under her breath. I gave her arm a little pinch to try to shut her up.

The house seemed to be empty but there was a creaking coming from somewhere upstairs.

'Fab's up here, I expect.' said Jules. 'I said I'd introduce you, so I will. Keep my part of the deal.'

Upstairs he knocked on a closed door and opened it without waiting for a reply. We followed him inside. Jules's brother was sitting on a sofa wearing headphones. He had been playing an electric guitar.

'Fab,' said Jules, waving his hand in front of his brother's face, 'we're back. This is Annie and June.' He stood back to reveal us standing behind him. Fab took of his headphones, laid down his guitar and stood up. He towered above us.

'Hello,' he said. 'Jules said you've come from Essex. Welcome to Devon.'

June positioned herself slightly in front of me.

'Fab,' she said 'is that short for something?'

'Yes, Fabien,' he said.

'Not a nickname, then?'

'No.'

'Well, anyway,' said Jules. 'You've met them. You know where we'll be.' Fab nodded and went back to his guitar.

'Behave yourself,' he shouted as we left.

'The strong, silent type,' said June as we went back down the stairs. 'Very attractive.'

'He doesn't like to be disturbed when he's practising,' said Jules. He took us back through the kitchen where he took a number of different bottles from the fridge and some crisps from one of the cupboards and piled them into our arms.

'There, that should keep us going for a bit.'

Back up in the garage room Fred was still struggling with the fire. Jules took over and soon had a good flame going. Fred opened some bottle of beer and passed them around.

June worked her way through the records and picked out some Otis Redding.

'Good collection,' she said.

'They're mostly Fab's,' said Jules. 'One of the benefits of having an older brother.'

'You know,' said June, 'I think you must be just about the most perfect family.'

Jules laughed. 'You don't know us very well yet. We've got just as many skeletons in the cupboard as everyone else, if not more.'

258

'Yeah, but, this place.'

'It is nice, isn't it?' Makes it hard to leave home though. I'll never be able to afford anywhere like this. Not as a spray painter.'

But your work must be one-offs' I said. 'You ought to be able to sell them for loads of money.'

How many scooterists do you know who've got loads of money?' asked Jules. 'It's a labour of love, I'm afraid.'

'Talking of which . . .' said June, looking at me meaningfully. I had been wondering when would be good to get on to the subject of Perry's scooter. I hadn't expected it to come up so soon. I took a deep breath.

'You remember that lad who gave me grief about talking to you at Isle of Wight?' I said. 'The one who was looking to cause trouble with me and Lance at the pub in Weston?

'Yes,' said Jules uncertainly. I hadn't quite started in the way I had intended.

'Well, he had an accident, not long after Weston. He broke his pelvis and his scooter's a write-off.'

'He's okay though?'

'Yeah, sort of. He's in a body cast, in hospital, but he'll be okay eventually. Anyway we're building a scooter for him. Well Lance is building the scooter and we're providing the parts.'

'Sounds like a good plan,' he said.

'Yes. So I was wondering, we were wondering whether you would be able to do the paintwork? We'd have to get it to you obviously and we could pay something although I don't know how much . . .'. I trailed off. I could see June looking at him anxiously.

'What sort of a scooter is it and what do you want doing?' Jules asked.

'It's a Vespa, a 1968 Rally. We don't really know what he'd want. The scooter he had was just plain blue although he did talk about getting it done in metal flake.'

'I could do that,' said Jules thoughtfully. 'You'd have to get it here like you say, and pay for the paint. I'd only charge you cost price though and I won't charge you for labour.'

'Thanks,' I said. June gave him a hug. 'You can give me a hug too,' he said to me. He enveloped me and I hugged him tight around his waist.

'Ah-hem,' Fred said to June.

'What?' she said. 'You haven't agreed to do anything for Perry's scooter.'

'I'll buy a can of paint if it gets me a hug,' he said.

'Deal,' said June. She gave him a heartfelt hug. 'Now we've got that sorted let's crank up the volume a little.' She switched the record for something with a livelier beat, kicked a rug out of the way and began dancing. Fred tapped his foot and after he'd got himself another beer, Jules joined in. I sat and watched.

'Aren't you dancing?' asked June.

'It's too light,' I said. 'I'm more used to dancing in semi-darkness or at least in a large crowd.'

'Well I can't fix the crowd,' said Jules, 'but I can fix the lights. He turned off the main lights and left a couple of wall lights on. A glow from somewhere outside shone vaguely through the window and seemed to merge with the light from the fire.

'Now you have no excuse,' said June and pulled me to my feet.

I lost my inhibitions once I got going. We pushed a sofa back to give ourselves more room and danced with abandon. Jules took on the role of DJ, switching between tracks on the records. There were speakers in all four corners of the room and the sound seemed to come from everywhere, centring itself in my ribcage. Tracks seemed to last for ever and yet time passed really quickly. I looked at the clock and it was half past eleven and yet a moment later it was one. I dropped first and not long after Jules collapsed next to me.

'You're on your own,' he called to Fred and June, stretching his arm across my shoulders.

'Was that a good evening?' he asked.

'Very good.'

'I'll show you around a bit tomorrow,' he promised. 'We don't have to spend all our time here.'

June changed records to one with a slower rhythm and turned the volume down. Fred had spread himself out over one of the other sofas and

June found a space next to him. I could feel myself beginning to drop off.

I became aware that the back of the sofa was giving way behind me.

'Don't move,' said Jules. 'I'm reconfiguring it into a bed.' I lifted my legs so I was fully stretched out. I felt him leave but he came back and spread a quilt over me. A while later he came back and laid down next to me, wriggling underneath the quilt. I could feel his body warmth, close but not touching.

There was some clattering over the other side of the room as June and Fred made themselves comfortable and then all was quiet.

At some point during the night. I woke to feel a hand on my skin, tucked into the waistband of my jeans. It didn't seem to be on the move so I covered it with my hand and drifted off again. A while later I woke again with Jules's breath hot on my ear. I turned away and he turned with me, fitting himself in behind me.

Much later I woke and he had gone and I wondered if I had imagined him there.

Chapter Nineteen

The light was shining through the large window behind me. Over on the other side of the room I could see body-shaped outlines on the sofa. June and Fred still seemed to be asleep. I got up and wandered over to the bookshelves. There were all sorts of books on all sorts of subjects. I picked up one I recognised the name of and took it back to bed. It was quiet except for the clucking of some chickens.

A while later I heard the sound of a scooter pull up and the engine cut out. Jules came up the stairs carrying a shopping bag.

'I've got breakfast,' he said. 'There's bacon, fresh rolls and some milk.'

'Sounds lovely,' said June who seemed to have been roused by the word 'bacon'.

'What are you reading?' asked Jules. I showed him the cover. 'A Room of One's Own. Sounds like your sort of thing. You can borrow it if you like.'

'Thanks,' I said.

We made tea and bacon rolls. I took mine to eat in front of the window. In the daylight I could see out over trees that had turned golden and red and were about to lose their leaves. I watched a squirrel scamper across the ground and up the trunk of one of the trees.

'It's beautiful, isn't it?' said Jules coming over to stand next to me. 'If you were to come back in a couple of weeks it would look completely different, all bare trees and you would be able to see over to the other side of the valley.'

'Yep, I could live here, I reckon,' said June. 'Let me know if your parents are looking for a lodger.'

'You couldn't,' I said. 'You think you could, but I reckon you wouldn't last a week. You'd be clamouring for bright lights and excitement.'

'We have excitement here,' said Fred.

'Oh, yeah? Paul from the sausage shop puts up a disco ball on special occasions does he?' asked June.

'He has been known to wear a flashing bow tie,' Jules admitted. 'That really pulls the punters in.'

'Does it? Really?' asked June

'No.'

'We've got more than Paul's, anyway,' said Fred. 'There are all sorts of things going on.'

'Fireworks on the beach?' I suggested.

'Well, that sort of thing,' said Fred.

'That's just an example of them having to make their own entertainment,' said June. 'That doesn't count.'

'Can you imagine if we tried it though?' I said. 'First we'd have to find a beach. We'd have to go to Clacton maybe, or Southend. The police would be all over us if we tried letting off fireworks in either of those two places.'

'We don't actually know that they're not going to do that here,' said Jules. 'We've never done this before and no one has checked whether there are any rules against it.'

'Best not to know,' I said.

'Exactly.'

'So, if it all kicks off, I'll see you in the cells,' said June

'Yup,' said Jules. 'It's a rite of passage, isn't it?'

'Anyway,' he continued, 'what do you want to do today? What can we show you that would impress you?'

'What have you got?' asked June.

'Beaches mostly,' he replied, 'and Exmoor. We could take a drive to Minehead. We do that sometimes on a weekend. There's a good pub on the front.'

'What do you usually do on a Saturday?' I asked.

'It depends,' said Jules. 'We might take a ride out or I might just stay in and read or listen to music. Sometimes if I've got a big job on I work through.'

'You're kind of self-sufficient then?' said June.

'Yes, pretty much. That's why it's good to have people over. You get to go out a bit and see your life from their viewpoint. Essex girls have quite a different outlook to Devon ones.'

'Is that why you invited us?' I asked.

'No. We invited you because we enjoyed your company, of course. Getting your view is just a side benefit.'

'And then you can come to Essex and see how we live,' said June. 'It's quite different from this.'

'Very different,' I agreed. 'I'd like to see something of your surroundings though.'

'Minehead then?' suggested Jules. 'You get the sights and a pub lunch. Which is about as good as it gets.'

The ride over to Minehead was beautiful. Even though it was November it was quite mild and there was a weak sun to warm us. Exmoor was really bleak in some places and otherworldly in others.

'There's not much wind, which is good news for tonight,' said Jules. 'We might have come unstuck with the fireworks if there was a strong breeze.'

At Minehead we rode up and down the front a couple of times.

'Just seeing if there's anyone about,' said Jules. 'But it doesn't look like it. Not to worry, we'll see them later.'

We parked up in front of a friendly looking pub.

'If anyone is about, they'll be in here,' said Jules. There were lots of people in the pub but they mostly seemed to be middle-aged men. A few greeted Jules and Fred and nodded to us.

'Are you regulars?' asked June.

'Enough that people recognise us.'

June and I found a table and Jules and Fred queued up at the bar.

'So,' said June, 'did you get up to anything last night? There seemed to be quite a lot of rustling coming from your side of the room.'

'No.' I was quite shocked that she had even thought we had. 'I need a bit more privacy than that.'

'Oh,' said June, 'I don't.'

'Don't tell me,' I said. 'I don't even want to know.'

She grinned. 'I do have a reputation to uphold.'

'What is Alex going to think?' I asked.

'What is Alex going to know, is the real question,' she replied.

'Well I'm not going to tell him,' I said. 'Unless he asks. You know I am no good at lying.'

'Let's hope he doesn't ask then,' she said.

'I still don't know how you are going to manage all of them at the party,' I said.

'Me either. It should be interesting though. Maybe I should say that whoever gives the best present gets to spend the night with me. Then I would see who was really keen.'

'Are we asking for presents?'

'I don't know about you, but I am.'

'You'll just end up with loads of champagne glasses with '18' printed on them.'

'Then I'll have to drink a lot of champagne, won't I?'

Jules and Fred showed up with the drinks.

'The pool table is free if you fancy a game,' said Fred. 'June and me versus Jules and Annie.'

'I hope you are a good player,' I said to Jules.

'I get by,' he said modestly.

We played four games at the end of which we were drawing two-all. I managed to pot the occasional ball and didn't pot the white so I was feeling quite proud of my effort. We were about to play a deciding game when I glanced out of the window and saw a couple of scooters pulling up. I pointed them out to Jules.

'Oh that's Drew and Si,' he said. 'Didn't you meet Drew's sister at Weston?'

'Is he the one who was going to join the army?' I asked.

'Yes, that's Drew. He's still here, as you can see.'

Jules lost interest in the pool game when Drew and Si came in. He went into a corner with Drew where they discussed something quietly. I took Jules's shots and lost badly.

Si joined us back at the table. He looked familiar but I couldn't place him. Jules and Drew were still huddled in conversation.

'Looks important,' said June.

268

'They always seem to have their heads together, these days,' said Si. 'I've no idea about what.'

'Are you coming to the fireworks tonight?' June asked Si.

'Yeah, I'll be doing the barbeque,' he said and I remembered where I had seen him before. 'Neither of you are vegetarians are you?' He looked at us suspiciously. We shook our heads. 'That's good. I can't face cooking those veggie sausages. They give me the heebie-jeebies.' He shivered at the thought.

Finally Jules and Drew finished their conversation and came over to join us. I went and bought a round of drinks and got a menu so we could order some food.

'Have something light,' Si said. 'I've got enough food for tonight to feed an army. He paused for a moment. 'Sorry Drew, no offence.'

Drew made a face, a grimace that involved crossing his eyes. He had obviously had to suffer a lot of army-related comments.

We ordered sandwiches. Jules came and sat next to me and put his hand on my knee. It was a bit unexpected and I jumped.

After we had eaten we went for a walk along the beach, skirting families who had bravely set up camp on the sand. Most of them wore jumpers over their swimsuits. Jules kept very close. At one point he put his arm across my shoulders and pulled me close. While I actually quite welcomed the closeness, it somehow seemed to be less about me and more about putting on some sort of a display for Drew.

I got an urge to phone Lance. I felt in my pocket but only found a couple of 2ps. Mid-afternoon on a Saturday was probably a bad time to catch him in anyway.

Jules and I had got separated from Fred and June who seemed to have got caught in a lip lock further back up the beach. I let Jules get ahead with Drew and Si and walked on my own for a while.

I thought a bit about Jules's lifestyle. It was very attractive. I imagined being surrounded by space and books and art. It wasn't anything I was familiar with. Mum owned a copy of the Complete Works of Shakespeare but although I had opened it a few times I had never progressed very far. At school we had got lumbered with Othello for O Level which was enough to put anyone off. I didn't feel as though I had squandered my education but I did think there was much more that I could learn.

Walking on my own on the beach it felt as though there were so many different ways I could go and so many people's lives I could use for inspiration. It would help, I thought, if I didn't feel as though there was one right path and that all the others would eventually lead to disappointment or failure.

Up ahead of me I could see Jules and the others turning back in my direction so I walked up to meet them. Jules caught hold of my hand as we walked back up the beach.

'Are you okay?' he asked. 'You looked a bit sad just there.'

'Not sad,' I said, 'just thoughtful.'

'In a good way?'

'Well not in a bad way,' I said. 'More, uncertain, I suppose. Everyone seems to be so much more sure of themselves than me.'

'Or maybe that's just how we present ourselves?' Jules suggested. 'You probably don't come across as half as unsure as you think you are. I see a girl who owns a scooter and goes on scooter rallies. That's a fairly confident path to take. You've got a clear identity there.'

'I suppose.'

'I'm not much for giving advice,' said Jules, 'but one thing I would say is, don't mould your life around other people and their lives. You've got to find what's right for you and then you can share it. You can be the person that people want to be like, not the other way on.'

Up ahead of us June was attempting to show Fred how to cartwheel.

'I don't suppose many people point June out as a role model,' Jules said, 'but I reckon she's as good a one as any. She knows what she wants and she goes and gets it and it is probably as simple as that.'

Fred was lying on his back in the sand, having fallen out of his cartwheel.

'It's not my fault,' he said to June, 'they never taught us this stuff.'

271

'Why not?' said June. 'That makes no sense. What do you do when you see a wide open space, walk across it?'

'Well,' said Jules, 'boys are supposed to have a football to hand at all times, so if they come across a wide open space they can kick the ball across it.'

'Have another go,' June said to Fred. 'If I don't teach you now, you'll probably never learn.'

We sat down to watch.

'I can't do it with an audience,' Fred grumbled. June pulled Jules up to have a go too.

'I can't cartwheel,' he said, 'but I can do this.' He launched himself into a handstand and walked forward about three steps on his hands.

'I've got a bad hip, or I'd show you my crab,' said Drew.

'And I don't want to damage my burger-turning fingers,' said Si.

'I can do a tree,' I said. I stood up and lifted one foot on to my thigh. I instantly lost my balance and fell over. 'Oh well, maybe not.'

We wandered back up to the scooters.

'We should head back,' said Jules. 'I said we would meet on the beach at seven.'

We rode back the way we came. The sun was starting to drop in front of us, turning the sky orange and pink like early slow-motion fireworks. I thought about how it was due to the rotation of the earth rather than the movement of the sun and started to feel as if we were riding in to the daylight.

If we kept up the right pace we might never need to experience night time.

Back at Jules's, June began bothering him about his planning for the party.

'The way I figure it,' he said, 'is we need six things in this order: people; fire; drinks; music; food; fireworks. Si's in charge of the food and the music. Curly's got a van full of wood, drink and fireworks. So all we need to do is make sure we get there on time.

We didn't have a lot of time so we took it in turns to use the shower and then set off west again. The beach was wide and long. There were a couple of cars parked up at one end. We went down the far end where there was no one. There were no street lights and so we turned off the scooter lights and sat there waiting for our eyes to adjust. Just as I felt ready to go and explore, Curly showed up in his van with his lights blazing and so I had to start all over again.

We helped to unload the wood while Jules chose a spot for the fire and marked out an edge with stones. He built it up while Fred sorted out the music and Curly unloaded cases of beer and lemonade. Other people began to arrive, some I had met at Isle of Wight and Weston and some I had never seen before. Most came by scooter and parked alongside each other as if it was the seafront at a rally. Others came by car and unpiled more wood and drink from their boots.

I felt a little overwhelmed by the number of people. I'd begun to think of it as our party rather

273

than a much bigger event that we were just attending. I grabbed June's arm.

'Don't leave me on my own,' I whispered.

'You'll be okay,' she said. 'If it all gets a bit much just go and sit by the fire. Someone will come and talk to you.'

I busied myself helping to dish out drinks and downed a can of lager much more quickly than usual which left me feeling both gassy and more relaxed.

June stamped down an area of sand to make it more suitable for dancing on. Si turned up and set up his barbeque. He had a tray full of potatoes wrapped in foil that he threw directly on to the fire.

Jules came up behind me. 'Having a good time,' he asked.

'Yes, not bad,' I said.

'We're trying to decide,' he said, 'should we let all the fireworks off one after the other, or should we set off a couple every twenty minutes or so?'

'I'd do two lots,' I said, 'an early and a late show.'

'Good plan,' he said, 'I'll suggest it to Curly.'

I lost Jules for a while after that. Billy and Sandy came over to say hello.

'Shouldn't you be at university?' I asked Billy.

'Yeah, I should be. I rode down especially,' he said. 'For the music mostly. It's all pop and rock in Aberystwyth. They've never heard of soul. I need a fix every now and again.'

'You should have chosen your university better,' said Sandy. 'If you had gone to Manchester you'd have been laughing.'

'Yeah, if they hadn't beaten me up for my west country accent.'

'Are you dancing then?' I asked.

'Are you asking?' replied Billy. He didn't wait for my answer, he just grabbed my arm and led me over to where June and a couple of others were showing off their best moves. The sound from the player was a bit tinny so we grouped ourselves round it to try and get the rhythm.

'It's a bit like dancing round your handbags, isn't it?' I said to June.

'Shh,' she said, 'or I'll lose my step and I'll be all over the place.'

I left her to it and went off to look for Jules. Without warning there was a small noise behind us towards the sea. I watched as a row of roman candles were set alight and began to glow faintly in the darkness.

'Ooh, and, indeed, aah,' said someone in front of me and there was a smattering of sarcastic applause.

When the last roman candle had fizzled out there was a silence amongst the crowd. No one quite knew whether that was the end of the display or not. Just as people began to turn back towards the fire, there was a whizzing noise and a light that seemed to hover above the ground. It began to spin round wildly and it became clear that this was a Catherine wheel nailed to a post. There was a row of these and they were given a small cheer.

They were followed by a whooshing sound and we all looked up trying to guess the trajectory of the rocket. It exploded in a shower of green and red sparks that were reflected on the sea and briefly lit up the faces of the people in front of me. Several more rockets followed and we oohed and aahed appreciatively.

When it was clear that the last rocket had been launched, Si shouted 'Grub's up' and we began queuing for his burgers and hot dogs. I couldn't see anyone I knew well enough to talk to. I thought I saw Emma but she was with a group of girls and I didn't think she would recognise me anyway. So I ate my food alone, sitting by the fire as June had suggested.

I wondered where Jules was. It was possible that he had gone off to help Curly with the fireworks. It seemed a bit strange that he had invited me to a party and then left me to it. I sensed a distance between us that I hadn't felt before but I couldn't pinpoint when it had started or what the reason for it was. Perhaps he just regretted inviting me and was counting the minutes until we were on our way back home.

And then I saw him, coming back to the party from where the scooters were parked. I was about to wave when I realised that he was with Drew. Something about the way he was touching Drew's arm reminded me of how Lance had touched me in the few weeks after we had got together for the first time, that period when you can't believe the person you are interested in is interested in you too and you have to keep touching them to make sure they are real and suddenly I understood about Jules. My first reaction was a sort of jealous sickness but as I thought about it I began to feel a warmth towards him and an urgent need to protect him.

Then there was a bang and a cry from over where the fireworks had been launched which caused a commotion and half the crowd ran off to check on Curly.

Later, much later, after Curly had been bandaged up and the fire had gone out, Jules took me, not Drew, back to his house and curled up with me, not Drew. I held him close until his breathing slowed, inhaling the smell of smoke on his clothes, and willed him the courage to do what he had advised me, to be himself.

Chapter Twenty

We all slept in the next morning. I woke to Jules gently shaking my shoulder.

'Do you want to go with me to collect the eggs?' he asked.

He lent me a pair of wellington boots that were several sizes too large and I flumped my way through long grass to the chicken house. We felt for eggs as Jules crooned quietly to 'the girls' as he called them. I put the eggs in my pockets where they sat like little hot water bottles.

On the way back up I decided to tell Jules about Lance.

'We got back together,' I said, 'when I saw him last weekend.'

Jules stopped for a second and looked confused.

'You didn't say.'

'No. Well I was going to. If you had asked, or if it had happened that I had needed to. But it didn't, so I'm telling you now. Just so I don't feel as though I'm covering something up.'

'I suppose you didn't need to,' he agreed. 'It was nice though, just sharing a bed, wasn't it?'

'Yes, it was lovely,' I said. 'You're welcome to come and share my bed anytime.'

Back inside, we poached the eggs while they were still warm and even as I ate I thought how I would remember the meal for a long time.

June downed her eggs without comment and had clearly woken up in planning mode.

'So,' she said to Jules, 'we need to work out how to get Perry's scooter to you.'

Jules looked at me. 'Do you want to give Lance a ring now?' he said. 'Then we can find out if he's stripped it yet and if he has transport to get it over here.' I was a bit reluctant to phone with everyone listening but couldn't think of a good excuse to get out of it.

I picked up the phone and dialled the number hoping that no one would answer it. It rang for a long time and I was about to hang up when it was picked up and Lance answered.

'Hello,' I said, 'It's Annie.'

'Hi, Annie,' he said. 'I thought you were in Devon. I've been thinking about what you've been getting up to. Are you okay?'

'Yes, I'm fine,' I said. 'I am in Devon. We're having a good time, we're heading back in a while. I just wanted to call you because Jules has said he would do the paint on Perry's scooter and we thought this would be a good time to find out where you are with it.'

'Well, paint's the next bit really,' he said. I've got all the parts that need spraying together, ready to go.'

'Do you want to speak to Jules then?' I suggested.

'What? Oh okay.'

I handed the phone over to Jules. 'He says it's ready to go,' I said.

I listened to Jules's side of the conversation. It sounded a bit stilted at first, as if he was slightly suspicious of Lance, but once they got onto the technical conversation they seemed to find a lot of common ground and I saw Jules relax. They discussed paint finishes and Jules made some suggestions for what should go on it. Eventually he wound the conversation up by exchanging phone numbers and addresses and I expected him to pass the phone back to me, but instead he just hung up. I gave him a look.

'Sorry Annie,' he said. 'I forgot I was talking to your boyfriend. Call him back if you want.'

'No, it's okay,' I said. 'I'll phone when I get home.'

'He sounds like a good bloke,' Jules said. 'He's going to borrow the work's van and bring it over himself next weekend.'

'Good old Lance,' said June.

'He agreed with the metalflake,' Jules said. 'It's not classic, but it will look good.'

'How long is it going to take?' asked June.

'Well he says he's done all the prep, sanding and filler and such like, so not that long really as I'll just be doing the one colour. A week or two tops.'

'Only, I'm thinking,' said June, 'if we can have it ready for our party. We've got five weeks. You reckon the paintwork will be done in three weeks or less. If we were to get it back to Lance straight away, could he get it finished in two weeks?'

'You'd have to ask him that,' said Jules. 'It depends how much time he has to spend on it. If something goes wrong, it can throw the whole project out.'

'But it's possible?'

'Yes, it's possible.'

'Right,' said June, 'that's what we're going for then.'

'Will he be out of hospital by then?' I asked.

'If he isn't, we'll bring the party to him,' she said.

Once Junes was set on a plan there was no putting her off. 'Time is of the essence, of course,' she said. 'Jules, you'll have to let me know as soon as you've done your part and I'll see if I can get Alex to come and get it and deliver it back to Lance. We'll pull an all-nighter if we have to.'

'Who's Alex,' asked Fred suspiciously.

'Oh, a good friend of mine,' said June. 'You can meet him at the party. You're all scooterists, you'll get on. Alex can deliver the accessories at the same time and then we just need to get the scooter back up to Essex.'

'Simple,' I said.

Leaving Jules was both easy and hard. He said he was planning to come to our party so I knew I would see him again. Our goodbyes at the station were all about the scooter and the party. At the same time, I didn't think we would keep the closeness that we had had at times over the weekend.

On the way home I found I couldn't talk about him. If June brought him up I changed the subject. I didn't want my thoughts of him altered by someone else's opinion. I knew I would never speak of what I had seen on the beach, a little moment that now I seemed to have imagined. Time would tell as whether Jules made that part of his public life. I wondered if I would be gone from his life by the time he did.

June spent a lot of the journey home talking about Perry's scooter. I felt quite disconnected from it as if I was just hearing about a group of people coming together to create it. While Lance was the driving force, June and Jules had become the other main players and I couldn't see how I could have a role in it beyond giving some money towards it.

'How do you think we ought to give it to him?' June asked. 'It ought to have a ribbon round it really, with a big bow on top. What if it rains though? Do you think we could get it into the Red Cow?' She stopped talking and looked at me.

'Was that last point actually a question?' I asked, since she mainly seemed to be having a conversation with herself.

'Yes. You have a scooter. Could you get it into the Red Cow?'

'Up the stairs?'

'Preferably, yes.'

'Well, it's possible, I suppose. They're not that heavy, just awkward and oily.'

'I had a boyfriend like that once,' said June.

'Of course, there's another problem,' I said, ignoring her, 'you would have to get Perry up the stairs too. I don't know how mobile he is going to be.'

'If we can get a scooter up there, we can get Perry up there,' sad June. 'We can figure out afterwards how to get them down again.'

'What if he doesn't want it though?' I said.

'What do you mean?' asked June. 'Why wouldn't he want it?'

'Well it might all be a bit too much,' I suggested. 'He had a perfectly good working scooter, maybe a bit temperamental and scruffy,'

'I had a boyfriend like that too,' interrupted June

'Temperamental and scruffy,' I repeated, 'but his. Now he'll never see it again and he's probably mourning it a bit. And we come along with this beautiful, perfect replacement. It's a little bit like your mangy but well-loved moggy died and someone has bought you a pedigree Persian or something to replace him. You'd have a hard time loving it for a while, wouldn't you?'

'I see your point,' said June. 'So how do we get him to love it?'

'I don't think we can,' I said. 'We just have to not be disappointed if he doesn't.'

It was late by the time I got home. I was planning to phone Lance on Monday evening, but he called me just as I was about to get in the shower. I heard Mum saying: 'It's a bit late,' then, 'I'll see if she can come down to the phone,' so I ran down the stairs half dressed.

'Alright?' he said. 'I thought I was going to get to speak to you again earlier.'

'Yes, me too,' I said. 'Are you okay with the plan?'

'Fine. He sounds like a good bloke. I think I can trust him with the work.'

'He'll do a good job, I'm sure,' I said. 'His scooter looks great. Did you know June is talking about getting Alex to go and collect it as soon as he's finished so you can get it done in time for our party?'

'No, that's news to me. I'm not rushing it to fit in with her plans though.'

'No, of course not.'

'I am coming up to Essex though.'

'For the party?'

'Well, yes, but before then. Mum asked if I would come up and help sort out the house ready for Perry, so I'm coming up the weekend after next.'

'Is he coming out, then?'

'No one knows really. It's a bit like prison, you don't know they're going to let you out until the day they do, then you're left standing on the steps wearing the clothes you went in with on, wondering what happened.'

'You seem to know a lot about it.'

'Only from talk. So shall I come and see you then?'

'Yes, or I could come and see you at your Mum's.'

'I'll come to you, Mum's will be full of furniture in odd places.'

'Okay, well let me know when you're coming. And you are coming to the party?'

'Yes, I wouldn't miss it.'

June spent the next week alternately flapping about the party and the scooter.

'Will you call Lance to check he's got the scooter to Jules,' she asked me, more than once.

'I will,' I said, 'if I haven't lost my marbles by then. You're driving me mad.'

'Yes, I know, sorry,' she said. 'I think I need more projects so I can stop fretting about the ones I have got.'

'Well, find me a career then,' I suggested. 'Do some analysis, find out what I should be doing with the rest of my life.'

'Hmm,' she said. 'Are you even sure you are suited to the world of work?'

'No,' I said, 'but who is? You've got to bring in the money somehow I suppose.'

'Yeah, but working? There has to be a better way.'

'I know. I could put it off. I could become a student, live in a hovel off a grant.'

'Yeah,' said June. 'I reckon that would suit you. Me, I want to be out there, doing stuff. You're better at thinking. You should have a look at some of the polytechnic brochures, see what they do.'

'I could have a look at least,' I agreed. I'd never really thought of myself as a potential student, but that didn't mean such a thing wasn't possible.

'I bet there's a polytechnic down in Portsmouth too,' said June. 'If you know what I mean. Now have we discussed recently what you're going to wear to the party?'

We had of course and in great detail. I wanted something understated and classy. Something I could dance in and that would fit in with being a scooterist.

'Well you're not going to find that in Top Shop,' June had said.

I had decided that I wanted something vintage, preferably from the sixties and June had suggested that we take a trip to Carnaby Street. As it was such an important trip we felt justified in bunking off college and going up for an afternoon.

In the depths of a shop selling second hand suits and dead foxes that you were supposed to hang around your neck, we found a treasure trove of shift dresses and spent ages trying and retrying them all on.

286

I went for a midnight blue velvet dress that hung to just above my knee and was edged in a slightly lighter blue satin.

June went for the whole mod look. Her dress was striped vertically in black and white and she found some white patent leather boots to go with it.

'Some lace tights, loads of eyeliner and an alice band and I'm sorted,' she said as I looked on, open-mouthed in admiration.

'We should have put a dress code on the invites,' she continued. 'Everyone else is going to look really scruffy compared to us.'

'Yes,' I agreed, 'I'd like to see Lance in a suit.'

'And with a haircut,' said June. 'You wouldn't recognise him, would you?'

I was under strict instructions from June to phone Lance as soon as I thought he would be back from Devon. 'I need updating regularly,' she said.

He was supposed to be driving over there on the Saturday morning and was planning on coming straight back. When I phoned on Sunday morning though, Ed answered.

'I don't think he's back,' he said. 'Just a minute, I'll go and check.' I listened as he stomped off down the hallway.

'No, he's definitely not here,' he said. 'I shouldn't start worrying just yet. I'll get him to give you a call when he gets in. By the way, can I come to your party? My invite seems to have got lost in the post.'

'Yes, of course,' I said. 'Get Lance to wear something smart, would you?'

'I'll try,' he promised, 'although you don't want to put him off.'

I waited in all day for Lance to call me back. I kept walking near the phone willing it to ring and I was nearly on the point of calling Ed again when it finally rang.

'I stayed over,' Lance explained. 'Got up there by lunchtime and Jules was so hospitable I didn't leave until lunchtime today. That's a great place he's got there, isn't it?'

'It's lovely,' I agreed. 'Did you have enough to talk about?'

'Plenty. We've got a lot in common.' He sounded as though he was on a bit of a high. 'We didn't talk about you, if that's what you're wondering. Well, not much, anyway.'

I hadn't really thought about the possibility of them discussing me. I wasn't sure I liked the idea of it. I decided I'd rather not know the details and changed the subject.

'So you dropped the scooter off okay then?' I asked.

'Yes. Jules showed me his garage. We did a test run on the paint on a bit of waste metal. I think it should look good.'

'You two should go into business together,' I said. 'You can fix the scooters, he can paint them.'

'Yeah, we talked about that. Not seriously though.'

'It could happen though?'

'We could make it happen.'

'Well,' I said, 'maybe you should.'

The talk at the Red Cow on Wednesday was all about Perry's scooter. Everyone wanted an update on progress and June was organising payment for the parts.

'Are you going to tell Perry who bought what?' asked Ben who had brought Katie again.

'I don't think so,' said June. 'I'll have a list, but it's better if we just tell him it came from all of us, isn't it?'

Even people who barely knew Perry, including Phil'n'Col, were coming up to make a donation. Someone had ridden up especially from a Southend scooter club to hand over money collected from the club members.

'We think it's great what you're doing,' he said. 'You never know when something like that might happen to you.'

When the rush seemed to be over, June counted out the money. 'Well we've got more than enough,' she said. 'Perry's going to have a fantastic scooter. I'll give you what needs to go to Lance tomorrow so you can give it to him this weekend.'

Dave came over to give us an update on Perry's progress. 'He's out of that body armour,' he said. 'He's still got leg casts and has some sort of brace, which he wouldn't show me. If he gets on alright with those, he could be out in a week or so.'

'No one has said about the scooter have they?' asked June. 'If he's out there's more chance he might hear about it before we give it to him. Whatever happens, it has got to be a surprise.'

'It will be,' said Dave. 'It's not like he's going to be roaming the streets. We ought to be doing some customisation of his wheelchair to keep his mind off scooters for a while though. Ask Lance whether he's got any tyres for a twenty four inch wheel.'

'Someone must have a whip aerial and squirrel tail, mustn't they,' said June. 'We could at least attach one of those.'

'And paint a target on the back,' I said.

'Good idea,' said Dave. 'Then he'll think that that's our welcome home present and he won't even think about anything else we might be doing.'

Lance phoned on Thursday to say he would come over on Friday evening.

'I'm riding over in the afternoon,' he said.

'Won't you want to see your Mum?' I asked.

'I'll have all of Saturday for that,' he said. 'She wants you to come over for lunch on Sunday.'

'Okay,' I said. 'I can do that.'

He arrived at about half past six, looking tired.

'Are you alright?' I asked.

'Yes. I've just been putting in a lot of late nights. I thought I could ignore June's demand that the scooter be ready in time for your party, but it turns out I couldn't.'

'Yeah,' I said. 'She has that effect on people.'

Lance came in and sat for a while with Mum and Dad. Dad asked him about his work and made approving noises.

'It sounds as though you've got a good business there,' he said. 'And I don't suppose you have to limit yourself to scooters, do you?'

'No,' said Lance. 'I've never stripped a motorbike, but that's not to say that I can't. I've just been lucky so far to work on what I love.'

'That's a good way to operate if you can make it work financially,' said Dad. 'It means you're always happy to get up for work.'

Having done our duty, we escaped. I decided to take my scooter and we rode out together to a pub near the river where we sat at a window seat and looked out at the lights on the opposite bank.

'So,' said Lance, 'we didn't take it seriously when we spoke about it, but what would you think if I did go in to business with Jules?'

'I think it's a great idea,' I said.

'Yeah, what was it he said? I think he said we have 'complementary skills'.'

'You provide a complete service?' I
suggested.

'Exactly.'

'But where would you base it?'

'Well, maybe one or both of us could move.
Jules has got a good set up there, but we should be
where the scooters are. Or where they can get to us
easily.'

'There are lots here,' I said. 'In Essex.'

'True. But do you think we could get Jules
to move here? He might not last long if he ended
up living in a poky flat.'

'Oh well, you'll work something out,' I said.
'Could you let me know though if you're going to
move. I've been looking into doing an HND at
Portsmouth Poly. It'd just be my luck that I start
there and you leave.'

'Really?' he said. 'You mean you're not
about to jet off to some exotic beach never to be
seen again?'

'Not for now.'

Lance looked as though he didn't know how
to react. I watched as several emotions washed over
his face. I wondered if I had made a big mistake
and he really didn't want me that close. I stood up,
feeling embarrassed.

'I don't have to,' I said. 'It was just
something I've been thinking about.'

'Oh Annie,' he said, 'sit down.' I sat.
Under the table he grabbed one of my legs between
his and held it there tightly.

'I'd love to have you close by,' he said. 'You know that, or you ought to by now. It's just that I've been preparing for your announcement that you're going away and then you tell me you're planning the complete opposite. I don't know quite what to feel.'

I reached my hand out across the table and he took it in both his hands.

'But you should know too,' he continued, 'that I've been thinking quite a lot about this business and how we could make it work, and suddenly I get it, I get how you feel about going abroad, that sense of possibilities. I don't think I have ever felt it before.'

'You feel confident,' I said.

'Yes, it is a confidence, I think. I'm starting to realise that actually I am good at something. I know lots of people appreciate what I do, but that's because they couldn't do it themselves. I make life easy for them. But working with the Portsmouth lot and meeting Jules, they do know what they're talking about and they still tell me that my work is good.'

Lance shifted in his seat and looked at me a little harder.

'A lot of it is to do with you too,' he said. 'You don't doubt me and that makes me feel that I shouldn't doubt myself. It's not easy all of this. It's as though I've got to become a completely different person. Maybe one that you won't like. Maybe one that even I won't like. So I don't know . .'. He tailed off.

293

'Well I suppose if we want to make it work, whatever 'it' is, then we will do, won't we?' I said.

'Yes,' he said. 'We just have to work out how.'

'Wow,' I said. 'You've no idea how much I want to go to bed with you right now.'

Lance grinned. 'That's supposed to be my line.' He thought for a moment. 'We should be having sex in inappropriate places at our age shouldn't we?'

We left the pub quite hurriedly. Holding hands we headed along the side of the river until we came to a boat shed. Lance tried the door but it was locked. Round the back there was a small extension to the shed which created a sheltered corner. We backed up into there and I felt the edges of the wood panels against my head and my back as Lance kissed me urgently. Even as I thought 'Not here,' I knew there was no way to back out of it. We did what we could to remove the clothing that was hampering us and Lance lifted me up, holding my weight under my thighs. It was short but it was exciting, my need carrying me to places I never thought I would go.

'You know the wait makes it better?' said Lance as we walked back to the scooters. 'Perhaps we should always live in different parts of the country, if it could be that good when we do meet up.'

'You don't mean that, do you?' I asked.

'No.'

Chapter Twenty One

Lance left for his Mum's with nothing resolved beyond the desire to make something work between us. I didn't think we would have a chance to talk about anything at his Mum's but I rode over there on Sunday morning looking forward to the prospect of a nice lunch at least. There were three scooters parked out the front when I got there. Lance's was lined up alongside Dave's and Bertie's. The boys were all squeezed into the kitchen, drinking coffee and smoking. Mrs Morales was working round them, trying to do the vegetables for lunch.

'Oh good,' she said, when she saw me, 'I can get one of them out of the kitchen. Lance, show Annie what we've done to the house.'

We walked through to the living room which now resembled a hospital room. It had a single bed and an armchair in it.

'That's different,' I said. 'Where's the sofa?'

'Up in the spare room,' he said. 'We've turned the house upside down.'

'So do you have anywhere to sleep?' I asked. 'I mean, can you come home, if you want to?'

'I can, but I won't, or at least not for longer than a weekend or something.' We walked through to the hall and Lance shut the door behind us.

'Annie,' he said, 'you ought to know that I don't plan to move back home, just in case you were thinking that was a possibility. I'm finished with living with my family. That's not to say anything bad about my Mum, but it's time I stood on my own two feet.'

'Okay,' I said, 'that's okay.' I was tired and Lance's statement made me feel as though he was moving away from me, even though he'd already done that. I could feel tears begin to pool in my eyes.

'Don't cry,' said Lance as he pulled me to him. 'This is a good thing, a positive step.'

'Yes, I know,' I said as I snuffled into his jumper. 'I just wish there was one thing I could be certain of, one thing that I know will still be the same in a year's time.'

I broke away from him and went and sat on the stairs. Lance came and squeezed in next to me.

'I can't say for certain,' he said, 'because you can't say what will happen, but I reckon there'll still be you and me in a year's time, don't you? We've both thought about how much we want to be together and we're both committed to it, aren't we?' I nodded.

'Well then. Anyway I need my own space, you don't think my Mum is going to let you stay here overnight, do you? Actually ignore that, my

Mum would do anything to keep us together, so she probably would.'

I smiled and wiped my eyes.

'Anyway, let's go back in, see Dave and Bertie before they go.'

Back in the kitchen, Mrs Morales had got Bertie to peel the potatoes which he was doing very badly.

'It's not even as if I'm getting to stay to eat them,' he grumbled.

'I said before,' said Mrs Morales, 'it's not that I don't have enough, it's that I can't fit you all round the table. I'll do you a plate and you can come back later for it if you like.' Bertie brightened at the idea.

'So did you tell Annie about Perry?' Mrs Morales said to Lance.

'No, not yet,' he said.

'It's good news,' she said.

'Yes, I went to see him yesterday evening. They've given him a pair of crutches and they're getting him to move about a bit. He reckons he might be out at the end of the week.'

'Well, we're ready for him, aren't we?' said Mrs Morales. 'Dave's going to come and help me get him settled, aren't you?'

'Yes,' he said, 'I'm primed and ready to go.'

'And then it's open house,' she said. 'He'll be needing company of his own age, so let anyone who wants to visit know where we are.'

'He should be able to come to the party then,' I said.

'It's looking good,' said Lance.

'And you're coming too?' I said to Lance's Mum. 'Did you get an invite?'

'I did, but you don't want an old person like me there.'

'Well my Mum and Dad will be there and June's bringing her parents and her Nan, so you'd be very welcome.'

'Oh, well, perhaps then. It would be a good excuse to get my hair done.'

Lance had to ride back to Portsmouth in the afternoon so we said our goodbyes after lunch.

'So you'll be busy until the party,' I said.

'I expect so,' he said. 'If I can get the frame back next weekend I reckon I've got a chance to get the scooter finished in time.'

'Do you ever regret coming up with the idea to build it in the first place?' I asked.

'When it's going wrong, I do swear at myself a bit,' he admitted. 'But I know this is a good thing, so it makes me feel good to do it. I've probably got more out of than anyone else, maybe more than Perry will.'

'You'll keep me updated?' I asked.

'I will. You know some of the work doesn't take much brain power and that gives me a lot of time to think. I'll put my mind to how we can make you and me work.'

'Okay,' I said. Lance pulled my coat around me. He kissed me gently and then lifted my scarf so it covered my mouth. 'Ride safely,' he said.

June was waiting for me when I got into college the next morning. It was getting cold now and I thought about catching the bus but I liked having the freedom to travel when I wanted without having to fit in with a timetable. She hopped about impatiently while I took off my gloves, my crash helmet and unwound my scarf.

'I phoned Jules last night,' she said. 'He says the frame will be finished by Wednesday evening. So I phoned Alex and he thinks he can get the van for Friday. Can you phone Lance and ask him if Friday afternoon's good for him?'

'I will do. I'm sure it will be. He wants to get on with it too,' I said. 'And it looks as though Perry will be out next weekend.'

'So it's all coming together then,' she said. 'I knew we'd pull it off.'

The days before the party seemed to go really slowly. I tried to keep up with what was going on with the scooter and with Perry. He had been kept in a few extra days it seemed and was now due out on the Wednesday. Lance phoned on that evening to say that Perry had been discharged and was settling in in Mrs Morales's living room.

By the following week it appeared that everything was in place for the scooter to be given to him on the day of the party. This plan had become so important I had almost forgotten that the party was being held to celebrate our 18th birthdays. June hadn't though and as soon as she had completed her epic journey with Alex to collect and deliver the scooter frame, she began planning the day of her actual birthday which fell on the Tuesday before the party.

'You had better come by bus, that day,' she said to me. 'Dad's giving me some money to buy everyone drinks, so I thought we'd go the college bar at lunchtime and then on to a pub in town afterwards.'

'Who's 'we'?' I asked.

'Oh, anyone who wants to come,' she said.

The college bar was usually quiet at lunchtimes, but not on that particular Tuesday. Our entire college class came as well as Phil'n'Col and some of the others from the class below and the secretarial courses. Some were very sensible and just asked for a soft drink but quite a few took advantage of June's Dad's generosity and ordered spirits and mixers. June said that she would choose my drink and came back with two glasses of something almost violently orange in colour. They both had little cocktail umbrellas floating on top.

'What on earth is that?' I asked.

'It's almost a tequila sunrise,' she said. 'Tequila and orange juice. It should have grenadine in it too, but really I was lucky to get the tequila. It's not something they have much call for, apparently.'

I took a small sip and almost choked. 'I'm not surprised,' I said. 'It's horrible.'

'Drink it slowly,' she said. 'You'll soon get used to it.'

I did try but I knew I would never get through it as it was so I added some lemonade when June wasn't looking. She was having a fine time flirting with the boys on the surveyor's course who were all older and usually ignored the likes of us catering students.

I watched as some people got steadily drunk and others went all red-faced and giggly almost immediately. In the afternoon classes it looked as though there were a few sore heads and some people who had planned to come on to the pub after college made their excuses and went home. That left a small hard-core group who could either take their drink or hadn't had much to drink. June and I were at either ends of this spectrum.

It was still early but as we were now into December there were lots of groups of office parties around town. We chose a pub that looked lively but not too crowded. Steve magnanimously bought the first round and made a toast to June:

'Who, now she is properly eighteen,' he said, 'will be able to frequent grown up night-time venues and will no doubt grow out of her silly scooter activities.'

'Never,' she shouted.

Later though, having downed a couple more drinks, she said to me a bit worriedly: 'What do you think? Will we grow out of our 'scooter activities' as he calls them?' 'I'm sure we will eventually,' I said. 'You can't tell how you'll think about things in the future, can you?'

'But I am grown up now, officially, that is. I mean, I can vote, for one thing.'

'I don't think you're going to change overnight,' I reassured her. 'At least, I hope you're not.'

'I'm not sure I want to grow up though,' she said, rubbing her fingers down the long red scar on her arm. 'I'm not ready to be responsible.'

She went off to phone Alex to let him know which pub we were in.

'Is Alex the one then?' I asked when she came back.

'Well he's lasted longer than most,' she said. 'Nearly three months, if you count from Weston.'

'And don't count Fred in the middle,' I said.

'Which I don't. It's going well, anyway. I think he might last a while. Maybe I am growing up.'

When Alex showed up I left them to it. I was fairly confident I wouldn't see June in at college the next day but she dragged herself in and only ran to the loos to throw up a couple of times.

'Shall we go and see Perry this afternoon?' she said once she was feeling a bit better. 'We ought to make sure he's going to come on Saturday.'

'I don't know,' I said. 'Shouldn't you be spending your spare time working on my cake?' I had been spending my spare hours moulding shapes out of brightly coloured balls of fondant icing. I planned to make the cake on Friday night and put it together on Saturday morning. 'It's all in hand' said June with an airy wave of her arm.

I drove her over to Lance's Mum's house. There was a wheelchair blocking up the hallway. We gave the squirrel tail dangling from the whip aerial a tug as we squeezed past. In the living room, Perry was sitting in the armchair watching tv. He still had a cast on one leg but the other was free. He was wearing shorts and his good leg looked thin and pale. He looked a bit tired.

'I'm feeding him up,' said Mrs Morales. 'Lots of chicken and steak.'

'And I'm feeling much better already,' said Perry loyally.

The bed had been covered with a crocheted throw to make it look more like a sofa so we sat on it.

'Well enough to come to the party?' said June.

'Yeah,' he said. 'I'll be there. I'll have my crutches and you can prop me up in the corner somewhere. I feel as though I've been out of circulation for too long. I need to get back to normality. It's been nice but I'm a bit fed up of everyone being kind to me.'

'Oh, they'll soon get bored of that,' said Mrs Morales, 'don't you worry.'

The doorbell rang. Mrs Morales went to answer it and came back with Sam in tow.

'Hi Perry,' she said. 'Hi June. I just popped in because I saw your scooter, Annie and I thought

you'd like to know what I've been up to today.'
She looked very smart in a skirt and jacket.

'You look like you've been for an interview,' said June.

'Correct,' said Sam. 'I've just been for an interview for an au pair agency. They're going to put me on their books and find me a family to work for.'

'An au pair?' I said. 'Here?'

'No. Somewhere in Europe probably. I've put down Italy as a first choice.'

'You're going for it then?' I asked.

'Yes. It's all thanks to you really Annie,' she said. 'I probably wouldn't have done anything about it if we hadn't have had that conversation and you hadn't lent me that book.'

'What about Dave?' asked Perry.

'Well, you know, now he's had a chance to think about it, he's actually quite for it. No one is an au pair for ever. I just need to get away for a bit, see a bit of the world, learn a language, you know?'

June and I nodded. We did know.

'I wish I had done something like that when I was your age,' said Mrs Morales wistfully. 'I might be a completely different person.'

'Exactly,' said Sam. 'Although you should never think you're too old.'

'I'm too old to be an au pair,' Mrs Morales said.

'Well maybe too old for that, but there are plenty of other things you could do.'

'I've got Perry now though.'

'For now. But you could be planning for when he's better.'

'Yes,' said Mrs Morales, 'maybe I should. There's not a lot holding me here.'

'Anyway,' said Sam, 'Dave says he'll come out for a holiday. Just between us, I think he's ready for a change himself. It might be the best thing that has ever happened to us.'

'Can I have your scooter when you go?' Perry said to Sam. 'Someone's got to keep the faith.'

'Can you? No.' replied Sam. 'I might take it with me, take it back home as it were.'

'It's not your style anyway,' said June.

'Perhaps not.' Perry seemed to sink into a bit of a sulk.

'Did you meet any nice nurses while you were in the hospital?' asked June in what seemed to be an attempt to change the subject.

'No,' said Perry. 'A body cast seems to be a bit of a passion killer, strangely enough.'

'Oh well, we'll introduce you to some nice girls on Saturday night. I'm sure we can get you back on the market.' I wondered what nice girls she was referring to. I wasn't sure any of the college girls would go for him. Perhaps we would have to give out some last minute invites.

I decided not to go to the Red Cow that evening. June was going though as she needed to get some agreement over what we could do with the scooter, so I dropped her off there and headed home.

'Lance phoned,' Mum shouted from the kitchen as I came in. 'He asked if you'd call him back.'

'Is he coming to the party?' she asked, coming through into the hall.

'Yes. He's bringing Perry's scooter up, we hope. That might be what he's phoning about.'

'Does he want to stay here?' Mum asked. 'He could use Julia's old room. I keep thinking I ought to turn that into more of a spare room.'

'I don't know, Mum. I expect he'll stay at his Mum's, if anywhere.'

'Well, I just thought, as it's your party, maybe you wanted to stay together?' I wasn't sure what she was offering. The whole subject of whether I was sleeping with Lance was one we hadn't discussed and it wasn't one I was prepared to discuss without some preparation.

'Thanks, Mum,' I said. 'I'll ask him, shall I?'

Lance was indeed phoning about the scooter.

'We're all ready to go,' he said. 'Well the scooter's ready anyway, and I've got the use of the van. You did tell Ed he could come to the party, didn't you? He's claiming you did.' I had forgotten about that.

'I did,' I said.

'That's okay then, he's coming with me. We're coming up on Saturday morning.'

'Er, where are you planning to stay?' I asked.

Oh, yeah, that's the other thing. Ed's booked a couple of hotel rooms. One for him and one for us, you and me, if you'd like to stay over.' I heard some shouting from somewhere else in the flat.

'He says to tell you that it's your birthday present,' said Lance.

'Tell him thanks,' I said. 'My Mum had asked if you wanted to stay here, but a hotel room will be much more fun.'

'I agree,' said Lance.

June came into college on Thursday with a folder marked 'Party' in large colourful letters.

'I've got all the schedules and stuff,' she said, 'so you know what you're doing when.'

'I know what I'm doing when,' I said. 'I'm going to my party in time for half past seven and I'm going to eat, drink, dance, chat and maybe snog until they chuck us out at midnight.'

'Oh Annie,' she sighed, 'if only it was that easy.'

At lunchtime we holed up in the common room so she could give me my orders.

'Right,' she said. 'I spoke to the guy at the Red Cow and he refused point blank to let us take Perry's scooter upstairs. I had to use my best negotiating skills. .'

'You mean you flirted,' I said.

'Yes, all right, I had to use my best flirting skills and he has finally agreed to let us put it in the corner of the pub downstairs. So then I phoned Salty and he's going to drop it off there late afternoon. He's going to cover it up so someone can do a big reveal.'

'Who?' I asked.

'I don't know. Salty says he's not doing it.'

'You, then?'

'Maybe. Or you and me together.'

'We'll see.'

'Anyway, you are coming to mine to get changed aren't you?'

'Of course.' I had planned to spend the afternoon at June's so we could get ready and psyche ourselves up.

'Right, and Salty's at the hotel?'

'Yes. I'm going there afterwards.'

'Okay, well he says he's going to come and pick us up from mine at about seven.'

'Us? Is he taking us in the van?'

'No. Apparently we'll need crash helmets.'

'And parkas as well then. I'll be in my party gear. And someone else must be coming unless he's planning on riding three up. He won't even have his scooter if he's coming up in the van.'

'Well he wouldn't be drawn on details, I'm afraid. He just said we should be ready.'

'Right.'

'So then we get to the Red Cow. Spend twenty minutes trying to make ourselves look presentable, after which people should be arriving so we say hello and all that, get a bit of dancing going. Then Mrs Morales is going to bring Perry at about eight. Everyone should be there by then. She's going to run up to us, saying she's going to get someone to help him get up the stairs but instead we all come down and we give him the scooter.'

'And then we go back upstairs and dance the night away?'

'Pretty much. The buffet's at half eight and then we should do the whole cake thing and then we can get down to some serious dancing.'

'And have a good time?' I asked.

'I hope so. You forget that that's what it's supposed to be all about really, don't you?'

'No,' I said. 'Maybe that's just you being all grown up.'

'I hope not.'

Chapter Twenty Two

I spent Saturday morning putting the finishing touches to my cake. I was quite pleased with it. It didn't look exactly as I'd imagined but I thought that June would like it. I left it with Dad to bring to the party later and rode my scooter over to June's house. It was cold and already dark but the buses passing in the other direction filled with Christmas shoppers looked cheerful with their lights and steamed up windows and quite a few houses already had their decorations up.

June was opening a bottle of fizzy wine when I arrived.

'It's only lightly alcoholic,' she said. 'I am pacing myself.'

We took it in turns to have a shower and then did each other's hair and make-up. June put on a Motown mixtape and we sang along as we worked.

'I feel like a Sindy doll,' I said as she sprayed liberal amounts of hair spray at my head.

'You look fantastic,' she said, 'even if I do say so myself.'

When I looked in the mirror I agreed that I didn't look like myself, but I did look good.

About twenty minutes before Lance was due we got dressed and went downstairs to parade in front of June's nan who was parked in front of the tv watching the Generation Game.

'Ooh, I am looking forward to this,' she said. 'Will there be music we can jive to?'

'There will, Nan,' said June, ' although I can't promise I can find you a partner'

'Shame.'

'I'll dance with you Mum,' said June's Dad. 'Keep you in check a bit, we don't want you putting a hip out, do we?'

There was some noise in the driveway followed by a knock at the front door.

'That'll be our lift,' said June. I was curious to see what Lance had planned and got to the door before June. I opened it to see Lance stood on the doorstep wearing his parka but with his hair neatly brushed and gelled down.

'Your carriages, ladies,' he said and stepped aside so we could see onto the drive. There were five scooters, all displaying leg shield banners that said 'Happy Eighteenth, Annie and June.'

'What do you think? I had them made up especially,' he said.

'They're brilliant,' I said. I gave him a kiss. 'Thank you.'

Lance's scooter was parked at the front and behind him was Dave and Sam, Bertie and Suzy.

'We wanted you to arrive in style,' said Dave. 'So we've planned a bit of a parade. We'll drive a bit slowly through town and see if we can get anyone to wave to us.'

'But you've got your scooter,' I said to Lance. 'You didn't ride it up, did you?'

'No, but I did have a bit of spare space in the van. I only brought it to do this but I might let Ed take the van and ride back tomorrow.

He turned to June. 'It's all in place,' he said, 'the scooter's ready for us.'

'I just hope Perry is,' I said.

June and I wrapped up as well as we could then I climbed on the back of Lance's scooter and June got on Dave's. Lance moved the scooter as if he was going to lead.

'Could we go at the back?' I said. 'So I can watch the others, you know, feel like I'm part of a ride out?'

We stretched out in a thread as we rode through the windy country roads but once we got into town we bunched up and rode slowly along the High Street, past the college and the station and up the road to the Red Cow, waving to anyone who glanced in our direction. I inhaled the smell of the exhaust fumes of the five scooters and listened to their similar but different engine noises creating a sort of mechanical symphony. It brought back memories of the rallies we'd been to over the summer and made me long for Easter and the new run season.

At the Red Cow we rode slowly into the car park where all the other Sessex Girls and SeaDogs revved their engines, flashed their lights and tooted their horns. With them were Jules and Fred, Ben and Katie, and Phil'n'Col.

'I feel like royalty,' said June, waving regally whilst dismounting from Dave's scooter.

'Thank you,' I said to Lance. 'That was really special.'

'Well we didn't want the evening to be entirely about Perry,' he said.

'I don't know how you got everyone together like that,' I said.

'I just asked them,' he said. 'It's amazing what you can do when you pick up the phone.'

Everyone headed inside. My Mum and Dad were already there and I found them a table in the corner where they were joined by June's family.

'You'll make sure you look after Lance's Mum when she comes, won't you?' I said to Mum.

'You've only asked me that a dozen times,' she said. 'Of course I will. I'm looking forward to meeting her.'

June's Dad came out from behind the bar with several bottles of champagne and proceeded to force a glass on everyone. The DJ began his set with some of the more popular soul tracks, ones by Wilson Pickett and Aretha Franklin.

'Play something from the Blues Brothers,' called June's Dad and the DJ played 'Can't Turn You Loose'. June pulled her Dad onto the dance floor and they got everyone around clapping and eventually joining in.

I stood with Lance at the edge of the floor.

'You look lovely,' he said.

'So, do you,' I replied. He was wearing suit trousers and a smart shirt.

'Do you think?' he asked. 'I brought a tie, but decided it was a bit much.'

Jules joined us. He gave me a kiss on both cheeks and shook Lance's hand. This was the first time I had seen them together and I was interested to see how they would react to each other. Jules had already laid his arm across Lance's shoulders and put his other arm around me, drawing us in together. Lance didn't seem to mind.

'My two favourite Essex people,' he said. 'Happy Birthday, Annie.'

'Thanks,' I said.

'I think we're staying in the same hotel as you,' he said. 'So we can continue the party back at yours later.'

'Sounds good,' I said. 'Thanks for coming.'

'Wouldn't have missed it,' he said. He turned to Lance.

'I had a peek at the finished result,' he said. 'She's looking pretty good.'

'You wait until you hear her,' said Lance. 'She's got such a lovely throaty sound.'

I looked over at June who had now got Fred on the dance floor.

'Does he know she's got a boyfriend and he's probably due any minute?' I asked.
Jules didn't look bothered. 'I'm sure June can handle it,' he said. 'I mean, look at us. I gave in gracefully to Lance over you, didn't I?

I wasn't sure that that was quite how it happened, but I let it lie. It felt like Lance stood a little taller as a result of his comment and perhaps that had been Jules's intention.

'Are you two dancing?' asked Jules.

'Maybe in a bit,' I said. 'I think Perry's due any minute.' I glanced over to Lance who was looking a bit anxious.

'Don't worry,' I said. 'He'll love it.'

I saw Alex in the doorway and some of the college lot behind him. The girls looked like they were ready to run so I went to greet them and get them a drink.

'You'll be fine.' I said. 'There are a few single boys here, I'll point them out if you like.' I was about to go and get Fred when Mrs Morales appeared behind me.

'We're here,' she said. 'He's here. At the bottom of the stairs. We'll need to be quick I think or he'll start tackling them on his own.'

I explained quickly to the girls what we were doing. Everyone involved in putting the scooter together was gathering nervously at the door.

'You go down first,' June said to Lance. 'Take him in the pub and we'll follow you down.'

'Why me?' said Lance as June practically pushed him towards the stairs.

'Who else could it be?' she replied.

We gave Lance about a minute before we followed behind him. I got lost in the crowd of people heading down the stairs and couldn't see

Perry as we entered the pub. The SeaDogs, anticipating the unveiling of the scooter gathered themselves around it. I saw June get pulled forward and someone find her a chair to stand on. Standing up there in her black and white dress and boots with her bleached blonde hair, she looked magnificent, like a ship's figurehead.

'Um, Perry,' she said. 'On behalf of everyone,' she waved her hand over us, 'in particular Lance and Jules, all the SeaDogs and the Sessex Girls, and lots of other people. Well we were all upset to hear that your scooter had to be written off. So we got together and we've got you this.

The crowd parted between the bar and the scooter. I could see Perry now, his arms in his crutches, looking a bit bewildered. June jumped off the chair and led him forward. He hopped unevenly alongside her. She looked back for Lance who was trying to lose himself in the crowd. She gestured at him to come forward. The three of them stood in front of the tarpaulin.

'No mate, you haven't . .' said Perry.

'Where's Annie?' said Lance looking back, 'she should be doing this too.'

Someone pushed me forward from behind.

'Why me?' I said. 'I haven't done anything.' Lance just looked at me.

'Come on then, Annie, you and me,' said June.

Seeing there was no way out, I grabbed one corner of the tarpaulin and June grabbed another

316

and together we carefully unveiled the scooter. The lights caught the flakes of metal in the paint and reflected off into the crowd. We all looked at Perry anxiously.

'No mate, there's some mistake,' he said, taking an arm out of a crutch and leaning on Lance instead.

'No mistake,' said Lance. He drew Perry gently forward. 'It's yours, we built it for you.' Gingerly, Perry lifted his good leg across the floor of the scooter and sat down on it as well as he could. A ripple of applause went through the crowd. Perry had tears in his eyes and I could see that Lance did too.

We watched as Perry ran his fingers gently over the headlight fairing and across the handlebars. He put his hands on the grips and experimented with the clutch and brake levers. Finally he spoke.

'Thank you. Everyone.' There was silence for a moment. 'That's as much as you're going to get out of me for now,' he said. 'Go and enjoy the party.'

Towards the back of the crowd, people started to drift away.

'We should go up,' said June. We left Perry on his scooter with Lance and the other SeaDogs.

'We'll bring her home tomorrow,' I heard Lance say to Perry. 'Wait till you fire her up, she's beautiful.'

I walked back up the stairs with Ed.

'Well did that go as you expected?' he said.

'It went as well as I'd hoped, I think,' I said.

317

'Good. Lance has put no end of hours into it. I suppose he'll be hanging round the flat now. We need to find him a new project and quick. In the meantime though are there any single ladies you can introduce me to?'

I took him over to the college girls, who had also been joined by Phil'n'Col, and left them to it. Jules was hovering nearby.

'Didn't you want to tell Perry about the paintwork?' I said.

'There's not a lot to say about it,' he said.

'But you could give him a chance to say thank you.'

'I saw the look on his face,' he said. 'He'll never put that adequately into words. I don't need any more thanks that that. Now, are you dancing?'

'It's about time I did,' I said.

We joined June and Alex on the dance floor. 'So,' I said to Jules over the music, 'you got on okay with Lance then?'

'Yes,' he said. 'I always knew I would. He's my kind of bloke.'

A thought occurred to me, 'I'm not getting involved in some weird triangle am I?'

Jules laughed. 'I don't fancy him, if that's what you mean. I think we could do some business together though. We created a good scooter there.'

'You'd have to be in the same place though,' I said.

'Not necessarily. We'd just have to have a good system of transporting the parts from one place to another.'

'So Lance could stay in Portsmouth?'

'If he wanted.'

'Only I'm thinking of going on to the Polytechnic there.'

'Yeah? Good plan, if Portsmouth has the course you want to study.'

June came over. 'They say the food is ready. I'll go and get the others up from downstairs, shall I?'

She disappeared down to the pub and I went to see how everyone was getting on at the old folks' table.

Mrs Morales was sat in the corner regaling Mum with some story about Lance. It looked as though they were getting on well.

'The food's ready,' I said. 'You'd better get in quick.' We let June's Nan go first and Sam got a plate of food for Perry. Lance joined me in the queue.

'Was it okay?' I asked.

'You mean does Perry like the scooter? Yes, I think he loves what it is, he's just not ready to accept that it is his yet.'

'Make him give it a name, that'll help,' I said.

We got our food and went to sit with the SeaDogs and the Sessex Girls. There was only one chair left so I sat on Lance's knee. He put his spare arm around me and absent-mindedly rubbed a patch of velvet on my thigh with his thumb. June was on a table over the other side of the room. She had Alex on one side of her and Fred on the other.

Everyone looked happy and I wondered what miracle she had pulled off there.

'That's a big pile of presents,' said Dave, pointing at a table next to us.

'Yes,' I agreed. 'I suppose I should wait until my actual birthday to open mine though.'

'You have to open this one,' said Sam, picking up an envelope. On the front it said 'To Annie. To be opened on the day of the party'.

'That's my Mum's writing,' I said. 'I wonder what that's about?' I put it on the table and looked at it for a bit.

'Aren't you intrigued?' asked Sam.

'I am,' I said, 'but I'm enjoying the anticipation.'

June came over. 'Alex and Fred seem to be getting on well,' I said.

'Yes, although I'm not sure either of them knows of my relationship with the other, so it all might go off yet,' she said. 'In the meantime, shall we do the cakes?'

'I don't know, is that next on the schedule?' I asked.

'You'd know if you had studied it, like I suggested,' she said.

'Well, okay, let's do the cakes,' I said. 'But there's something I want to do while everyone's eating them so don't let the DJ start straight away, will you?'

I went and put the envelope in the pocket of my parka and brought my cake out of the kitchen. It was a rectangular cake and I had covered it in coloured squares of icing so it looked like a disco floor. I'd sculpted various oddly angled people and placed them on top so it looked as though they were dancing. The one in the middle had yellow hair and a black and white dress.

'Wow, that's great,' said June as I put it on the table. 'I like me. I hope no one eats me.'

'I'll try and save you,' I said. She brought hers out from behind her back. It was in the shape of the top part of a scooter: the legshield, the headlight and fairing and the handlebars. It was coloured to match mine. Where the Vespa name badge would be instead it said 'Annie' and the logo badge said '18'.

'That's brilliant,' I said. 'Are you sure we shouldn't be opening a cake shop?'

We posed for lots of photos and then lit some candles. Everyone sang 'Happy Birthday' and we blew the candles out.

'Have a piece of cake,' June shouted.

'Then I've got something to say,' I added. I'd had an inkling that June was planning to make a speech and I knew if I was going to make one too, I'd have to do it first. I went over to the DJ.

'Can I stand on your speaker?' I asked him.

He looked me up and down. 'Well you probably could,' he said, 'but once one person does it, it's open season, so I'd have to say no. You can use my microphone though, if you're wanting to make a speech.'

I took the microphone from him and tapped it experimentally. Now I had it in my hand I wasn't sure I wanted to carry my plan through. I saw Lance looking at me though and decided to go for it.

'Hello?' I said and my voice came through the speakers behind me, making me and everyone else jump. Everyone was now looking at me. I took a deep breath.

Um, yes, well, you know,' I said. 'I do have something to say. You know that this is our birthday party, June's and mine, and I just wanted to say something about June, what she means to me. I hope that's okay.' A few people nodded and someone clapped.

'Okay then,' I said. 'I met June on my first day at college and we became friends straight away. Maybe that's June, I don't know, but there's not been a minute since when I've had a cause to doubt her friendship. I think we're quite different, two sides of the same coin, perhaps, but somehow we work together. I'm sure you all know how fantastic she is, what a positive force she is. June,' I found her in the crowd and locked eyes with her, 'I just wanted to say, in front of everyone here, thank you for being my friend, I hope you always will be.'

June came over and enveloped me in a hug and everyone applauded. There were lots of things I had planned to say that I had forgotten when I'd actually stood up there but I hoped she had got the message.

June took the microphone from me. 'I'd like to say something about Annie too,' she said. I tried to move away a little but she held onto my

hand tightly. 'Annie is really the best friend a person can have. She's loyal and she's honest. She's always there for you. But there's something else too, something I don't think even she is aware of, and that's how she brings people together. Perry's scooter wouldn't be the scooter it is, if she hadn't brought the skills of Salty and Jules together. Perry might even still be in the hospital if she hadn't thought that he could stay with Mrs Morales. These aren't the big and flashy things that people see and value, but maybe they should. The world is a better place with people
Annie in it.'

'Thank you June,' I whispered.

'Thank you for coming,' she said into the microphone. 'Thank you for the presents. We hope you'll all join us on the dancefloor.'

Lance came over. 'June's right you know. You said you didn't do anything for Perry's scooter, but it wouldn't have happened without you.'

'Without all of us,' I said. 'This is our party so we get to say nice things about each other, but everyone has their part to play, don't they. Things would be different if even one person was missing.'

There was a clatter behind us. We turned round to see Perry lying on the floor, it looked as though he had fallen off his chair. We went over to help but Andrea got there first.

'Oh, who let him have a drink?' she asked. Perry got to his feet and grinned.

'I feel like I'm getting back to normal,' he said.

Much later, after everyone else had gone home, the last few of us made our way to the hotel. June had brought a few of the most interesting looking presents and our parents had taken the rest home. Everyone ended up in one room. Lance and I made room for ourselves on one side of the bed and Alex and June took the other. Jules lay down in the middle of the bed. and Fred and Ed were left with the chairs.

'No one copped off then?' asked June.

'I don't think the girls of Essex are ready for the charms of a suave Hampshire guy,' said Ed.

'Or a slightly rough Devonian one,' said Fred.

'Their loss,' said Jules. 'Did you enjoy your party girls?'

'I did,' said June. 'And I think my Nan did.' Her Nan had got up on the dance floor and joined in on a couple of numbers, with some of the boys taking her hand.

'And Perry,' I said. Perry had gone home quite drunk and very happy.

'Are you going to come with me when I take the scooter up there tomorrow?' Lance said to me.

'Can we come too?' asked Jules. I still haven't heard her ticking over yet.'

'Yes, we'll have another party, shall we?' Lance said. 'See if we can keep it going until Annie's birthday?'

'Talking of which,' I said. 'I have this envelope I'm supposed to be opening.'

I went and got it and sat on the end of the bed with it.

I opened it carefully, trying not to tear the paper. Inside was a piece of paper. Unfolding it, at the top I could see it said 'Sales Receipt'. The rest took a bit of working out.

I saw the word 'Acapulco' and some dates in December and it became clear.

'It's a receipt for flight tickets,' I said. 'My Mum has bought me a flight to Mexico, leaving the day after my birthday.'

At the bottom, Mum had written, 'To Annie, We hope this helps with your wanderlust. Julia will look after you. Happy Birthday, Love Mum and Dad x x x.'

'I'm going to Acapulco,' I said, feeling quite dazed.

'But you're coming back?' asked Lance.

'Yes, it's just a holiday,' I said.

'Good,' said Lance and I heard the word echo round the room as the others agreed. At that moment I knew that I didn't need to go abroad to look for what I needed, I had it right there at home.